CITIZENS MILITIA

Book 2 in The Curtain Series

DAVID T. MADDOX

Made for Grace
PUBLISHING

DAVID T. MADDOX
Made for Grace Publishing
P.O. Box 1775
Issaquah, WA 98027

Library of Congress Cataloging-in-Publication data
Maddox, David T., date,
Citizens Militia / David T. Maddox.
p. cm.
ISBN-13: 9781613398487 (pbk.)
LCCN: 2017905988

To contact the publisher please email
service@MadeforSuccess.net or call +1 425 657 0300.
Made for Grace Publishing is an imprint of Made for Success, inc.
Printed in the United States of America

THE CURTAIN IS dedicated to four people who have had most influenced my life and ministry over these many decades. There have obviously been many others that God has used, but these people have changed my life and I want to acknowledge them and affirm how God has used them.

RICHARD OWEN ROBERTS – In my life Mr. Roberts has been like "the Bookseller" in this story – the one who opened God's word and revealed hidden truth. He taught me about revival and awakening and showed me what it means to walk without compromise at a high cost.

DR. HENRY BLACKABY – Henry (as he prefers to be called) opened my eyes to what it means to walk intimately with the Lord – to hear Him speak, to discern what He has said, to see Him working around me. He has encouraged me in the way of obedience, made me aware of the cost of my obedience to those I love, and so much more.

KYLE & LAURA MARTIN – This couple opened my eyes to what we are called to in the Great Commission, what it means to put no limits on the Holy Spirit, the importance of the Jewish people in end times, what it means to be prepared for the return of Jesus, what it means to walk in faith in total dependence on God, and so much more. Time to Revive, the ministry they began, is the only revival ministry I have encountered that David T. Maddox doesn't' just study revival or pray for revival, but actively seeks to gather churches together in revival. I have been privileged to be a small part of this ministry for the last five years. Here God is mightily at work.

JANET WHITEHEAD MADDOX – My bride, my completion, the one God uses to keep my focus and to confront me when I get off the path.

No man was ever more blessed than I have been in sharing my life with her, our kids and grandkids – sharing our relationship with God. To minister together with the same heart has been the joy of my life.

ACKNOWLEDGMENTS

WRITING A BOOK is a long journey which for me began in 2007 when the Lord inspired me to try and take the truth of Scripture about the invisible conflict that goes on around us and picture it in such a way that people could have a better understanding of this reality which affects their daily life. My attempt has in some cases been futile, but hopefully what is shared within the pages of the book is Biblically accurate and will open eyes to help answer the why questions for much of what we face today.

Many people have encouraged and helped me along the way. In 2007, Matt and Kim Clark read each chapter as the book progressed giving me valuable input and perspective as the story and characters developed. As a trial lawyer, I was used to telling stories and being sure that the stories matched the evidence, but as this book continued the characters took over the story and drove it in surprising directions. Later others including Mel Sauder and Jerry Jagoda would read revisions, there were seven in all, and similarly gave input and encouragement.

For me, the "hero" in this process has been my editor, Catherine Barrack whose insight and discernment was invaluable. Her maturity as a Believer enabled her to ask the right questions to be sure that the story did not go beyond what was Biblically possible as have others who attempted to write similar stories. Her skill and sensitivity gave new life to some of the characters at critical points in the story and gave me insight that only a third person reading the story can give. It is a much-improved story because of her partnership in the process.

Special thanks must also go to Buzz Leonard, who introduced me to Bryan Heathman and Made for Success Publishing. They quickly understood what I am trying to do and have been helpful at each stage of the process working patiently with a first-time author.

Ultimate thanks go to the Lord, who despite me having stage four cancer has enabled me to finish the book in between this past year of chemo treatments. I am hopeful that the book will bless the reader even as writing it has blessed and taught me. If it does bless you, please share it with others.

CHAPTER 1

THE ANNOUNCEMENT
AND THE RESPONSE

Wednesday, February 6 – MD minus 109 days

THE PRESENCE OF the Lord was very real to the four men as they shared and prayed together that day. It had been over a decade since there had been a sense of holy awe in the chaplain's office at the Williams College campus. The events of the past few hours only made them more passionate to obey the four-word command given by Gabriel to their Iranian brothers, "Stand together and pray."

"I sent a message back to them acknowledging God's command and hoping to encourage them in their search. I told them we would stand with them and pray and call on all believers to join together and pray." Looking around the room and knowing that Chaplain Forrest contacted all the pastors of true churches in Williams, the Bookseller observed, "It is clear that the message hasn't yet been received by the local church leadership."

"Today may change that and you will have an opportunity to obey the command tonight when you are interviewed for the ITN special," Chaplain Forrest commented. "Pastor Wilson's church is meeting to pray tonight. Not all the leaders have closed ears."

"Yes," responded Pastor Wilson, "and I contacted the archbishops in Rwanda and East Asia, and they have issued a call to prayer for the churches affiliated with the Anglican Mission in America. They also issued a call to pray for America to their churches in Africa and East Asia. Much faithful prayer is being raised around the world but sadly little here in America — the subject of that prayer."

"Chaplain Forrest, would you be willing to open the chapel at noon and at night for prayers? I would be willing to join other believers to lead prayers for our nation," Paul Phillips suggested, even surprising himself. "Perhaps other students would join with believers in the community and pray together."

Turning to the Bookseller, Paul asked, "Mr. White, maybe you could come the first evening and share and answer questions. After what happened today, people would come to hear. Maybe you could even say something about it in your interview tonight and we could start tomorrow."

"Yes, yes, yes!" Chaplain Forrest responded with enthusiasm. "The chapel will finally become a house of prayer as Jesus said the church should be."[1]

"This is important," the Bookseller interrupted, "Do you see what God is doing? The formal leadership of the local church has not responded to God's call, so He is going beyond them to find others with a heart to obey Him. That has always been God's way. If those called to lead will not lead His people as He commands, He will first give them a chance to repent and obey, and if they refuse, He calls others. God's plan waits for no man or institution and is dependent on no one. His will be done."

There was silence as those present considered the words spoken by the Bookseller. The message seemed clear — they must go beyond formal church leadership and into homes to reach believers and lead them to prayer by the Holy Spirit.

"You are right Mr. White," Pastor Wilson said breaking the silence. "Remember, Jesus told the parable of the tenants against the religious leaders of His day who refused to walk in obedience. His closing statement to them has always been a cold warning I have never forgotten. He said, 'I tell you that the kingdom of God will be taken away from you and given to a people who will produce fruits.'[2] I fear we may already be there, or getting close to that in America. That is one of the reasons for the Anglican Mission in America."

"Don't forget Jesus crying over the city of Jerusalem," Chaplain Forrest added. "In seventy years the whole city and nation were crushed by the Romans 'because,' Jesus said, 'you did not recognize the time of God's coming to you.'[3] Clearly, God has come with His message, and we must respond or expect no better from the terrorists than Israel suffered at the hands of the Romans in A.D. 70."

"I do not know whether the formal leadership can be awakened," the Bookseller answered with deep sadness and concern in his eyes. "Only God knows, but the command is to call all believers to join together and pray. All we can do is obey, pray, and appeal to the leaders to lead people in prayer. The rest is in God's hands."

The President Speaks to the Nation

Tom Knight stepped to the podium to make the formal introduction, "Ladies and gentlemen, the President of the United States." Those in the press room of the White House stood and became quiet as President Strong approached the microphones.

"Thank you, ladies and gentlemen, please be seated.

"My fellow Americans, I have asked the networks for time this morning to comment on recent events which concern all of us, and to ask for your help. Earlier this week, we were shocked by reports of the killing of seven young Arab men in seven American cities and the dumping of their bodies in dumpsters. As you have likely heard in the news, these seven men carried no identification and the forensic analysis here and abroad have revealed nothing about their identities or country of origin. These are non-persons who arrived illegally and died unknown and for an unknown purpose.

"This morning in Williams, Illinois, another unidentified young Arab man was killed as he attempted to detonate an explosive vest. Again, the body carried no identification, and forensic evidence has thus far given no information on his identity or country of origin. Thus, we have another non-person who arrived unknown and died unknown.

"It is important that we all face—without alarm or fear—the reality that some groups are trying to infiltrate our nation with terrorists and equipment for terrorist attacks.

"The full resources of this government are being employed worldwide to find and eliminate this threat. While I cannot discuss the specifics because our enemies monitor our broadcasts just as we monitor theirs, I can assure all of you that our anti-terrorism measures are as comprehensive as possible. However, The American government cannot succeed without your help and without Congress addressing border security immediately. We need the eyes and ears of every American watching their neighborhoods, workplaces, and cities. We need everyone to inform law enforcement and Homeland Security of any unusual activity or the presence of any unusual person. We are not on a 'witch hunt' against Arabs or anyone based on race, religion or nationality, for terrorists are not limited to any religion or nationality and we know that not all Muslims are terrorists. However, we do need everyone to unite and stand against those who seek to harm us in our own nation, and we need to close the open doors on our borders.

"We are obviously concerned, but not alarmed. We know that if we come together as Americans we can protect one another and make it impossible for aliens with evil intentions to walk freely among us and do us harm. Please, take these efforts seriously as your duty to your fellow citizens."

The President paused, sighed, and then continued in a quieter voice, "Unfortunately, we must expect that a day may come when, somewhere in the United States, an attack will be launched; perhaps even several. We will be prepared to respond appropriately. If we work together, we can eliminate most threats. However, it would be dishonest to tell you that we can prevent every killer sent to the US from carrying out a hate-filled mission.

"Last weekend an old man in Williams, Illinois, stepped up to a microphone at the end of a press conference, asking that believers in America pray together for God's deliverance and for the wisdom to understand why God has allowed terrorism to happen on American soil. This morning that old man became the latest target of terrorism. They obviously did not like what he said and sought to silence him by killing him. That is their way, not ours.

"I would like to close this morning by adding to what Mr. White said, and ask all Americans to join with me in prayer for God's wisdom and deliverance from this threat. Thank you."

The president took no questions as he walked soberly back to the Oval Office.

An Unexpected Reaction

The White House press corps were stunned. There was something about the way the president had spoken with frankness and honesty that traversed politics and agendas. Here was the leader of the free world standing before his people humbly and honestly, seeking their help in facing a common danger. The mood changed instantly, and the desire to criticize was replaced with a desire to be a part of the effort to encourage the people to stand together against an unknown threat. Their reports and commentaries began to reflect the changed attitude.

In New York, George Murphy, a reporter at the *Times Daily* began to reconsider the leak from Commissioner Matthews regarding Press Secretary Knight's secret work at a presidential commission. Something was obviously going on within the government to address what the president considered a very real threat. This morning's statement was part of a much larger effort of some nature. There was a story there to be mined.

The networks scrambled to determine how to deal with the new candor about a possible threat. At ITN, work on tonight's production continued to change as the news required shift after shift in focus. There was now unconfirmed word of a military deployment of some nature to the Chicago area. How did all of this fit into the reality of a shooter still at large and another dead terrorist? Why had they targeted the Bookseller and why would the shooter protect him?

Around the country, law enforcement organized to receive and process thousands of phone calls that people were making shortly after the president concluded his address. People who had seen things that troubled them finally had the chance to step forward and share their concerns with the authorities. Most of the initial calls seemed insignificant, but they were all well cataloged, briefed, and forwarded to Homeland Security for analysis even as they were being investigated at the point of origin.

As the news organizations combined news reports on the president's address with local announcements by other political leaders, citizens began to think over things they had seen and wondered about previously. In Carmen, Arizona, teenager Juan Martinez decided to change his way to school. He decided to ride his bike in front of the old Craig place every morning so that to see what was going on with the road trucks from Mexico. Retired truck driver Sam Will, who headed the Citizen's Militia in Williams, decided to follow up on stories he was hearing from some of his old trucking buddies about an operation called Brother's Trucking. Even Chaplain Forrest was rethinking what he had seen of the car with the strange moving license plate before the shooting in front of the warehouse. He had been wondering why the car did not show up on the ITN video taken of the shooting.

The call for prayer had not gone unnoticed in America or in the invisible realm. It reinforced what the Spirit had been saying to those with the light inside them, and created a sense of need among many who remained under the influence of the forces of darkness. God enabled the blind to see and the deaf to hear and become searchers. Keepers and Guardians waged war over every soul as God called many to Himself. All who had watched the President's address had heard the president admit that he needed God's help. If he did, then perhaps they did too.

The president's statement had reinforced the importance of the upcoming security fair in Williams. For some unknown reason, this little town became the center stage before all America. The ITN commitment to continue the series they were doing—combined with the reality of the attempt on the Bookseller's life by a terrorist—made the threat of terrorism real in Williams. Officer Sally Johnson had been advised of the raised terror threat in Williams, and she had been planning to incorporate the Citizens Militia into the police deployment without telling them of the threat. She understood why that information needed to be kept confidential within law enforcement, but it was hard for her personally to withhold that information from Tom Campy whom she had come to like and trust.

A Different Response

The reaction to the president's address was not universally favorable. In the office of the Senate majority leader, the legendary temper of former President Cox once again erupted, and he threw a book through the television screen accompanied by a stream of profanities as he stomped around the room. The spotlight had been taken from them in a moment. They would have to completely reorganize the effort and redirect it to counteract the president.

"That man is impossible, and worst of all he believes that garbage," the former president screamed continuing his rant.

"Calm down Leonard," Majority Leader Howard interrupted. "Remember your own advice. All we have to do is turn the perception and join in the fight against terrorism. We will make the Together Tomorrow agenda the way to fight terrorism and he will have to join us. When we met with him, he warned us not to ignore the terrorism threat. He knows something is going on and we need to take advantage of that; we need to take the initiative away from him. Rather than following him, let us lead. He has admitted that he does not have the answer and needs God to tell him what to do. Let us provide the answer, and the American people will follow us and ignore his God language.

"A president is supposed to have the answer. He has shown weakness. We need to take advantage of that."

"What specifically are you thinking?" Cox asked.

"Let us call our own press conference and not only make a statement but also take questions and appear open. We will acknowledge the president's call for citizen involvement and offer congressional cooperation in the effort to confront the threat. Do you remember George Murphy's article in the *Times Daily* regarding the press secretary's involvement in some secret presidential commission? Let us call Tom Knight to appear along with others from the intelligence community before the Senate Intelligence Committee, in closed session, to report on the crisis. We can find out what is going on and arrange a few convenient leaks as needed to take the initiative away from the president."

"Well, if we are going to take him on, let's take him on," Chairman Crow added. "We need to take advantage of this moment to present the opportunity as an antiterrorism package. None of us believe that fighting terrorism does anything apart from creating more terrorists, but we can pitch this as self-defense on the homeland—which even the peace movement would have to agree with. We can blame the current policy for creating the problem and we will have the answer the president does not seem capable of providing. That will make him a lame duck, even in his own party."

"You are absolutely right!" Cox said excitedly. "Sorry, it's hard to be on the outside when a couple of years ago his office was my office. I resent this mouse of a president and his calls for prayer. That bunch wraps themselves in religion claiming a divine right to lead. We have to get religion completely off the public stage. We have made a lot of progress, but the job is far from complete. The cry must remain, 'Freedom from religion!'"

"It is not that difficult," Majority Leader Howard added. "At the press conference, we will present a quick fix for the threat. First, the North American Union as a way to have unified control over the whole continent on matters of security beginning with control of the roads by controlling the issuance of driver's licenses. We can sell that as an anti-terrorism tool and as a way to fight the importation of drugs and illegals. We also sell it as the way for greater economic security for Americans. We can open the roads, relying on Mexico and Canada to regulate licenses before the North American Union develops its own regulations as a first step. That would enable us to meet the Together Tomorrow timetable and open the way to the political money tree."

"The other major thing would be to deal with religion. We have to be smart and present it as a way to fight terrorism without disclosing how it would affect any religion other than radical Islam. The amendment to the Hate Crimes Act is an easy sell if we present it as a definition of terrorism and a way to control the hate speech by the Mullahs. The terrorists have made hate and violence a religious act. To encourage terrorism by sermons is the same as running a recruitment campaign for suicide bombers. What we stay away from is talking about the consequences that would overflow to other religions. If we are successful, we can take religion off the public stage as the invisible police officer and stop its interference, allowing people to make their own choices without condemnation. That after all is the definition of freedom—the right to do what you want as long as you don't hurt someone else."

"Agreed, but we need to do this quickly. What about the subpoena on the old man?" asked Chairman Crow.

"Simple. Let's use the press conference as an opportunity to mourn the loss of the innocent process server and ask that the old man appears voluntarily. He would look bad if he refused. It would take some work, and we would have to be careful, but I bet we can organize a show before your committee that would be nationally televised and would make the case to the public for controlling all forms of radical religion."

"Sounds like a winning formula to me," the former president added with glee. "How soon can you take this production public?"

"I will schedule it for noon tomorrow. I want to see what comes of the ITN special on Williams city before we go public. Oh, and by the way, Mr. former president, that Together Tomorrow crowd owes me a new television set."

"Done," Cox said laughing. "It will be here on time for you to watch the show tonight."

"Hold on just a minute please," said House Majority Whip Eric Besserman, "I have sat here quietly and listened to this discussion. I have been considering the North American Union proposal and the strategy to negate religion as a political force, but some questions remain unanswered. Who or what is behind this Together Tomorrow group? In addition, why hurry to open the roads?"

"You sound like Strong," Cox angrily responded.

"Perhaps, but these are legitimate questions that someone is going to ask, and I want to know before I support this effort. Where is the money coming from?"

"Together Tomorrow is a PAC organized by two naturalized Saudis," Cox responded. "I don't know or care where the money comes from, but I assume it is tied to Saudi princes or relations tied to the ruling family. I don't know for sure."

"Why would the Saudis want to put money into opening the roads to Mexico, and why now?" asked Besserman.

"I don't know why, but their money follows their interests so it has to be for their own purposes. I understand they own some trucking companies in the States and in Mexico. What difference does it make if it does not hurt us? This is politics—we all have supported efforts we considered foolish to keep some group or money source. It is the nature of the beast," Cox answered.

"What about the timing issue? What's the hurry?" Besserman continued. "I don't understand the timing issue either," Cox responded. "All I know is that if we don't have at least the open roads piece in place by Memorial Day, the money goes away. Look, Eric, I know you have a tough race coming up, and you need their support."

"I just don't know about this one," Besserman responded. "I may have to step aside and let someone else carry it. I am not comfortable right now. For me, it does not pass the smell test, and I do not like the back-door attack on religion. I know it's not popular, but religion is a real part of my life and I am kind of partial to having a standard beyond any of us out there as the guide."

Majority Leader Howard finally broke the long silence. "Eric, think about it. This could be a problem for you. It could cost you your leadership position."

"I will think about it," he answered. "You can have my resignation as majority whip any time," and with that, he left and the mood turned somber.

CHAPTER 2

ANOTHER CLUE, ANOTHER OPPORTUNITY

Wednesday, February 6 – MD minus 109 days

A FAMOUS MAN ONCE said, "War always goes per plan until the first shot is fired. Then chaos reigns." So it was in the visible world as people with vastly differing agendas prepared for their next move. It was no longer a celestial chess game, but a battlefield. Those in the fight had a will of their own, making manipulation by forces in the unseen realm difficult and complete obedience unusual. One side sought to control by deception, passion, and cunning; the other looked for people willing to seek and submit in obedience to revelation.

In a human sense, the sides were a total mismatch as the forces of darkness understood what drove the human creatures, and used that to accomplish the Dark Master's purpose. The forces of light did not seek to drive or motivate the flesh, but rather to sanctify the human creatures so they became children of the light; then the Father's will would become their life purpose.

Although the waging of the physical fight was with weapons of death and destruction, the real battle was for the hearts and minds of everyone. Without capturing those, the people would not soldier. It was in the flesh that emotion trumped intelligence, ability, and common sense. The change within brings forth new spiritual birth, which Paul Phillips had been born into.

Unfortunately, even those changed within could still fall prey to manipulation when they took their eyes off Jesus and allowed their emotions to rule. Fear is the greatest of these emotions and the most powerful opposition to the faith.

Creating fear and panic is what Abdul Farsi intended to do in Williams. How would these Americans react to the daily threat of indiscriminate death and destruction? Much had been learned from the shooter, but even that was not a measure of the fear and despair caused when large numbers of innocent people are killed on a regular basis. Farsi hoped that the assassination squads should be able to kill as many as the shooter's total kills with each attack. Sunday would be the test. It should be easy unless the Citizens Militia were deployed to College Church. He had to know for sure.

Grabbing his cell phone, Farsi dialed Tom Campy's number, written on the card he had been given following his interview. "Mr. Campy, I think I am done. I was told that my identification badge would be ready tomorrow and I am available for assignment this weekend when I am out of class. What is happening Saturday and Sunday?"

"Don't know yet about Sunday," Tom answered, "but the security fair is on Saturday and in light of the shootings this morning and the president's statement, I would like you to partner with me in the security detail for that event. After you get your identification badge, give the office a call, and go and get your red jacket. I am thrilled to have you on our team."

"I am equally thrilled with this opportunity," Farsi responded as the call ended. He then returned to the old rent house off Bell and 17th to post a response to Demas Assad and to meet with Sunday's team.

Tom Campy suddenly remembered he should save Farsi's cell phone number in his cell phone directory in case he would need it in future. He took a minute to do that. Getting the number from the incoming calls directory, the area code surprised him. Where is 617 from?

Deployment Completed

In Chicago proper, the Alpha Force had arrived with its equipment. An AWAC aircraft patrolled high above the city, providing independent military intelligence regarding movement of aircraft and the ability to respond almost instantaneously to any threat. Military aircraft were hot and ready waiting on runways in and near the city. Other aircraft capable of monitoring cell phone and radio communications were in the air seeking to intercept any attempt by the terrorists to relay instruction by this medium. Orders had been issued for a pre-dawn deployment and the unmarked radiation detection vans had begun to scour the city.

Major Luther Hedges, the commander on the ground, had completed meetings with state and local leaders and had advised them of the threats. The police in Chicago, Williams, and the surrounding communities had been briefed. Communications were tied together so that any response could be coordinated. The governor had prepared orders to call the National Guard if needed. All was as prepared as possible, and for that moment, at least no one was seeking to benefit politically from the threat. They were all working together to protect the people.

"Mr. President," General Hedge communicated by phone. "Our forces are deployed and ready."

"Thank you General," the president responded. "I pray they are not needed."

Getting Closer

Elsewhere in Washington, a home phone rang. Because of the crisis, additional secure lines had been installed in the homes of all key participants. "Hey David, Geek here again. Sorry to bother you at home, but I got the other one," Darrell Reed blurted out excitedly. "These people are sophisticated but careless. This J-14 fellow posted from Cambridge, Massachusetts, and if you have looked at the website recently, amidst all the gibberish, he got a message from someone in Williams, probably the same guy that sent the last one."

"I haven't looked. What did the message say?" David Barnes asked eagerly.

"Well, it's not much and doesn't seem to go with any other communications I have seen," Reed answered.

"Darrell, what is it?" Barnes insisted.

"Oh, sorry, now I'm playing the analyst. It was only two words, 'J-14. 0-1. All mine.'"

"That makes no sense," Barnes responded in frustration as he mentally sought to decode the message's inverse meaning. "A message without any ties to a prior communication. What is that about? It seems he's denying responsibility, but for what and why?"

"Hey, it's not my league, but maybe someone got in trouble for the shooting in Williams. You know, like all those dead people in dumpsters. Maybe this guy is covering his backside not wanting to join his pals, and he denied responsibility to stay alive. Maybe there was no prior written communication. Maybe someone panicked and made a phone call," Reed suggested.

"You know, this is kind of fun. I see the opposite of the message, 'All mine' means 'none mine,' or 'all someone else's.' Maybe there is hope for me yet if I ever need a different job."

"Can it, Mr. Geek! You are the best at making the box talk. Leave it to me to figure out what it says," Barnes responded. "Got to go and pass this on. Thanks for the great work."

Picking up the phone, Barnes called Tom Knight and passed on the information concluding, "It appears their leader was in Cambridge, Massachusetts, when he posted and he was obviously concerned about the attack on the old man this morning. He must have called the leader in Williams and got a written denial in response. That would confirm the theory of rogue attacks by some of those sent here for MD, or the other type of attacks we are anticipating in Williams."

"Any chance that cell communication could have been monitored?" Knight asked expectantly.

"Not likely," Barnes replied. "We do very little domestic surveillance and what we do has been severely limited by law and by the courts. If this J-14 fellow had called from out of the country, there would be a good chance that the call was monitored... but not from Massachusetts to Illinois, unless there were special circumstances. That is not true over the Chicago area tonight because of the deployment of the Alpha Force, but unfortunately, that call was most likely made before Alpha Force was operational based on the timing of the web posting. I will check anyway and we can put them on notice to watch for calls from Massachusetts."

"Can we do anything from the Cambridge end to monitor calls and catch this J-14 person?"

"I don't know, Mr. Chairman, that is over my head. Perhaps the Attorney General can help. Maybe we can subpoena cell phone records and trace the call by looking at calls made from a 617 area code to a 630 area code. That would be Cambridge to Williams."

"Good idea, David. That just might work. I will call the attorney general and see if we can't get that done tomorrow."

"What do we know about the J-10 person, Chairman Knight asked?"

"We have seen only that one post from Iran," Barnes answered. "Apparently he was there for the MD planning session. That is it right now. We have no confirmation that there are two people. It could be the same with a different mission emphasis. I don't know, but my best guess is that there are two leaders and two very different missions. What we face tomorrow or Sunday in Williams is J-10's project. The whole effort may be under this J-14 in the States. We all know who is running this thing from afar. I wish… "

Interrupted mid-sentence, they both heard, "This is the White House operator. The president wishes to speak to you."

"Tom, David, glad I got both of you at once. You saved me a call. I wanted to invite you two to the White House to join Janet and I for dinner and watch the ITN broadcast if it is not too late. Sorry I didn't call earlier. We have been pretty busy up here with the deployment."

"Thank you, Mr. President," both said at the same time.

"Mr. President," Tom Knight added with a more serious tone, "there is news on the location of the leader and on these rogue attacks. Let us brief you quickly and then we will join you for dinner."

Alexander's Chance

Molech had barely survived his encounter with the Dark Master. Argon was now a mere wisp banished to Europe. Unless something changed, he would not even be allowed to see MD in America. Gone was Molech's arrogance and confidence. It was replaced with anger, hatred, and a new commitment to focus on the real foe.

Molech had been reminded who the war was against. The Enemy's book had laid it out clearly in those visions given to John the Apostle in the years of John's exile on the island of Patmos.

The war is against "those who obey God's commandments and hold to the testimony of Jesus."[4] The real foes are the committed ones; that is why the failure to kill the Bookseller and his young friend was monumental. "There are not that many," he seethed, "but the committed ones are all extremely dangerous to the Dark Master's reign. Somehow, they must die," he screamed into the darkness.

The Dark Master himself had carefully selected and anointed Argon's replacement. It was Alexander, an assistant to the Legion. Alexander had served faithfully in the Middle East. He knew the importance of what was beginning in Williams and had the right darkness in his heart. He had earned his name from the influence he exerted over the human called Alexander, the metalworker of whom the Apostle Paul had written in his last letter, who "did me a great deal of harm."[5] Molech smiled, remembering the pain Paul the Apostle had suffered as he awaited his execution in a Roman prison. Those were good days that he hoped could be repeated.

The relationship had changed. Molech could not treat Alexander with the same disdain he had treated Argon. This one was dangerous because of his historic success, and the fact that he was the Dark Master's selection. He had agreed to take a lower position only because of its importance. Molech would have to watch his back, for Alexander could easily replace him—of which Alexander was well aware. They could not fail again. "It would be easy if we did not have to work through the human creatures," he thought to himself.

Fight for the Message

The world eagerly awaited the clock to strike eight o'clock New York time. That was the time selected by ITN's Carl Stern as the best viewing opportunity for the greatest audience. In an unprecedented decision, the network had decided to broadcast simultaneously on a free feed online, making the show available to anyone with an internet connection, anywhere in the world.

All day long, the promos had played using the portion of the video from the morning shootings and the president's statement, along with a contrast of the Bookseller's comments at the press conference and conflicting statements from pastors. Some thought it was a stretch of the imagination, but ITN had broadcasted some promos with video from 9-11 asking if another such attack was in our future. The title had not changed. It remained, "Williams Fights Back — A City Under Siege," but events had obviously expanded the focus and the opportunity.

The other networks responded with competing specials focusing on the dead terrorists and the president's statement, or they went to the old stand-bys and scheduled a popular movie, reality rerun, or special athletic event, to draw away the audience. All prepared commentaries to respond to anything in the ITN broadcast that threatened their political agendas or worldview. No one other than ITN wanted to give the Bookseller a platform from which to speak, but they were all prepared to criticize whatever he said.

In the invisible world, Molech had gathered the leadership of the forces of darkness to coordinate their response. Keepers and Tempters were being sent to exert influence; either to keep their subjects away from the broadcast or to translate it and use it as a means to inspire evil and hate against religion. If they could not kill the old man, they could perhaps negate his message and make him the target of insults and ridicule. If Chemos really had the control he thought he had over those meeting in the Senate majority leader's office, then soon the Bookseller's conduct would be illegal and he would either have to stop or be arrested.

Alexander scrambled to steer the people of Williams away from the broadcast and to try to interrupt or stop the transmission itself. Unfortunately, he had not been on the job for long and was still assessing those whom he could trust among the human creatures to carry out the Dark Master's will. No one had given serious consideration to what to do about the old man and the broadcast, because he and his young friend were supposed to be dead. Alexander looked in Williams for scoundrels to form a mob, much like he had inspired against the Apostle Paul in Thessalonica thousands of years ago. They did not succeed to kill Paul, but forced him out of the city.[6] Perhaps that would work again. The old man had nowhere to go.

Areopagus, the leader of the forces of darkness in Chicago, volunteered to help by persuading one of the street gangs under his influence to break up the broadcast. He had heard of Alexander's need from scores of dark wisps who had been in Williams, and overheard Alexander's frustrated cries as he searched among an unfamiliar people. Keepers were instructed in what to do, and soon a mob was in cars and vans on their way to the warehouse for a little fun.

They would silence this "holier than thou" old coot.

The forces of light watched the light within begin to burn brighter in believers as the Spirit's influence and guidance were distributed throughout the earth, calling believers to hear God's message — that was even now being given to the Bookseller — and instructing those who had been chosen to act. Guardians heard their instructions to protect believers from the influence of the Dark Master, but also to contest for the hearts and minds of those who were without the light inside. No one would be abandoned to the wishes of the Dark Master this night. The battle would be for every living human anywhere on the planet. There was great excitement and anticipation among the forces of light.

Together Again

Tom Campy literally got up from eating his dinner mid-bite to call Officer Sally Johnson. He realized that his decision to add Abdul Farsi to the Citizens Militia had damaged their relationship, and she was his police contact. Therefore, he felt compelled to act immediately.

"Sally, I have a real concern about the Bookseller's safety during the broadcast tonight. According to the ads, He is to be interviewed live from the warehouse, and I have a fear that the same crowd that tried to kill him this morning may seek to strike during the broadcast. What a set up to send their message to the world — a live broadcast! I just don't have peace about not protecting him, regardless of what he says."

"We are ahead of you on this one," Sally answered. "We have dispatched a force to protect the warehouse during the broadcast as well as after. I will be there shortly. If you want to join us with several of your red-jacketed friends that would be fine, but you may not bring Farsi. I don't trust him."

"I am leaving now," Campy replied sheepishly, "and will call some of the leadership to join with me. They will all be people you know. Thanks for being ahead of me on this one."

"Don't sound so surprised Tom. We serve the same God who has the same will for all of us. He just spoke to me first. See you there."

A Surprise Guest

Those who had gathered waiting to watch the ITN broadcast that night included a crowd in Senate Majority Leader Howard's office surrounding the new television set purchased by Together Tomorrow. Fifteen were also watching in the old rent house off Bell and 17th, one in a garage apartment close to the campus, two in a house in Cambridge, Massachusetts, and several in a room far beneath the earth on the Pakistani/Afghan border. There was also a group meeting in a rented high school auditorium with Pastor Wilson. They had set up TV monitors so that everyone could see the broadcast and hear what the Bookseller said, and then pray together.

In Iran, both Hushai and Ittai had made separate arrangements to meet secretly with other believers with whom they had been praying in response to Gabriel's message to watch together. It was dangerous. They knew the leadership of Iran would also be watching as well as many members of the State Security Forces. There would be few, if any, of the SSF available to search for believers that night.

The dinner in the White House residence had followed a private meeting in the Oval Office where David Barnes and Tom Knight had brought the president up to date on the latest intelligence findings and the need for cooperation from the attorney general in the continuing investigation. Orders had been issued to the AG and the three assembled for dinner. They ate together while watching the ITN special. Barnes and Knight were surprised to find that there was a fourth guest for dinner. Senate Majority Whip Eric Besserman had been invited to join them. "This president never ceases to amaze me," Barnes thought. Tonight would be a night to watch, answer questions, and not volunteer information. Just maybe the president could begin to build a bridge to the other side. There was always hope and it was worth a try. Besserman was a man of character who always placed the country first.

CHAPTER 3

LIVE FROM WILLIAMS

Wednesday, February 6 – MD minus 109

"GOOD EVENING AMERICA. This is Walter Murrow for ITN news. I stand at this moment before Williams College, adjacent to its sign on the front lawn that proclaims to the world that this college is different. It's stated goal is to prepare men and women to serve Jesus Christ: a goal not much different from that originally proclaimed by the founders of Harvard University, who in 1636 declared that every student should 'consider that the main end of his life and studies is to know God and Jesus Christ who is eternal life.' That philosophy has changed at Harvard, but Williams College continues to proclaim the purpose for which it was founded.

"Williams College is arguably the most prominent feature of the city of the same name, which reflects something of the independent character of the college. Williams has recently been a city under siege afflicted by a plague of deaths brought about by an unknown and still at large shooter who kills randomly and seemingly without purpose. Over the past five months, there have been forty-one shootings in this small Midwestern city. The most recent killings occurred this morning and two died. One was a suicide bomber seeking to kill an old man who spoke at a recent press conference here to call on American Christians to pray. The other was a private process server seeking to serve a congressional subpoena to that same old man. Forensic evidence confirms that the Williams' shooter killed them both.

"This morning's shootings were accidentally filmed by employees of this network as they sought to obtain background film for this broadcast. As has been widely reported, the video did not reveal what some eye witnesses say they saw. Did angels actually appear in front of the old man and his young friend to protect them from the shooter? That is a question you will have to answer for yourself after seeing the video and hearing the eye witnesses, who we will present before you this evening.

"Earlier today, President Strong called on all Americans to join together to watch for those of us who have entered our country illegally to do us harm. His statement comes after the bodies of seven unidentified young Arab men killed execution-style were found in cities across the country. That, combined with the explosive vest found on one of the shooting victims here this morning, confirms the president's warning. There are terrorists among us now that have been sent here to do us harm. How should we respond?

"We have come here to Williams because the people of this city have joined together to fight back. This represents the best of America, a people standing together. Williams is an example to all of us of how a people subjected to terror can come together to overcome fear and strike back at the threat. It is an example we all need to consider as we answer the president's call. It is an example we will be watching in the coming days to see how it works in practice to eliminate the threat.

"We also recently heard a controversial call from this city for Americans to pray. It is controversial because it was accompanied by an implied plea that America be what it professes to be, 'one nation under God.' A nation that means what it says on its money, 'In God we trust.'

"Does America really need God's help in this crisis? Is the terrorism we have experienced, and that which threatens us, some form of judgment from God on America?

"Tonight, in a live interview with Samuel Evans White, we will explore these and other questions. Mr. White is the old man from Williams who recently made press conference comments that have caused much controversy. Apparently, he was the terrorist's target this morning. In Williams, he is affectionately called the Bookseller. We will hear from him after hearing from the others, and then you can decide for yourself what God is saying to America, if anything.

"We begin with a history of the threat Williams faces."

Standing behind a large picture board showing all 41 victims, Murrow gave an overview that melted into interviews with surviving victims describing their experience and murdered victims' families telling of their last moments together and how their loved ones died. It was hard to hear the experiences of the victims. The interviews were difficult to conduct.

The focus shifted to law enforcement, not critically, but seeking to understand why this killer has been so difficult to catch. That discussion opened the connection to how this siege was like what Israel faced from terrorist attacks on its civilians in the recent infatida, and how these kinds of attacks were possible across the United States. Experts gave their input on the risk America faced and commentators reviewed the meaning of the president's statement.

Having established the threat Williams faced and the reality that it was the kind of threat that all of America faced, the broadcast shifted to the effects of the siege on the citizens of Williams. Interviews showed how the fear generated by the constant and indiscriminate nature of the killings had changed the people and the city. Experts explained the long- and short-term effects of such a level of fear on any community, and how terrorists can use that to accomplish what they could not by direct military means.

The focus then shifted to the question of what the city of Williams has done to confront the threat of terrorism and reassure its citizens of their security. Murrow provided an overview of how the citizens organized a militia on their own, and how that militia affiliated with the police department. Interviews were shown of representatives of the Citizens Militia and the police. The background checks and training required to be a part of the group were emphasized. Video was shown of red-jacketed groups on patrol and interviews with parents talking about the relief it brought to see their armed neighbors protecting schools, parks, and other public places.

Outside the Warehouse

As the broadcast continued, a crowd began to gather outside the warehouse. ITN had set up large TV screens so that the people who came could see the broadcast. Some prayed, some shouted, and others just watched. There were signs of support and jubilation. The whole scene appeared like the United Supreme Court grounds on an anniversary of Roe v. Wade.

The police and the Citizen's Militia had formed a line in front of the warehouse to keep the crowd back from the entrance, and were prepared to act if required. A caravan of cars arrived from outside the city, with a group wearing gang colors. They carried weapons and began to shout, "Stop the broadcast! No more talk from the old man. End it now!" The gang boldly began to close the distance between themselves and the police.

Officer Sally Johnson, who was in command, immediately ordered the Citizens Militia representatives to stand behind the police and not to leave the entrance to the warehouse regardless of what the police did in response to this new group and their threats. They would be the final line of defense to protect the Bookseller if required. Every police officer was prepared to respond with the level of force necessary to hold the ground. They were not going to be intimidated. They were not going to allow these thugs from the big city control what happens in their town. The police force suddenly brandished automatic weapons and shotguns. The Citizens Militia wielded their firearms. The crowd began to run from the site to a safe distance from where people were gathering to watch the broadcast.

Officer Johnson closed the distance between herself and the apparent leader of the gang quickly with her weapon pointed at his head. She spoke clearly, without fear, and in a firm tone. "You have thirty seconds to clear the street and leave these premises or you will all be placed under arrest, your vehicles searched for illegal substances, your weapons examined forensically to determine whether they have been used in other crimes, and we will run every individual here and their families for outstanding warrants and immigration status. If anyone discharges a weapon, we will shoot to kill and you will die first. Leave now and we will forget you were here and do not come back. You will be arrested on sight."

The gang leader, no fool, turned immediately and said, "We don't have the hardware for this fight. Let's leave this dump."

As they left, they filled the air with curses and obscene gestures, but the air was also filled with applause as the crowd returned, amazed with the courage of the lady cop. She wondered too. Those had not been her words but they were the words the gang leader needed to hear, spoken the way they needed to be said for him to get the message and leave. Evil, when resisted, always flees.[7]

The broadcast then continued uninterrupted, and those in the warehouse had no idea of what had happened outside.

The Interview

While the confrontation outside the warehouse was happening, the broadcast was exploring the concept of the neighborhood watch program. This program entailed citizens providing information on suspicious people and activities in their neighborhood. The police officials interviewed expressed the need for help in preventing crimes and terrorist attacks. Civil rights groups expressed concerns. They cried out against what they saw as the invasion of privacy. There were differing opinions on the matter. The consensus among the citizens interviewed was that they wanted this opportunity to be an integral part of their own security, and they wanted to know that their neighbors were looking out for them.

The interview with Tom and Sally about the upcoming security fair was played after the phone numbers of those desiring to join the Citizen Militia or the neighborhood watch program were placed on the screen. The crowd outside of the warehouse cheered when Sally and Tom appeared on the TV screen. The atmosphere changed to one of excitement and hope that threats would be met with the maximum force possible just as the gang members were confronted.

Everyone closed in for a better view as the discussion shifted to that morning's shootings and the mysterious men in red jackets — that either were there or were not, depending on who you asked and what you believed. The video of the shooting was shown and the witnesses interviewed. The sidewalks and the streets were still marked with the outline of the bodies. The bloodstains were still there. It was eerie to stand where these sad events had occurred only hours before.

The broadcast shifted again as final preparations for the live interview concluded inside the warehouse. The subject became why America faced these threats, and what part religion might have to play in the ultimate solution. The Bookseller's comments at the press conference were played and the world heard him say once again, "I wonder if we could add another dimension to this effort and call on believers everywhere to pray for God's deliverance and for the wisdom to understand why God has allowed this to happen. Allowing 9/11 and its progeny is, after all, His judgment on His people. We must understand why He is angry and change."

These comments were followed by excerpts from sermons, either agreeing or attacking what was said. Included was Pastor Elkhorn's declaration, "Jesus said blessed are the peacemakers for they will be called sons of God, but the person we have all heard from in Williams is anything but a peacemaker. He might be more correctly labeled as a troublemaker."

Pastor Elkhorn's opinion was contrasted with excerpts from the sermon of Pastor Wilson, who said, "What did the Bookseller ask us — his Christian brothers — to do? He asked us to join together and pray. Nothing is more biblical than believers praying together. What did he ask us to pray for? There were two things. First, we were to pray together for God's deliverance. Can anyone take issue with a prayer for deliverance when, in the Lord's Prayer, Jesus specifically instructed us to pray that the Father 'deliver us from the evil one?' You will find that in Matthew 6:13.

"The second prayer request was that we join together to pray for wisdom," Pastor Wilson continued, "specifically wisdom to understand why God allowed 9/11 and has allowed Williams to be terrorized by the shooter. Is that biblical? Wisdom is what James told us to pray for. He wrote, 'If any of you lacks wisdom, he should ask God, who gives generously to all without finding fault and it will be given to him.' That is found in James 1:5. A more significant inquiry might be why we didn't ask for wisdom sooner. Clearly, no one has the answers to that."

The excerpts from Pastor Williams were followed by an interview with the chairman of Senate Homeland Security Committee, Mr. Crow, who said, "I'm in Pastor Elkhorn's camp. The old man is anything but a peacemaker. He incites violence against himself and others. The process server who died this morning was seeking to serve him a subpoena from my committee. We are considering an amendment to the Hate Crimes Act to make religious language that incites violence a hate crime. It is time we stop foreign and domestic terrorists who motivate with religion. You can be assured we will serve that man with a subpoena if he will not come to Washington voluntarily to testify."

Murrow, then live, added, "By contrast, this morning the president had this to say about the Bookseller: 'I would like to close this morning by emphasizing what Mr. White said and ask all Americans to join with me in praying for God's wisdom and deliverance from this threat.'"

Murrow continued, "The views regarding what this man said or meant are polar opposites. Is he well-intentioned seeking to share what he honestly believes God is saying, or should he be seen as a criminal inciting violence and unlawful conduct? You decide. Mr. White is here and we are interviewing him live. He has not seen my questions and we have not discussed the interview beyond the ground rules. Those ground rules are that I can ask him anything I want but we must allow him to complete his answer and may not cut anything out from his answer. There it is. This is reality TV — live with no edits.

"Mr. White, thank you for accepting to be interviewed as part of this broadcast."

"Thank you for the invitation, Mr. Murrow. I certainly do not want to leave people as confused as some of your interviews indicate. Before you begin, I do want to say that the first time I heard that one of the men killed this morning was seeking to serve a subpoena to me was when I heard the Senator's comments. I am so sorry that he was killed trying to get to me. Please tell the senator that he does not need a subpoena to talk to me. I will be glad to talk with him just like I am talking with you, and say again to the family of that man: I am truly sorry for your loss. Do you know his name?"

"I'm embarrassed to say I don't. We really should know that. Doug, can you find that out before the broadcast ends?" Murrow said to an assistant off camera who rushed to call the police to get the name.

"Mr. White, you were almost killed today. Are you afraid?"

"I don't fear physical death. We all know that death is inevitable since man's fall in the garden, but in the Bible, Jesus reveals that He holds the keys of death.[8] I cannot die until He allows me to die and if I am faithful and there are still things He has for me to do, I will live. What I fear is not being faithful and missing the opportunity to do the things He has planned for me to do.

"I also don't fear physical death because it is not an end for believers. It is a beginning, where believers are finally made into what they are intended to be. The Bible teaches that we will become like Jesus when we die. When we are freed from these deteriorating physical bodies by death, that process is completed and we live in His presence.[9] Not a bad future to look forward to. Had they succeeded in killing me today, I would have been like the thief on the cross who went to be with the Lord in paradise.[10] That is certainly not an unhappy ending.

"But I'll tell you what I fear most, Mr. Murrow. I fear for those who are not believers who die physically. It brings me great sorrow. The Bible teaches that they die apart from the Lord, and that on the last day there will be a judgment on everyone.[11] We are all guilty in the sight of a holy God for no one is without sin, but in that moment of judgment, believers will have Jesus standing for them and pleading their case. The defense will not be that they are innocent; it will be a request for a pardon because Jesus has already suffered the penalty for the sins of believers.[12] An unbeliever will have no defense; having rejected Jesus they will not be eligible to receive a pardon. Unbelievers will suffer what the Bible calls the second death —an eternity apart from God living in a just punishment for their sins.[13] Jesus said that is the kind of death we should fear, not physical death."[14]

"Mr. White, you have become controversial, to say the least. How do you explain your sudden prominence and the response of your critics?"

Sighing, the Bookseller answered, "Please, it is important to understand that this is not about me or any other believer. I am not important, and I am not the real target of those you call my critics. I am merely a messenger; one of many. It is the message that they are criticizing because it declares that there is a sovereign God before whom we are accountable. He rules over the affairs of men and He cannot be overcome by any man or nation. The Bible declares that ultimately every knee will bow before Him and acknowledge Him as Lord.[15] My critics are fighting against this truth. I am their target because I am publicly affirming it."

"Mr. White, if believers are being made to be like Jesus, how do you explain violence in the name of serving God? That seems to be contradictory. Jesus was a man of peace."

"Jesus was much more than that, Mr. Murrow. Jesus was not of this world.[16] He was a man of flesh like you and I, but He was also so much more than that. He was God in flesh.[17] When Jesus prayed at the conclusion of the Last Supper, Jesus declared that His followers had become citizens of His Kingdom not citizens of this world.[18] In addition, when He stood before Pilate, Jesus affirmed that.[19]

"The battle Jesus and His followers continue to fight is not a battle in the flesh; it is a battle for the hearts of men and women. That battle rages across the earth, but it is not being fought with physical weapons to injure or kill. The conflict is evident in every person's life. Jesus said, 'Do not suppose that I have come to bring peace on earth. I did not come to bring peace but a sword. For I have come to turn a man against his father, a daughter against her mother, a daughter-in-law against her mother-in-law — a man's enemies will be the members of his own household'.[20]

"The reason this is true is that people have to make a choice in their heart as to who they will follow. Some will choose to follow Jesus, making Him their Lord, but most will follow their own way. Jesus never advocated violence to change an opinion or to force different behavior. In fact, on one occasion when some of His disciples asked Jesus if they should call fire down from heaven on a Samaritan village that had rejected Him, scripture records that 'He turned and rebuked them.'[21] Jesus commanded people to love each other, and one of the ways we can express love is to tell people the truth about Jesus. Only then can people make a knowing choice, and they will live with the consequences of that choice in this world and on the last day. For Jesus said, 'no one comes to the Father except through me.'[22] When someone makes the wrong choice and rejects God, the believer's response should not be anger but sorrow, just like when Jesus cried over Jerusalem."[23]

"Help us please Mr. White. With all the confusion, it is difficult to know what you were trying to say to America. What was the message?"

"I actually did not come with a message for America. I came with a call for the believers in America — and now in the world — to join and pray for God's deliverance and for the wisdom to understand why God has allowed these things to happen. The message for America was really delivered by the president this morning as he called on all Americans to join with him in praying for God's wisdom and deliverance from this threat. What has become controversial is what I said about 9/11 and other terrorist's attacks. I said that 9/11 was a judgment by God on believers, and that believers must stand before Him to find out why He is angry so that they may repent and change. That is a truthful message.

"My critics among believers and unbelievers alike did not listen from their hearts. If they had, and if they had read their Bible, they would have agreed that judgment always begins with the people of God.[24] God is not surprised that unbelievers act like unbelievers, but when believers act like unbelievers, God must act to protect His good name — which they are destroying by their lifestyle. If you were to ask any group of ten people in America what single word best describes those who call themselves Christians, the unanimous answer would be 'hypocrite,' and they would be right.

"Here is a simple truth: God will do or allow whatever it takes to reclaim His people for Himself. Unfortunately, for those who are unbelievers and live in America, the 'whatever it takes' will fall on them as well as on the believers among them. God will allow many horrors and natural disasters until His people seek Him in prayer and are changed. When they are changed, the nation will be changed and God will again extend His arm of protection."[25]

"Mr. White, our time is almost up. One last question, how should we as a nation and as individuals respond to the threat of terrorism?"

The Bookseller was silent for a moment in prayer before answering, and then he said, "You will find the answer in 2 Chronicles 20:12."

"Well, what does that say?" Murrow asked.

"Look it up and you will remember," the Bookseller answered.

Frustrated and out of time, Murrow sought to close when his assistant, Doug, called out, "James Harper. That was the process server's name."

"Thank you," the Bookseller replied. "If you have a phone number, can I have it after the show ends? I would like to call the family and pray with them."

"I am honestly at a loss for words," Murrow declared to his unseen audience of millions.

"There is so much more I would like to ask, Mr. White, and so much more I would like to say about what is happening here in Williams... but we have to close this broadcast. ITN will stay in Williams reporting on future events. Perhaps we will have another opportunity to continue this discussion with Mr. White and let you, our audience across America and around the world, submit questions. Back in New York, please put a question up on the website to see if people would like to hear more from Mr. White and have a chance to ask him questions.

"One final thought: tonight has been unusual. There were no commercial breaks in this presentation. The companies that banded together to sponsor this special broadcast made that decision. We at ITN have listed these sponsors and their products on our website. As this broadcast ends, we ask you to take a moment now to view the list and to express your appreciation to these sponsors by purchasing their products or services.

"For now, from Williams, this is Walter Murrow for ITN News. Good night."

Off camera, Murrow was heard yelling, "Doesn't anyone have a Bible?"

CHAPTER 4

THE AFTERMATH

Wednesday, February 6 – MD minus 109 days

AS THE BROADCAST ended, the president turned off the set with the remote, turned to Janet and said, "I know that passage. I read it in the Oval Office. Do you guys remember?"

"Yes, Mr. President," Tom Knight replied, "and frankly I was shocked at the time."

"It is a cry of desperation from Judah's king who faced an overwhelming force," the president continued. "It was an acknowledgment of the nation's need for God's intervention if it was to survive. I feel that way with what we face. They cannot defeat us with an army, but they can destroy the willingness of the people and the politicians to stand against them. Then they will not need an army to win."

"What exactly does the verse say?" asked Senator Besserman.

The president reached over to a coffee table by the couch and picked up his Bible and turned to 2 Chronicles 20:12 and read:

> *O our God, will You not judge them? For we have no power to face this vast army that is attacking us. We do not know what to do, but our eyes are upon You.*

"God sent an answer to the prayer. In verse 14, He spoke through one of His servants.

'Listen, King Jehoshaphat and all who live in Judah and Jerusalem! This is what the Lord says to you: do not be afraid or discouraged because of this vast army. For the battle is not yours but God's.' That next day as they marched out for battle, they were led by singers appointed by the King who sang and praised God. When they arrived at the place of battle, it was already over. Their enemies lay dead."[26]

Pausing to let that sink in fully, the president turned his full attention to the Senate majority whip. "Eric, you and your colleagues on the Hill are unaware of the serious nature of the threats that have been discovered by our intelligence community and on which we have been laboring mightily. What I tell you now is completely confidential and must not be shared with anyone until we are prepared to respond."

"You are asking that I listen to what you have to say and not share it with the majority leadership in Congress? Do I understand you correctly?" Besserman responded.

"You do perfectly, and when I am through you will understand what I am asking you to do and why."

"Mr. President, for some reason I trust you on this one. I agree to maintain confidentiality until you either advise me that I am at liberty to speak or you go public with this."

Knight and Barnes sat open-mouthed in shock at what was playing out before their eyes. This senator was in leadership with the group that was trying to destroy President Strong and the president was taking him into his confidence. It made no sense, however, what makes sense in a world where people want to kill you simply for being an American?

"Eric," the president continued, "We believe that right now we face a two-pronged assault, one of which is pure indiscriminate terrorism for the purpose of destroying America's will to stand and fight in the Middle East. The other, much more dangerous, has been designed to neutralize our ability to respond militarily beyond nuclear, and would effectively destroy our way of life for years, if not decades.

"As we speak, the Alpha Force has been deployed to Chicago to counteract a possible terrorist attack tomorrow or Sunday. We believe that our intelligence is good, but we don't know the specific target or the nature of the attack. We have taken every precaution we know, and the call for public involvement was actually a call for citizen's eyes and ears to help us locate and eliminate the threat before they can carry out their plans. I say this to you so you can measure my request by what happens over the next few days.

"My request is for your help in dealing with the larger threat. You probably saw the *Times Daily* article by George Murphy on Tom Knight's involvement with a secret commission. That commission is privately known as the Survival Commission because we believe that our survival as a nation is what is at risk in this second effort. We believe one of our original commissioners, Pete Matthews, is leaking information to Murphy and we risk disclosure before we are prepared to respond. I want to remove Matthews and replace him with you. That is the request. I trust you and your experience. I know that you will make independent judgments on matters the commission is considering and will also be invaluable at providing us with guidance on how and when to bring in congressional leadership.

"Think about it, Eric. I need to know by tomorrow morning as the commission will be dealing with critical matters as the week progresses, particularly if we are correct on an attack tomorrow or Sunday. If you are going to be on the commission, I need your involvement and input now."

"Mr. President, you need to know that I may not be your best choice if the purpose you have in mind is a bridge to the opposition. I am not on the same page with the Senate leadership and may be resigning my post as majority whip. They have a program that will likely be announced tomorrow that I cannot support. They are going to confront you head-on with this issue."

"Eric, the American people know and trust you because of your independent judgment. Whether you have a formal position or not, the country will still listen to you when you speak. More importantly for me, you will have something to say. The only bridge I need from you is the bridge to the answer of how to fully identify and eliminate this threat. I believe you can help me there, and in the process, provide some guidance on how to communicate with more reasonable members of the majority."

"I can do that, Mr. President. This is clearly bigger than any political party or election." He was surprised at his trust in someone who had been his political enemy for so long. It was unnatural and he knew the cost would be high. Cox and others in leadership were vindictive, but he felt compelled to invest himself fully for the good of the country.

"Tom, I want you and David to meet with Eric first thing tomorrow morning and brief him on all facets of the investigation to date," the president responded. "We need him brought up to speed as quickly as possible. I want his input on the Iranian threat and how we can involve Israel to both gain their help and warn them of what may be coming to help them prepare. Eric knows Prime Minister Zimri. Perhaps he can be our conduit — someone they know and trust."

" Mr. President, you wouldn't say that if you knew the majority leadership was prepared to sell out Israel to make peace with the terrorists," Besserman responded.

"Yes, but you have been consistent on standing with Israel, and as long as I am president, America will stand for Israel without standing against the independent Arab states. I do not believe that to be an inconsistent policy. There are two sides to every story, but the answer is not to the destruction of one or the other."

"Joshua," Janet Strong interrupted quietly, placing her hand on her husband's. "We just heard another call for prayer from Mr. White, and you men have been discussing the very survival of this nation and Israel. That passage of scripture spoke to me. I agree that what Judah's King said so long ago also applies to us today, 'We do not know what to do.' So our eyes better be on God. Can we take a few minutes to pray as we have been called to do by our brother in Williams?

"I don't know all of you and hope I am not embarrassing you, but I need to pray right now," she continued, her voice deep with emotion. Taking the president's hand, she began to pray and the others joined. Some silently and some aloud. The point had been well made. Don't just talk about prayer — pray!

Response in the Invisible

The reaction across America and around the world was as had been before: millions reached for their Bibles to find out what the Bookseller meant by his last answer, while those who had no Bibles turned to their browsers and apps. In countries that deny access to the Bible, there were tears as people faced the reality that they could not know what the last answer meant. Fortunately, in the New York office of ITN, the computer technician assigned to put Walter Murrow's question up on the website intentionally decided to first post the whole interview, including all of the 20th Chapter of 2 Chronicles. Suddenly, anyone in the world with internet access could see the Bookseller's interview and the answers in one place.

In the invisible world and across the darkness that had blinded much of humanity, it was as if a gauntlet had been thrown down. The passage of scripture the Bookseller had shared declared that there was a God and only He could deliver humans from the threat they faced. That passage was a declaration that the god of the terrorist was not the one true God. The forces of darkness and those under their influence understood the risk of such declarations and the opportunity they presented. This was a Mount Carmel moment, where the people of old had to choose who they believed was God and the real God evidenced Himself by action in response to their prayers.[27]

The forces of light rejoiced at the challenge for they knew the Holy Spirit would not have given that scripture to the Bookseller unless the Father was prepared to answer the prayer of His people — if they would pray and stand before Him to be changed. In the physical world, the test would be viewed as a contest between competing deities or religions. In the invisible world, it was solely a test of whether God's people were ready to return to Him. God remained sovereign and omnipotent.

Even the darkness had to admit that truth, but not visibly. That was the advantage of living with a language of lies.[28] They could know the truth but proclaim a lie. The lie would always prevail unless someone stood for the truth. The president and the Bookseller had begun to challenge the lie. But would that be enough? Would it be in time?

The Dark Master called together his leadership counsel including Molech, Chemosh, Legion, Baal, Asherah and Ashtoreth to deal with the challenge. His voice seethed venomously, "We need to infuse our followers with anger and hatred at what that cursed old fool proclaimed," he declared. "They need to all become like Demetrius, who would have eliminated the Bookseller had Molech's plan not failed with the shooter. The Enemy won that battle, but not the war. These Christians talk, but they don't pray and they don't really trust the Enemy in their personal lives. They believe in Him for eternal life — fire insurance — but they don't believe in Him for the here and now. The simple fact is that they do not obey. All but a few will ignore the call to pray and they can easily be driven to silence, living in fear.

"Everything needs to move forward quicker and with more violence. Kill Christians and Jews and anyone who even expresses interest. Destroy that pretentious Christian nation, America. Now get out of my sight until you succeed. No excuses. This is my victory. Even the Enemy will help us destroy them if we can keep these people from praying. Do whatever it takes."

The World Responds

In the aftermath of the broadcast, a gathering in a room far beneath the earth on the Pakistani/Afghan border pondered on what they had just heard in light of the planned execution squads and MD. "America's leader has been awakened," the Sheik observed, "but he has no idea what to do. He is grasping for answers. This Bookseller is the ultimate infidel, but he will soon be silenced by the coming events. Do not fear this man or the God he says he serves. There is no power that can overcome us if we do not stop the fight. They cannot walk in fear or with pain for many days. That was proven in Vietnam and again in Iraq and Afghanistan. These Americans are cowards. They will run from violence on their own shores and elect leaders who will give us what we want. Just watch."

In Iran, two believers prayed and excused themselves from their separate meetings for the flag was up and there was news.

Elsewhere, a member of the SSF concluded a discussion on a plan to find and identify Iranian Christians. It should work, he thought.

In Cambridge, Massachusetts, the two known as J-10 and J-14 faced more pragmatic issues. On the one hand, in response to the president's call, the Americans would now be looking for their operatives. On the other hand, the operatives were frustrated with waiting. Not everything was in place. The final piece — the open roads legislation — was not even out of committee. They would both know more after Sunday happenings in Williams, but the reality was that they might need to change the

MD plan and move the date forward. How soon could things be ready here and in Iran? They had to make decisions quickly and coordinate with other leaders here and abroad. They were thankful for the coming AEA Convention when they would all be together once again. That would be the opportunity to coordinate a revised schedule.

The fifteen watching in the old rent house off Bell and 17th understood that their world had changed once again. Now they would have to be even more careful because of the call for citizen involvement. They were concerned with the development of the Citizens Militia, but most were thankful that Farsi was now on the inside. They would know before Sunday whether Citizens Militia forces had been deployed to College Church. Doeg did not care much about the Sunday discussion. His thoughts remained on the attack he planned at the Security Fair on Saturday. No one with a red jacket would be safe there that night.

"You saw for yourself the challenge of the old man," Farsi said. "Did you hear what he said? He has declared on two occasions now that there is no god but his God. He says the reason for the violence is that his God is angry with Christians. He has the 'angry with Christians' part right but not whose god is God."

"When our attacks are completed, these Christians will experience real fear and see for themselves that this God they serve cannot rescue them from our hands. It is god's work we do and we must not fail. Sunday we will begin. Prepare yourselves to kill these infidels."

In the garage apartment close to the campus, Susan had watched in stunned silence. The film of the attack did not reveal what she had seen. Her car, which was in the direct line of the filming, was also not shown. It was as if she had been protected even as the Bookseller and his young friend were protected. She remembered the flash of light shown on the video. That was how she escaped. Had the angel protected her even though she had missed her targets? Nothing in what the old man said that night made him sound like a religious fanatic. She was confused and troubled. It seemed that the angel was lying to her. The game had become a never-ending nightmare as she considered what she had done. In desperation, she began to pray — to whom, she did not know — but she wanted to understand and know what to do.

In Washington, former president Cox was again in a rage, but he kept his shoe on and the new television survived. "Where is Besserman?" he asked. "Why isn't he here? Have we lost him on this one?"

"I don't know, but the signs are not good," Majority Leader Howard replied. "We better be prepared to announce a replacement for him tomorrow when the push begins."

"That low life SOB," Cox answered. "If he backs out on us, I will run against him myself. A former president can be a senator. I would slaughter him."

"You might want to think that one through a time or two," Chairman Crow added. "Unlike former presidents, we senators have to disclose sources of income and have other ethical limitations which would require you to change the way you live. I don't think you are ready to give up Together Tomorrow's little retainer just yet, are you?"

"You are right, of course," Cox admitted, "but we can't let these people win. Somehow we have to take the initiative and restore some sanity to this government. How did that silly old man ever get on national TV anyway?"

"I don't know and I don't care," Howard answered. "He isn't running for office and his audience will soon evaporate if we present an alternative. All he has done is present another way to confront terrorism using religion. The terrorists use religion to move their agenda. There is no difference. Let us get back to the game plan and push the agenda of peace while attacking those who use religion to stir up hate and violence. Now, who do you suggest as a replacement for Besserman if we have lost him?"

What Now

The website at ITN was deluged with hits. Many web visitors were seeking more information on the broadcast and they wanted to answer the question on whether the bookseller should be interviewed again. An unprecedented multitude overpowered the website from across America and around the world. It would take hours for everyone seeking the opportunity to express their opinion to do so. The early compilations showed over 80% of the listeners wanted to hear more from the Bookseller and have their questions answered. The majority of listeners with questions were along the same lines: "Are you telling us that God is no longer on

America's side?" Jim Hunt and Carl Stern were already reviewing their success and planning what they were to do next.

The mayor of Williams was also considering his options. He liked the publicity given to the city as a place that stood together against violence, but could not personally stomach the violence. Forty-one shootings were hard to comprehend, even living through them. Picking up the phone he called the police chief. "Harold, I don't care what the Bookseller says, put 24/7 security on him and in the warehouse. He has become a national figure who represents Williams. There has already been one attempt on his life. We cannot allow another shooting, particularly after tonight's broadcast. He must be protected."

"I will certainly follow your orders, Mr. Mayor. Though, based on what happened this morning, he seems to be well protected without us."

CHAPTER 5

NEW DISCOVERIES AND CHANGES

Thursday, February 7 – MD minus 108 days

ITTAI DROVE QUICKLY back to the hotel, reviewing in his mind the events of the past few days and trying to organize his thoughts. He carried with him the message from the Bookseller and information relating to the possible attack in Williams or Chicago. He struggled to understand the seeming contradiction of MD and recent events. He wanted to know what Hushai had learned, but was afraid of what he might hear. Events were moving too quickly. He could not help but wonder if they would hear again from the angel Gabriel. He had sought to obey God's command by gathering groups of believers to pray. It was dangerous but wonderful to join together. They were so isolated from one another in this land of oppression. To be together filled him with joy.

"My brother," he said as Hushai entered the cab and they departed to their secret place of meeting and prayer, "I must share with you the message from the old man. He answered us immediately," and he handed him the note still in the envelope marked Top Secret Eyes Only.

Hushai read the note and paused silently, taking in the message and the instruction to not be afraid. "The words read differently than they would have in light of what he said tonight and the attempt on his life. What is Hebrews 4:13?"

"That is the real encouragement for me," Ittai answered. "I have memorized it and repeat it often when I am discouraged as we seek to discover the details of the MD plan. It reads, 'Nothing in all creation is hidden from God's sight. Everything is uncovered and laid bare before the eyes of Him to whom we must give an account.' He is telling us that God knows of this plan and is faithful. If God's people are faithful to turn back to Him and pray, it will be disclosed in time. If not, we will have brought this on our own heads."

"That is a frightening truth," Hushai added, pausing again to consider the full implications of what had been said. "I am afraid the old man's call to pray the prayer of King Jehoshaphat is truer than he knows. Ittai, do you know of Nicholas Vandenberg and Joseph Krenski? Are those names familiar to you?"

"I know the names," Ittai responded. "Isn't Vandenberg a former Russian general and Krenski former head of the KGB?"

"You are correct. Vandenberg and Krenski remain forces of power in today's Russia. They have the ear of President Sorboth and are part of the leadership group that has never gotten over the demise of the Soviet Empire or the loss of its position as a player in world events. They would reestablish the Soviet Union by force if they could. They hate what they see as the arrogance of America in the world and Israel in the Middle East. Like the terrorists, they are enemies motivated from their hearts. Both were here yesterday at the invitation of the Iranian president."

"Have you been able to find out why?" Ittai asked.

"Not specifically, but it appears to be connected to Iran's response to MD. Whatever they learned when they detained and searched the crowd leaving the meeting at the training camp in Kerman Province has convinced them that MD is real and can happen. They continue to plan for a post-United States world. To get there, they have to negate the US nuclear option so they can go after Israel and have a free hand in the Middle East. The information I have obtained is that they are offering Russia an opportunity to become the lead outside player in the Middle East. I believe they are exploring some form of defensive alliance which they hope would keep a crippled post-MD America from striking back with nuclear weapons and gives the Soviets the excuse they have been looking for to be a part of eliminating the nation of Israel."

"You cannot be serious," Ittai responded. "This president would never surrender Israel to a nuclear threat and he will not allow Iran a free hand in the Middle East. It will not happen."

"You are assuming that President Strong survives the MD attacks, politically as well as physically," Hushai answered. "He has the character to stand but the issue is not his character, the issue is the character of the American people. Does this generation have the courage and perseverance of prior generations who suffered significant defeats over long periods but stood together fighting until there was a victory? Those generations had praying leaders like Washington and Lincoln, but they also had the foundation of a strong church — believers throughout America who prayed and were willing to sacrifice for the sake of victory. I fear that is missing today, which is the reason we heard what we heard from Gabriel and why God has given the old man opportunities to call His people to pray and stand before Him. God wants to restore what has been lost in America and around the world.

"You have heard of the political opposition President Strong faces from the majority party. It is worse than you think. I am told that Saudis working with the terrorists are financing and influencing the opposition who are furthering the terrorists' goals with the politicals advancing that agenda in complete ignorance. Politics in America have become so short sighted that the politicians consider only the next election — what it will cost to win and what the people think or can be manipulated to think. That may be the way to power today but it is not leadership. The poll-driven agendas sacrifice long-range vision for today's election win. God has no place in the 'what I want now' system, which is where America is heading at full speed. I believe that what we are seeing is God saying, 'Stop or live with the consequences of your folly. I will no longer allow you to use My name in vain.'"

"I didn't realize you were such a student of the American folly," Ittai answered. "Unfortunately, you are right on with what has happened to their political system. It started out as a republic and has been transformed into what they now call a 'democracy'. People forget that fools and tyrants have been elected over the centuries when election alone is the goal. Hitler was elected because he said what the people wanted to hear. Then he proceeded with his real agenda that the earth has yet to recover from. They got what they wanted and suffered the consequences. America may be next."

"Enough of this frustration, we are not American politicians. What have you learned?" Hushai asked.

"Before we go there, let me ask: Hushai, what do you know about these Saudis?"

"Very little," Hushai answered, "but it is clear they are both the financiers and active facilitators of MD. They are equally as terroristic as Ahmad Habid, the Iranian who commanded attacks against Americans in Iraq. They are evil people who intend to see America crushed and forced out of the Middle East. Is there any further leak on how MD is to proceed?" Hushai pushed. "What weapons? What targets? How will they be delivered?"

"All I can tell you is that they know," Ittai answered gravely. "Whatever they got from the planners lays everything out in extreme detail. If we can get our hands on what they have, we will know the answer to all the questions and the Americans should be able to stop the attacks. Unfortunately, that information is not in the hands of those I work with. Access has been limited to a few who are out of my circle of influence. That is why I say we are like King Jehoshaphat. We do not know what to do and our eyes better be on the one who does."

"What about the Americans?"

"There has been some real progress, but not enough," Hushai responded. "What I tell you now is for you alone — unless you need it to bargain for other information.

"The Americans think they have made some progress in locating one of the means of communication and may have broken some of the code used by the leaders. They have identified what they think are two different leaders of two very different strategies. One is MD, but the other is some type of terrorist strike not necessarily connected to MD. They will know more in the next few days. If they are right, there will be a terrorist attack in Williams or Chicago by Sunday at the latest. If that does not happen, then it is back to square one, starting all over again.

"They believe their intelligence is good. That is why the president made his statement regarding citizen involvement. They are hoping someone will see something and report it to local law enforcement in the

Chicago area. They went national to cover their knowledge of the Chicago area threat and to get people in place to start looking for unusual signs created by preparation for MD. They had to say something after the execution of the seven terrorists and the attack on the Bookseller resulting in a terrorist being killed."

"Wasn't it amazing how God protected him?" Ittai interrupted. "It must have been angels dressed as members of the citizen's military group shielding him. I almost had to laugh when I heard what happened. Evil destroying evil, only God could do that."

"Yes, and we, of course, have no trouble believing in angels after our last time together," Hushai agreed.

"I will tell you this: they believe that 'MD' is Memorial Day and that is when the massive attack is scheduled. They are seeking confirmation, but that is the tentative timetable."

"Tentative may be right," Ittai inserted. "With the need to execute some of their own operatives, don't be surprised if they move it up. I seriously doubt that the terrorist killed trying to blow up the old man was sent by anyone connected with the MD operation. One of their real problems is that their killers can't be controlled. I believe they are running out of time. I know we are.

"My contacts within the SSF tell me that they are going to strike out hard against Christians gathering to pray or study the Bible. He was candid with me. If I am caught with such a group, even though they have valued my services, I am dead. They wouldn't even give me a second thought."

"On that somber note, I think it's time to pray," answered Hushai.

Once again, the forces of light surrounded the car, creating an impenetrable barrier to the forces of darkness and causing the vehicle to be invisible to the human eye. Together, these two watched the sun rise as they closed their little prayer meeting and sped off to return to the hotel and another day to obey the instructions given by the angel Gabriel.

The Battle for Hearts

The president and Bookseller's call to prayer was heard by believers throughout America and around the world for whom prayer was not a new experience. Spiritual leaders in churches and home Bible study groups were all sent the same message as the voice inside echoed the call given through the angel Gabriel: "Stand together and pray." Their numbers were few, relative to the number who claimed to be Christians, but their faith was great and the call was clear. As they prayed, each began to seek guidance on how they could obey and gather others to pray. While praying, they all encountered the Holy Spirit who began to deal with them individually regarding anything which God saw as sin in their lives. There was shock and sadness at the reality of sin they had for so long overlooked or covered up. It was not about others, but about their own sin. They saw clearly that they needed to be changed, and their response was to cry out for forgiveness. When they did, they were both heard and changed.

In the invisible, scores of thousands of Tempters were physically removed from believers and their return blocked by Guardians. The light within began to burn brightly as Providers were dispatched to encourage and enable the committed ones to stand together and pray. The specific individual direction came with the commitment. They had stood before the Lord and been changed. Separately they all began to pray the prayer of Jehoshaphat, "We don't know what to do, but our eyes are upon You."

Decisions were being made in the invisible as many who held formal leadership positions in churches and Christian ministries ignored the call to pray and continued with their existing program and practices as before. Having rejected God's clear call, God now rejected them as leaders and passed the mantle of leadership onto others who may have held no position in the visible world but who had a heart like King David of whom God said, "I have found in David, son of Jesse, a man after My own heart; he will do everything I want him to do." [29] Those unwilling to change became like Saul, Israel's first King. He still held the position, but God had replaced him and anointed David as king. Saul's usefulness to God had ended. God's blessing went to David.[30]

The light burned dimly in the hearts of those unwilling to lead in prayer. In them, the Dark Master released Tempters and Keepers to draw them further away from obedience and into conflict with those who sought to obey the Spirit's leading. It was another front in the continuing battle within local churches and among those who called themselves Christians.

Susan Finally Sees

For Susan Stafford, it was a forced return to a place she did not want to be; but this time her eyes were wide open as Molech again assumed the visible form of an angel of light and her room was filled with the brilliance of an unnatural glow. She recognized the unearthly voice as he spoke, "You have failed in executing god's judgment. The young man lives and so does the old man who continues to preach lies and deceive many into the second death. You must attack again or serve the damnation of the second death yourself. The two will meet again at the warehouse Friday morning at 8:00 AM. You must be there waiting for them and kill them both. This time, the old man first. He has become more dangerous because of his access to the media. His lies are broadcasted worldwide. He must be silenced."

"Who are you anyway?" was Susan's disrespectful response. "I did exactly what you commanded, yet something more powerful than you protected that boy and old man. I could not even see them, and one of the people I killed was actually a terrorist with a bomb who also intended to kill them, along with many innocents. Did you send him too? You may have special powers and the ability to manipulate light, but from what I know you are not an angel and you have lied to me.

"I watched the old man on the broadcast tonight. He was not seeking to deceive and lead anyone to suffer the eternal judgment of the second death. All he did was call Christians to pray. No real angel would oppose that."

"Oh, you would like to know who I am? Indeed, I'll show you who I am," said Molech, his voice deepening with a harrowing insidiousness. The room suddenly became heavy with a darkness so unnatural and deep like that of a tomb. "I represent the Dark Master, the keeper of hell, the one who carries away the dead in the second death amongst screaming and gnashing of teeth. You, a mass murderer, have already reserved for yourself a place in the hottest part of hell. There is no hope for you. If you do not obey, I will take you there now. Obey or die."

Molech boldly spoke his lie, for God had not yet allowed for Susan to die. Suddenly, the Curtain was opened and momentarily Susan saw Molech for what he was. His hideous form looming over her, dark with fiery orange eyes, bright yellow skin and huge hands with enormous long fingers. She smelt of burning sulfur. Yet strangely, she was not afraid.

Looking evil straight in the eye, with tears streaming down her cheeks, she said, "I have killed or injured scores of innocent people for which I am accountable and for which I deserve the second death. I cannot change that reality, but I will not be your instrument for any more murders. I know now that it was you who lead me into devaluing human life, playing murder out like a game. I am as evil as you are. Kill me if you will. I deserve whatever comes."

As suddenly as it had been opened, the Curtain closed and there was silence. Susan knew that this leader of darkness had departed from her. She still lived, but wondered why. Had the Curtain remained opened, she would have seen what Paul Phillips experienced in the cemetery; for a Guardian had been assigned to her and it was he who overcame her Keeper, opening her eyes and freeing her from hordes of Tempters. Now she was free to become a searcher. However, was it too late?

Besserman Decides

The knock on the door was answered at the Washington DC apartment only because he recognized the voice. "Besserman, it's 5:00 AM," Majority Leader Howard complained. "Not even God is up at this hour. What do you want?"

"I have a letter for you and wanted to show you the courtesy and respect of delivering it myself first thing this morning. I know what you have planned for today, and I wanted you to know of my decision before you go forward with the press conference. I am resigning my position as Senate Majority Whip. I cannot support the policies former President Cox and Chairman Crow are pushing. I believe that President Strong is right on this one and we should be the loyal opposition and criticize where we disagree, but not to try to cut his legs off as he battles what I believe is the fight of this generation. We need to work with him, not try to destroy him."

"Eric, you better think this through and reconsider. If you do this and resign, it is over for you as a party leader. You will probably be finished altogether. You should expect to encounter a carefully selected, well-funded opponent in next year's election. Are you really willing to give up what you have worked for all these years? You are a man of position and power."

"It's not about me," Besserman responded. "It is about preserving

America and returning the nation to the principle of self-sacrifice rather than 'what's in it for me.' This is bigger than you or me. It is bigger than any party or the election. We cannot survive as a country if we continue to polarize every issue and divide ourselves into competing groups for selfish purposes. We must come together and stand against these enemies seeking to destroy us."

Handing Howard the letter, Besserman continued, "I am reminded of Benjamin Franklin's comments in Congress just before signing the Declaration of Independence. Remember what Franklin said: 'We must, indeed, all hang together or most assuredly we shall all hang separately.' That is how we must approach the threat this nation faces now. I am truly sorry that you will not join with the president. You will live to regret your decision more than I will my resignation."

Howard accepted the letter with sadness and concern. Eric Besserman had been a faithful public servant who had advanced the party's agenda for decades. What, he wondered, could have changed his mind?

The letter read as follows:

Majority Leader Howard:

It is with regret that I tender my resignation as Senate Majority Whip, effective immediately. I have consented to accept an appointment from the president to serve with others on a commission seeking to deal with the current threat this nation faces. I will retain my Senate seat and continue discharging my duties there for the people of my state, but the agenda currently being advanced by the party is inconsistent with my service on the commission and my belief in what is best for our country at this time. I have appreciated the opportunity to serve my country and party in this position and it is with great sadness that I have made this decision.

Eric Besserman

Shaking his head, Howard grabbed the phone and placed a call to the still sleeping former president.

CHAPTER 6

MAJORITY PARTY'S RESPONSE

Thursday, February 7 – MD minus 108 days

AS FORMER SENATE Majority Whip Besserman closeted himself with Chairman Knight and David Barnes to catch up on the activities of the Survival Commission, his Senate office released his letter of resignation to the press and copies were delivered throughout the Capitol to other members of his party. Moments later, the phone rang in his office to disinvite him to a party caucus and majority's press conference scheduled for later that morning. Not unexpected, he thought.

Later in the Senate Caucus Room, the whole protracted story was laid out with a definitive majority party spin. Leading the presentation was Majority Leader Howard and Chairman Crow. Attending by invitation was former President Cox.

"Here is our recommended way of proceeding," the majority leader continued. "The leadership has nominated Senator Caperton to replace Besserman. We cannot afford the time or diversion of a contested election in the process of filling the majority whip position, so we ask that this is approved unanimously by voice vote." They approved, but many were clearly not happy with the way this was being stuffed down their throats, particularly some who wanted the position themselves.

"Besserman is being stripped of committee leadership positions and is being reassigned to places where he will have less influence over policy and less opportunity to speak publicly. The leadership wants to make a statement here. We will not tolerate such disloyalty. There must be party unity on key party positions during an election cycle."

"Wait a minute. Don't you think that there should be a decision of the caucus after hearing his side of the policy disagreement?" inserted Senator Baker. "We all know Eric Besserman. He has been loyal to this party and he is a man of integrity. In his letter, he makes some strong public statements about our policy. He would not do that without a good reason. I for one want to know why he has taken such a strong position."

"Well, you for one can ask him," Howard responded. "He will get no invitation from leadership to create further division."

"Is it now considered division when a member of the caucus wants to talk through an issue?" Baker responded. "Are you saying that we who have been elected by the people of our states don't have a say in our party's agenda? I did not come here to be subject to some absolute authority to tell me how to think and vote. I worked hard to get elected and have been here four terms now. I will join in policy I agree with or which does not negatively affect my state or the country, but I will not be told I can't think or question a proposal put forward by anyone in my party," he said with increasing anger.

"I am not your political lackey! If you want to treat me like you have chosen to treat Besserman, do it, but you better think of the consequences to you and to this party of a real internal revolution. I am tired of it and ready for that fight."

The temperature in the room was rising as the open conflict threatened to spill over. "What I am saying is that without party discipline, nothing advances and we will not remain in the majority," Leader Howard responded. "If you want the privileges that go with being in the majority party, then you must follow the leadership or there will be consequences. Have I made myself clear?"

Almost in a rage, Senator Baker rose from his seat to leave the room when former President Cox jumped up and blocked his way out. "Hold on everyone. This is getting out of hand. Sam, please sit down and hear me out." Respect for the former president overcame Senator Baker and he sat down.

"The majority leader's bedside manner could use some work, but we all know that Howard is right in what he is saying. Sam is also right and has been here a long time. The two positions are not inconsistent and it is my understanding that the precise reason we are here is to talk through policy and confirm the party's positions and strategy. Besserman was warned of the consequences of publicly rebuking the party's position. He knew, and yet he chose to challenge all of us in this room. That cannot go unaddressed."

"Listen to me," Cox continued with gravity in his voice. "We are at a critical time in the future of our party. This president is vulnerable. Now is the time to crush him and render the religious right powerless. We have a source of funds to take him and every member of his party on in the coming election cycle. If we are careful, we can control Congress and the White House with a sixty-vote majority in the Senate, for at least a generation. We will be unstoppable. Listen to the plan. It has been well thought out. Join with us. It is good for America but more than that, it is the salvation of our party and the assured defeat of theirs.

"Mr. Majority Leader, take us through the plan," and with that, the power point presentation began.

"If we are to win this battle for control, we must take the offensive and lead in a new direction that accomplishes our purposes and captures the emotions of the American people so they will follow," Leader Howard explained. "Americans want to be passionate about something. We must both create and feed the passion. To do that we have to have a catch phrase that overcomes what they have been able to do with 'the war on terror.' That single phrase creates immediate thoughts in the mind of the hearer that prejudices them against any competing agenda. Our phrase must trump that.

"If we have been successful at anything, it is in placing the blame for undesirable circumstances on another. Americans do not want to look themselves in the eye and say that they are the cause of their own problems or that they deserve what they are getting. Americans want to point the finger at another and blame them for bad circumstances or for poor conduct. As a result, they don't really believe that people are inherently evil, they believe that people become evil because of something others do or because of their circumstances. Americans are prepared to excuse almost anything if they can find a way to justify the conduct based on something or someone. What we have to do is find a way to attack terror as the fruit of an enemy rather than as the enemy. Find the root cause of terror and make war on that.

"Our theme will then be, 'Through Their Eyes — Dealing with the Root Cause of Hate.' Our war will not be against terror, it will be against hate. This opens the opportunity for policy change as we want the policy to change. The idea will be to walk in their shoes and ask the question, why do they hate? If we can eliminate the reason for their hate, we can defeat terrorism and create allies. Here are the policy possibilities:

1. Legislate against hate engendered by religion — words or deeds. This will allow us to shut the mouths of those who preach hate, whether under the guise of the Muslim religion or from the Bible.

2. Normalize relations in the Middle East by a gradual military withdrawal. The Middle East should be treated like the rest of the world, with a focus on commercial relationships. Let them govern themselves as they choose to govern themselves. We should not seek to impose our system on them. Their form of government will evolve just as ours has.

3. From now on, equal consideration and treatment for Israel and the Arab nations. Nothing creates more hatred than Israel and the way it deals with its neighbors and Arabs living among them. We should deal with them no differently than we deal with the Arabs.

4. Allow the UN to be the UN. Eliminate the hatred of America by transferring the hard decisions to the world community. America should not impose her will on the world because of her military power. That only generates more hate, and hate is our enemy.

5. At home, we should create the North American Union to bring together our neighbors and make them family. That has positive security and economic implications as we develop a unified system of regulations, taxes, and licenses. It also opens roads and highways so that commercial traffic may pass without restriction. We need to do that as a symbol and begin now.

"What we want to present to the American people is a new vision of the world; a world without hate which will be the world without terror, because there will be no reason for it.

"This president will oppose our policy direction and we will probably not be able to get the votes needed to override vetoes in this Congress, but the focus will lead us to victory in the next election cycle. Also, we have discovered that we can do some of this without legislation. The open roads portion can be accomplished under existing legislation if the secretary of transportation will modify existing regulations. Fortunately, the current secretary of transportation is a member of our party and we have already begun discussions to encourage him to act quickly. He has asked that we pass a form of Congress resolution asking him to do that. We will begin with that and an amendment to the Hate Crimes Act to focus attention on our war against hate, and our efforts to make our neighbors family.

"We intend to move forward with this today if you will allow. We are prepared to hold a press conference and launch a media campaign to take control of the agenda from the president and change the target of the war from terror to hate. Our peace friends will support this approach because it accomplishes their purposes. Under the banner of 'make our neighbors family,' we can deal with everything from global warming to economic security. All we are doing is wrapping our existing agenda in a new package to neutralize the effect of the 'war on terror' phrase. This will work."

The debate went on throughout the morning, causing the morning events at the Capitol to be canceled unexpectedly and the press conference moved to the afternoon. In the end, the pressure of the leadership prevailed. The caucus voted to proceed as recommended, but there remained serious doubts among some within whom the light still burned. Parts of this new agenda were very troubling. The way Besserman had been treated still troubled some.

Justice Called In

Even as the majority party caucus was meeting to undercut his efforts, the president had called in Attorney General Felix Rodriquez to enlist the help of the Justice Department in the ongoing investigation of MD. "Felix," the president opened, "I believe you know Tom Knight and Eric

Besserman. Meet David Barnes who has been moved from the CIA to the White House to help with our terror investigation. We need the Justice Department's help to dig deeper into some of the leads and to protect the secrecy of the investigation. I want you to join the commission I have formed to coordinate the investigation and prepare our response to what we believe to be a threat to the nation's very survival. This is to be your highest priority. When we finish here, they will bring you up to speed on what we have learned."

"Yes, Mr. President. How can I help?" was the Attorney General's response.

"Tom, you and David can outline what the commission needs right now and I will have one more matter to discuss when you finish."

"Felix," Chairman Knight began, "we have isolated the location of the domestic leader of the planned attacks. Messages which are communicated through a website have been posted from a computer located in Cambridge, Massachusetts. One such message was answered by an operative in Williams, Illinois. We believe that there have been phone calls exchanged between these two. We need to find a way to confidentially obtain phone records in Cambridge and Williams to see if we can discover who these people are. The calls would be between the 617 and 630 area code. Additionally, we need to investigate any foreign calls into those area codes. If we find something, we need wiretaps on landlines and the ability to monitor cell phone communications. David will be able to give you additional detail.

"We have dates when a meeting was held in Iran to coordinate this attack. We need airline information on foreign travel and returns during a reasonable window surrounding the event. We also need information and comparisons on out of country reservations close to Memorial Day, which we believe to be the current date of the proposed attacks. Our intelligence tells us that the leaders of the planned attacks are not operatives who intend to die. They will send others to their death but will most likely leave the country before the attacks — or at least send loved ones out of the country. This may be a way to identify them.

"We also believe that the planning and placement for the attack have been going on for a number of years, and that the domestic leadership is American educated. They appear to be resident aliens. We need you to conduct a confidential investigation of all student visas issued to men or women from Middle Eastern countries other than Israel. In order to see who stayed in America and where they are now, track them to see if they graduated and cross-index the graduates with those who have green cards or work permits. Find out where they work. Then, if we compare this list with the airline information or identify some who live and work in Williams or Cambridge, we may find the leaders."

"If we can get a list, we can go to our allies and seek their help. Perhaps they will open their airline information and we can find the people who went to Iran. They probably went under false names and documents, but it is worth a try. We might be able to trace funds sent to support the attacks. There are lots of obvious possibilities if we can get identities."

"We also need to know what is legal regarding arrest and interrogation of a resident alien who is suspected of involvement in terrorist activities. Our intelligence indicates these are true believers, but only as long as they are not put at personal physical risk. If we find one and can move him to Guantanamo Bay, that alone might be enough to get the information we need. These people are the worst of cowards. They happily send others to their death without a second thought, but will not even stay in the country when the attack is launched if they can get out beforehand."

"Yes, but let me interject this before anyone gets carried away," the president added with a commanding voice. "I want whatever is done to be strictly within the law. We cannot expect God to open our eyes and provide us what we need if we cut corners. I am serious about this. I do not want the blood of innocents on my hands. Someday when this effort is investigated by our political enemies and history records what we did, we will not be found to have ignored the law."

"Mr. President, that may not be possible," the attorney general answered.

"Felix, it not only will be possible, but that is how it is to be. Stay within the law. Am I clearly understood?"

"Yes Mr. President," they responded together.

"Now, let's discuss my issue," the president said. "Confidentiality is absolutely essential on everything that is being done here. This is national security at the highest level. A leak could reveal to our enemy what we know and how we have obtained information. That would be catastrophic.

I want a team to be ready on a moment's notice to take legal action to stop disclosures and I need your help to plug an existing leak.

"When we finish here, Commissioner Matthews will be invited in. I am going to fire him because he has made unauthorized disclosures to George Murphy, a reporter at the *Times Daily,* who is now snooping around Chicago where we have deployed a military team in anticipation of an attack today or Sunday. I want to confront him in your presence and with your support. I intend to tell him that if he discloses any further information he learned from his involvement with the Survival Commission, that you will instruct the criminal division to impanel a grand jury to investigate him for a possible violation of national security laws. We will follow the law, but so must our political enemies."

"This is a meeting I will enjoy," the attorney general responded.

"Gentlemen, why don't all of you but Felix adjourn to a conference room and we will deal with Commissioner Matthews. After that, please fill Felix in on the details of the investigation so he can get started."

"Yes Mr. President," they answered and departed as Commissioner Matthews entered.

"War on Hate" Launched

The meeting with former Commissioner Matthews was short and blunt, and he got the message. He left quickly, pale and shaken.

The majority party press conference to launch their "war on hate" was laid out on the Capitol steps, much like the Republican party had done when they launched "the contract with America." It sounded good. Americans did not identify with anyone who was openly an advocate for hate, but upon reflection, the policies necessary to accomplish the stated goals did not receive universal acclaim. Those who advocated for Israel understood the message. If adopted, America could no longer be counted on as a friend or neighbor. America would leave the Middle East to fight their own fights and would support the last man standing with oil. Conservatives understood the message. If adopted, the road to the abandonment of American sovereignty and influence in favor of less conflict had been chosen. Religion, all religion, would be designated the enemy and be limited and controlled. This agenda would result in a very different America, in a very different world.

Watching the press conference on television, the president turned to Eric Besserman and said, "As bad as it is, that trash will sell if Americans are no longer willing to stand and bleed and fight for as long as it takes to win. We will know when we see how the people respond to the next attack on American soil, and unfortunately, we should have that answer soon."

"So far, nothing in Williams or in Chicago," Tom Knight added.

"Your key phrase," the president added, "was, 'so far.'"

What Next for ITN

In New York, Carl Stern was on the phone with Jim Hunt considering what to do in light of the massive response to the Williams' broadcast. The number of hits and email requests on their website was beyond anything they had anticipated, and continued flowing in. The story had caught America's attention. As a result of the president's warning, it all played together perfectly, and now with the majority party's announcement of a "war on hate" that included religion, the statements of the Bookseller were being combed with interest. The idea of another broadcast where people could ask the Bookseller questions was exciting. Already, the question of whether God was no longer on America's side demanded an answer. They had to get the Bookseller to agree to another live interview; perhaps several. Strangely, people wanted to hear what the old man had to say.

"Let's start out with something we can use to measure the interest and grow the crowd for a possible Bookseller special," suggested Jim Hunt. "Let me see if he will agree to appear at the end of the national news tomorrow night to answer the question, 'Is God still on our side?' His answer and the response of the viewers will show us if there is the level of interest we think."

"Go for it," was all Stern said.

CHAPTER 7

A Request and a Change in Strategy

Thursday, February 7 – MD minus 108 days

THURSDAY ENDED PEACEFULLY in Williams and Chicago. The fans at the Chicago Bulls game and people waiting to fly out of the city were surprised by the increased security, but most of them appreciated the new security measures and ignored the inconvenience. The unmarked radiation vans had found nothing. The monitoring of communications had revealed nothing unusual. The citizen calls were investigated and nothing radical was found.

George Murphy was in Chicago for the *Times Daily*. He had seen the military aircraft at the airport hot and ready. He knew something was up. The last time he saw such preparations was immediately after 9/11. Clearly, the administration knew much more than they were telling the American people. He was disappointed when he placed a call to Commissioner Matthews only to learn that he was now "former commissioner" and refused to give him any new information. In fact, Matthews had told him not to call again. What now?

Suddenly his cell phone rang. "This is the White House operator. Please hold for the president."

The next voice he heard began, "Mr. Murphy, this is President Strong. I apologize for interrupting your evening, but I want to speak with you briefly about your latest investigation regarding the commission of which Tom Knight is chairman and Eric Besserman just joined."

"Thank you for your call, Mr. President. Is this on or off the record?"

"For now, this is the background so you can better understand what you have discovered and why it is important to use some discretion so as not to inadvertently reveal information to our enemies that could thwart our investigation. When you return to Washington, perhaps we can sit down and have an exclusive on the record," the president responded.

"Mr. Murphy, you are a student of history, so I am confident that you are aware of the way some members of the Washington press cooperated with President Kennedy during the Cuban missile crisis. Although they discovered information relating to the investigation that was being conducted, when asked, they withheld publication until the administration fully understood the threat and was prepared to respond. Any early disclosure would have placed the nation at great risk and may have caused a different outcome.

"Today, the nation is in a similar place and I am making a similar request. We are involved in an investigation of what we believe is a plan for a catastrophic series of coordinated attacks intended to negate the nation's ability to project its power outside of our borders, one which could threaten our way of life for decades into the future. This commission which Matthews told you about is called the Survival Commission, because that is what we believe we are addressing. My request to you is simple — do not publish anything further about the commission and its investigation until we have successfully ascertained the targets, defined the threat, and are prepared to respond.

"If you focus the investigative reporters of the nation on this matter, there will be a feeding frenzy that will begin to reveal what we know and how we are conducting our investigation. Should that happen, our enemies will change how they operate and we may never learn what we need in order to prevent future attacks or minimize future damage."

"I hear you, Mr. President, but how does what you are suggesting relate to military aircraft hot and ready on runways in Chicago and the movement of some sort of elite military force here?"

"Still background for now," the president responded.

"Yes, with a protest," was Murphy's response.

"Under the guise of a training exercise, we have deployed a special tactical unit to Chicago in coordination with local and state leaders to be prepared to address what our intelligence believes may be a terrorist attack that will occur in Chicago or Williams within the next seven days, probably on Sunday. The attack in question is not what is being investigated by the Survival Commission, and it will be different from anything we have faced before. That is more than you need to know, but it should provide you with evidence that what I am saying is true."

"All I can commit to right now," Murphy said, "is that I will continue my investigation and hold any story at least until Monday. But, if there is an attack, the quid pro quo is exclusive information for an investigative piece."

"That isn't good enough," the president answered. "I need your commitment about the Survival Commission story; to hold it until we tell you we are ready, which we will do before we go public. Obviously, if someone discovers what we are doing and reports it, you would be released from your commitment. If you hold the story, we will give you details before we go public so you can be first. I will also commit to the first interview with you. In the meantime, if the attack occurs as expected in Chicago or Williams, we will provide you additional information for your story on our response, but you cannot publish information on how we discovered the threat. That would give our enemy the tools to modify their procedures so that we would have to start all over to discover their means of communication.

"I have told you more than I should, but my investigation of you reveals that you are a man of integrity whose word can be trusted. Although we have policy differences, I understand that you too are a man of faith. My advisors tell me I am a fool to even talk to you, but I sense I can trust you to do what you say and to keep your commitments."

"I too will be seen as a fool, Mr. President, but... I trust you. I will hold the commission story and wait to hear from your office."

"Thank you, Mr. Murphy. You will not regret your restraint. Please, as you pray remember to ask that we are given wisdom and discernment to know and be prepared to respond to this threat. The old man in Williams is right. We cannot do this alone."

Strangely, George Murphy found himself appreciating this president and feeling thankful that he was in the White House at that time. Praying as requested would come easily, for he too was one of those with the light inside. Suddenly it seemed to be burning brighter as the Spirit encouraged him to pray.

Darkness Prepares to Try Again

As multiple dark wisps raced back and forth across the earth, Molech became increasingly concerned with the messages he had received. The forces of light were on the move. The shooter was in rebellion. The Bookseller and the kid still lived. The number of believers who were available to pray was still small, but increasing. Those who unknowingly served the Dark Master and were essential to the success of his agenda were ignorant of the progress of the investigation and were getting careless. Discovery was now possible. The instruments of darkness needed a wake-up call. They needed their eyes opened to that fact and would have to change their plans so that they would be effective. He frantically searched for an answer in his inventory of schemes and deceptions that had always worked in the past. He needed to move quickly.

"You have become too attached to this to see clearly," Alexander said with a condescending tone. "You forget who rules this earth until the Son of the Enemy returns.[31] It is ours and we simply need to reclaim it. These humans are mere instruments. Use them and we will succeed. We have lost nothing. This battle by the few against us is a mere irritation. Do what always works. Infiltrate their groups and leadership with our servants who will turn them away from the light. We already have Farsi among them. Let us use him to discover their plans. Let us make him a hero in the eyes of our foes. Let us find a way for him to stop what will appear to be an attack by our people, and perhaps find a way for him to reveal the identity of the shooter. Then he will be exalted and trusted. This will make him able to get the information necessary to open the eyes of the fools we have to work through."

"Yes, that should work. We have influence over Farsi and have deceived Tom Campy into supporting him. The opportunity is available Saturday in Williams when the rebel Doeg has planned an attack on the red coat militia. We must sacrifice one of our own, but who really cares? There are always others to use. Legion seems to have an endless supply of bodies. If he will direct those under his control and Chemosh will continue to push the American politicians, we can influence those under our control and the plan will move up with everything in place before the Enemy's forces can be prepared to resist. We still must deal with those two in Iran, but that should not be difficult with the darkness of those we control in leadership."

"You have forgotten the Enemy and His chosen vessels there," Alexander reminded Molech. "We will be defeated by them — even as we were previously defeated in the attempt to eliminate the Bookseller and the boy — if we do not neutralize this prayer movement and its leaders. We have seen that the Enemy will not let us kill them, so we will have to attack them where they are vulnerable. You have studied them. Where are their weaknesses?"

"The old man has walked with the Enemy for decades," Molech answered. "He knows the words of the Enemy's Book and seeks to obey what it says. He cannot be easily deceived and stands against most temptations because he truly loves the Enemy. He has been overcome by this sickening humility and does not seek anything for himself which limits how he can be attacked. His body is aging and frail, but the Enemy protects him even from physical attacks... at least for now."

"If we cannot attack him successfully," Alexander continued, "can we attack his wife? That is every man's weakness."

"I see you have learned much in your service of the Dark Master," Molech responded cautiously, "but you obviously don't understand how the Enemy joins two believers in marriage. We have worked hard through the years to sell marriage as a license for people to have sex with others in a protected relationship, terminable at will, and no longer risky for women because of abortion rights. We have even succeeded recently in changing the definition of marriage so that two who marry can be of the same sex, something the Enemy considers an abomination.[32] "Nevertheless, regardless of all our efforts, when the Enemy takes two believers, a male, and a female, and joins them, he joins their heart and spirits. They become one before Him in a way that makes deception difficult and temptations ineffective, if the light burns brightly in both.

"Trying to get to the Bookseller through his wife is a wasted effort except to the extent that the Enemy allows us to attack her body. His love for her would limit his usefulness to the Enemy if he had to care for her. Unfortunately, the Enemy has placed limits on what we can do to her as well. Several years ago we tried to kill her and would have succeeded, but the Enemy awakened the old man to the reality of what was happening and she was allowed to recover."

"What about the boy. That has to be the way to get to the Bookseller," Alexander said, thinking aloud. "The boy has no sexual interest in other men so we can't use that to temporarily prohibit him for use by the Enemy. The girlfriend might work, though. Although she is a searcher who has learned much through looking at the Enemy's Book, she does not have the light inside. She is vulnerable to fear which can be used to end her search and turn her focus away from the Enemy and toward her love and concern for the boy. Fear paralyzes these weak creatures. Perhaps we can influence her in her fear to reach out to him physically to demonstrate that she loves him and seeks to protect him. She could be influenced to try and keep him away from the Bookseller because of the recent shootings. She would temporarily negate his usefulness in service to the Enemy by starting sexual relationship outside of the Enemy's definition of marriage. That could discourage and divert the Bookseller from his assignment."

"We tried to use sexual tempters once already and it failed," Molech said in frustration.

"Yes, but you tried it before there was a double attempt on his life and when you tried it, you attempted to make him the aggressor," Alexander answered. "This time, let's be subtle and create an environment where she reaches out to him in love with the desire to give herself to him. Women are sometimes thoughtless. You know that. A woman can be used easily to break any man if she presents herself as wanting to give her man the 'ultimate gift' of herself. It is a powerful set of emotions that we can use. We have presented sex for centuries as the way for women to exercise control over men. Her fear and the desire to give herself to him should succeed if we can provide the opportunity and influence the girl. That boy is a man and he can easily be made to cross the line when the girl he loves invites him.

"This should be fun. Think of all the so-called pastors and religious leaders who have been drawn into sexual relationships by their weakness and lust for a well-made body when we create the opportunity. Of course, this will be difficult and challenging. However, if the boy falls, the Bookseller will be drawn away from an absolute focus on what the Enemy is trying to do through him. Perhaps he can be discouraged, remembering all the times we have succeeded in having other so-called Christians put him down and reject the message the Enemy has given him to speak. Maybe we can drive him to depression, maybe even suicide. Oh, wouldn't that make even Legion envious," Alexander chuckled.

"It's worth a try," Molech answered, and calling a horde of dark wisps to him, he sent them off with messages to implement the new strategy. Keepers and Tempters were dispatched to those they controlled in Williams and Cambridge. He left the Washington politicians to himself and the Middle East leaders and operatives to Legion. They were advised of the strategy, but they were free to implement what they knew would work over those they influenced.

Attack through Samantha

She reached for the phone, half in defiance at the unearthly being that had tricked her and half in hope that she could make some positive contribution before paying for her crimes. She dialed 1-800-HELPNOW, and the cheerful voice on the other side of the phone at police headquarters was glad to take down her information and accept her application to join the Citizens Militia. She expected no difficulty in her application being accepted, for she was an 'A' student and had no police record. As silly as it sounded, she was not afraid.

The evening prayer gathering at the Williams College Chapel ended. The Bookseller had declined to attend with the comment that should have been expected, "This is not about me. It is about the message God has sent to his people. I don't want to become a sideshow distraction. This is too important. Just gather the willing and pray."

Paul and Samantha left together and headed back to Samantha's apartment to have a few private moments together. Things had changed after the shooting. Their drive was silent.

"Paul, you have got to get away from the Bookseller," she began as they entered her apartment. "It's too risky to be around him. You were almost killed yesterday! I stood over my Dad's grave not long ago and I do not want to stand over yours. Please, do this for me."

"Sam, Sam, why are you afraid? Have you not read of the Heavenly protection God gave us? We saw nothing, but the news crew saw what must have been angels dressed as members of the Citizens Militia, and so must have been the shooter if we were the target. Two different murderers seeking our lives and we were not touched. God protected us. After that, how can I fear for my life?"

"Paul, I'm not like you, I'm afraid. I want to know more about Jesus. I want to believe even as you believe, but right now I just can't and I'm afraid. I know we made a decision in that church on Sunday, but like the Bookseller said, it wasn't the real thing. This isn't just about eternal life; this is about your life here and now. Someone is trying to take the thing I care about most away from me — and that's you. Paul, I love you. I'm yours and I love you. All there is of me is yours; you can have it all. I want to give myself to you, right now. I cannot live without you," she said as they embraced and she took his hand and placed it on her breast.

What followed would be viewed differently by the forces behind the Curtain. The forces of darkness ambushed the two with emotions of lust, need, and fear while the forces of light responded with compassion, tenderness, and understanding. Paul was enabled to hear and understand what Samantha's heart was saying. Although he wanted to love her and not simply have sex with her, it took all the restraint he could muster not to consummate the excitement and lust legitimately racing through his body. He wanted her and he wanted her immediately, but somehow he restrained his passion, removed his hand from her breast and simply held her close.

Tears soon fell down Samantha's face and they kissed deeply because they loved each other, but the kissing was free from lust. Paul had refused what he knew was an offer made in fear. He just loved her and he prayed as he held her that she might be born again. "How can I share with her what she needs to hear to believe so that our hearts can become truly one and she is no longer afraid?" he thought. "Tomorrow, I must ask the Bookseller."

Future Risks

Elsewhere, high above the city, Barnabas heard it. He had heard it before. It was God's provision, a heavenly multitude crying out for the many who did not know how to cry out for themselves. He knew immediately that it was the angels of the children who Jesus had always said see the face of the Father in Heaven.[33] The little ones are at risk, he realized and listened carefully to instructions.

CHAPTER 8

UNVARNISHED TRUTH

Friday, February 8 — MD moved — now minus 77 days

"SLEEPING BEAUTY, AWAKEN! Geek here with news."

"Slow down Darrell. Let my brain at least shift out of the park. Don't you ever sleep?"

"Sleep, how can you sleep?" he responded, talking even faster. "The chase is on and there are more clues. I can't stop, it's too exciting! We have to find those guys and stop them!"

"Alright, already, slow down and tell me what's happening."

"I am close to having the signature for the particular computer the J-14 fellow has been using to communicate. If I can get that, I may be able to hack into the hard drive and download files and communications. Maybe we can get their plans and identities that way."

"Great!" David responded. "That would be monumental, but what about new clues? The commission meets later today and I need a solid update on anything definite that we have."

"Try this on for size, Mr. Barnes. We have two new messages, one of which is from another apparent leader. I have been trying to translate with no luck. I sense this one is important but I can't get there. I think the plan is changing because of the renegade attack in Williams and the killing of the seven earlier. I could be wrong, but I don't think so."

"What are they?" asked Barnes, now wide awake.

"The first posting was '00. MD down 1. J-14'. That posting came from Cambridge, Massachusetts. Several hours later, a second posting was made by a different leader in Pakistan. Maybe it was the big guy himself. It says, '00. Never MD. J-1.' They both obviously concern the plan identified as MD and have to be related somehow, but they are Greek to me. Now you have your homework and I am going to bed. Later."

"Thanks, Darrell. That should keep me occupied until the meeting. Great work again, as always. Keep pushing for a chance to hack into the hard drive of J-14's computer, or better yet, find it. You could make all of us sleep better… and longer."

"Believe me, I am trying my best."

"I believe you. Get some sleep and then get back to work later."

A Change of Schedule

"El-Ahab, you must leave at once and advise our Iranian brother Ahmad Habid of the change in timing," the Sheik instructed. "He must be prepared to move against the American forces in the Middle East in coordination with our strikes in America on the new schedule. See what you can learn of the Iranian's plans. Perhaps this will be the opportunity for him to strike at the Jewish abomination."

"I will leave as ordered, respected one," El-Ahab answered, "but what about the commandos in America. Will the posting be enough?"

"No, there will be many questions, but remember that we provided for that in the initial planning. The coordinators will all be at that convention in Phoenix next week. They will get their answers there from Assad and Aladr. Farsi will also be there to report on the execution squads. The initial attack is still scheduled for Sunday."

"These Americans may fold without the necessity of MD. They certainly did in Beirut when the Cole was hit. They have no stomach for blood. Look at the killings in Iraq. More people die on their highways in a single big state in a year than have been killed in Iraq and Afghanistan, yet we have been able to drive a movement to force the government to withdraw. They are cowards. At least in Vietnam they were really bleeding. This generation of Americans is overcome with ease and pleasure. They will soon stand for nothing in the face of a blood risk. The only exception is that stubborn president who will soon be driven from office. I hate him, but I also respect him for he is a formidable opponent."

Elsewhere in the Middle East, Israel's Shin Bet and Mossad were far down the road to understanding the coming threat from Iran and the potential Russian involvement. Prime Minister Zimri wondered whether it was time to inform the Americans about what they had learned and how they were preparing to respond. For both America and Israel, it was a question of survival. However, the recent majority party press conference had made it very clear that the leadership of that party could no longer be trusted with matters of Israel's security. "Thank God for the American president," Prime Minster Zimri thought, "He is in his last two years but he still commands the American military and is Israel's friend."

Paul's Mandate

"It was not what I expected or wanted, but that was Samantha's response to the events of Wednesday," Paul said as he shared the events of the past night with the Bookseller. "She acted out of fear and concern for me. Her love is real and frankly shared. I believe that I will marry that woman someday. I want to, but God is not finished with her and I know she will be different when she is wholly His. I do not understand because I do desire her sexually and emotionally, but I am not as I was. That is no longer enough. There is more, and we are not yet at the place where we can be of one heart as well as one flesh. I don't even understand what I feel."

The Bookseller was silent, thrilled at what God was doing in Paul's life. Excited and encouraged by God's activity, he did not want to corrupt God's message by speaking out of turn, so he waited for a question and prayed for the wisdom to answer correctly. He did not have to wait long.

"Mr. White, what is it I am feeling? What should I do?"

"Paul, you are experiencing real love for Samantha; it is a love beyond yourself and it is a timeless love that does not simply think about what you want or need. That is the love the Bible tells us we are to have for our wives. The Apostle Paul wrote in Ephesians that believers are to love their wives as Christ loved the Church and gave Himself up for her.[34] It is a sacrificial love that thinks of her first and gives to meet her needs while ignoring your own.

"But, Paul also wrote that believers should not be yoked together with unbelievers, pointing out that light cannot have fellowship with darkness.[35] You are living that conflict of sacrificial love for Samantha which she cannot receive or share because she is not yet born again. Your heart is crying out for her to be a believer like you so that your love can be made complete in Jesus. That is what you are feeling, along with your natural physical desires which seem to conflict with what your heart is feeling. God has given you those desires too, which are holy when expressed together in marriage with the sacrificial love of Christ."

"How can I explain that to her?" Paul asked. "I don't think she would understand."

"You're right," the Bookseller answered. "She wouldn't be able to understand unless God opens her eyes and ears. Do you remember your first dream of the dark beings blinding people, covering their ears, and reaching deep into their skulls so they could not see or understand the truth?[36] She has been called to search, and as a result, has been freed of complete blindness — but that search is not to find the truth about you. She has been called to a search to discover the truth about God which will also open her eyes to the truth about you. If you want the feelings of your heart to become the reality of your life, you must seek to lead her to Jesus."

"How can I do that? What do I say?" Paul asked with the intense sincerity of real love. "I want her to know the peace and joy I have in Jesus and to be able to share a love for Him together."

"Paul, listen closely, for there is so much deception and error being preached and taught regarding how one becomes a Christian. You and Samantha have experienced some of it when you went to that place of darkness called Faith Church of Joy. They convinced you both that praying a little prayer was all it took to be saved. You now know that is a lie based on what you experienced when you really got saved. You received a new heart and new Spirit within.[37]

"Samantha, like so many others, is still living the lie. They have been sold the equivalent of 'fire insurance,' and are as blind today as the day they prayed because they are not born again.[38] It is more difficult for them to see today than before they were led into error."

"Is there no hope then?" Paul cried out in anguish.

"Of course there is hope, for there is God. You were awakened and changed. She too can be awakened and changed."

"Again, please, what can I do? There must be something I can do or say," Paul responded.

"There is. You can first pray that her eyes be opened to the truth for we know that God wants all men and women to be saved and come to the knowledge of the truth.[39] He wants none to perish in the second death but all to come to repentance.[40] Since the Bible tells us that is His heart, we can pray with confidence knowing that is God's desire. He wants everyone to have the opportunity to make a choice as to who or what will be their god.

"Paul, you must live your faith carefully and openly before her so that she will see Jesus in you. However, that alone is not enough for one captured in deception. You must also confront the deception by sharing with her what happened to you — how you were freed from the lie and born again.

"Your testimony of what you have learned and experienced is something she will listen to because she knows and loves you and has seen the change.

"Begin by helping her to understand what it means that there is a God. It is here that most so-called religious people fail. Think about it for a moment. If there really is a God, He is sovereign over everyone and everything. If there is a God, He sets the 'rules' and He has the right to judge everyone according to the standards He sets. If there is a God, He is all-powerful and no person or nation can overcome Him or His declared will. If we try, we become His enemy.

"The God of the Bible is all of that. He is holy and just.[41] "That is another misunderstood concept. To be holy means that He cannot tolerate any evil, disobedience, or rebellion. He cannot make any exceptions, which is why all people are guilty before Him for all have sinned in thought, word, and deed and fallen short of the glory of God. All sin is equal in the eyes of a holy God.[42] "Since God is also just, He must punish all guilty people, which is everyone, for we all have sinned.[43] Justice demands that all sin be punished, but God is love, which creates a seeming contradiction. How can God be holy and just, yet love the one whom He must punish?

"The Bible tells us that a conversation occurred before creation in which it was decided by God to provide a way for a person to avoid punishment for their guilt, and for God to remain both holy and just. That plan was for God to become a man in Jesus Christ. The Son of God, equal to God the Father and Spirit in power and glory, would come to earth and be born of a virgin. He would live a life without sin so that He would carry no guilt, and then in love, He would willingly accept in His body the punishment God's holiness and justice required for our guilt.[44] That was the reason for the cross.[45] Jesus, God in the flesh, did what we could never do for ourselves. He suffered our punishment and in the process, offered us the opportunity to be cleansed from our sin.[46]

"Samantha has accepted this part of the plan. She has declared that Jesus is her savior, but there is a problem with that declaration. Jesus is not a person's savior until He is their God. The term the Bible uses is 'Lord.'[47] When Jesus becomes a person's God then He is their savior and they will be born again, given a new heart, and a new Spirit.[48] That Spirit will give them a desire to obey God and His word simply because He is God; and as such we owe Him obedience. The desire to obey will also be a product of their love for God, responding to the reality of what Jesus did for them on the cross.[49]

"Here is the cold truth: the Bible teaches that there is no salvation apart from obedience. There is no forgiveness of sin apart from obedience.[50] When Jesus becomes your Lord, you surrender any right to make decisions independent of His will. If you believe that you have the 'right' or privilege to disagree with God or with what He has said in His word, then He is not your God or savior.

"The 'pray a little prayer and then continue with your life as you wish' crowd rejects Jesus as their Lord who rules over them as God, and they continue to live unforgiven in darkness. They have sought insurance from the punishment of hell while being able to live their lives as their own god, independent from what God wants or what His word says. It is the greatest of all tragedies. They have believed a lie because no one will stand and tell them the truth. You must tell Samantha the truth before it is too late. God is seeking to draw her to Himself. Allow Him to use you as the instrument to confront her with truth."

"It will be hard to tell her that she is not saved after baptism and church membership," Paul said with some anguish and fear. "I could lose her."

"Paul, answer me this, would it be love to have the cure for a deadly disease from which Samantha is suffering and choose not to share it with her, rather than choosing to tenderly care for her as she deteriorates and ultimately dies?"

"Of course not. I would be compelled by love to share it with her," Paul answered knowingly.

"Neither then would it be love to fail to confront her with the truth about her need to make Jesus her God and be born again. Even if she rejects you and ends your relationship. When you stand before Jesus in judgment, you don't want to be the cause of why Samantha lived her life deceived and died physically only to suffer the second death because you did not love her enough to tell her the truth."

Paul got up and hastily grabbed his jacket saying, "I have to leave. I have to find Samantha and tell her about Jesus as God and what that means. She has to hear the truth and I have to share it with her now."

As he rushed from the room, the Bookseller knelt to pray, asking God to give Paul boldness and wisdom to speak the truth and for God to open Samantha's eyes and ears that she might hear and understand and be born again.

Congress Moves Quickly

Congress moved quickly after the majority party's press conference. Before the sunset on Friday, they had forced through a sense of Congress resolution requesting the secretary of transportation to open the highways to unrestricted Mexican and Canadian truck traffic. The economic benefits sounded good and the promised unlimited source of cash was too much for the politicians looking to the coming election to stand against. The Minority Party was divided, but the temptation of cash for the next campaign was simply too much to resist. The resolution passed easily with bipartisan support.

The amendment to the Hate Crimes Act was set for hearings. A formal request had been sent to the Bookseller asking that he appear and testify along with numerous religious leaders and educators who shared Chairman Crow's view of the danger of all religions.

The Senate Foreign Relations Committee had scheduled hearings on America's policy toward Israel and had invited among others Professor Daniel Thompson of Williams College to testify on why a change was needed. Together Tomorrow flooded the airways and print media with paid advertisements trumpeting the "war against hate."

Former President Cox began a cross-country series of speeches seeking to convince the American people that the time was ripe to attack the causes of hate as one of the ways to eliminate terrorism. America, he argued, must place its emphasis on economic relationships leaving the people of the Middle East and elsewhere to choose their own form of government and leaving conflict determinations to the United Nations. The effort was seen as a good beginning by those with an alternative agenda.

New to the Commission

The Survival Commission gathered in a conference room in the old Executive Office Building. After opening with prayer, Chairman Knight introduced President Strong who had a few announcements to make.

"Ladies and gentlemen, you need to know that I have removed Pete Matthews from the commission because he leaked information on our investigations to a reporter for the *Times Daily*. We cannot and will not tolerate leaks. Any leak is free intelligence to our adversaries, which weakens our ability to prepare to address terrorism threats and undermines our effort to eliminate MD. The attorney general has been asked to join the commission in order to help with the investigation and provide guidance on how to deal with issues within the law as they arise. He has been given a list of assignments directly related to following up on leads and information of which you are aware.

"I have also asked Senator Eric Besserman to join the commission, both because of the breadth of his knowledge on terrorism and his relationship with Israel's government. He will be our point man in coordination with Israel. They know him, and frankly, they trust him more than any person in this room myself included."

"Mr. President," Besserman jumped in, "You overstate my value and understate their view of you. The government of Israel has complete confidence in you and in your administration. They know you are a friend who will honor America's historic commitment to their security."

"Thank you for your kind words, Eric. I do not intend to be the American president who turns against a friend for oil or political favor.

"All of you have seen the news and know the political price Senator Besserman has paid for standing with us against the policies of the current leadership of his party. It is that kind of political courage that will be required if we are to be successful in defeating terrorism threats," the president continued.

"Tom, it is your meeting," and with that, the president left the room so the debate would not be limited by his presence.

CHAPTER 9

THE COMMISSION STRUGGLES

Friday, February 8 — MD minus 77 days

"TO BEGIN WITH, we need a report on the latest satellite imagery from the training camp in Northern Iran," Chairman Knight continued. "Director Crenshaw?"

"Early this morning, which was be the middle of the night in Iran, we picked up an explosion of some nature at the Iranian training camp. The explosion created a massive fireball which appeared to have a petroleum source. Since we have been watching this camp, we have seen nothing apart from an apparent oil terminal operation — complete with fuel trucks and oil storage tanks. What this has to do with a possible terrorist attack we have not been able to discern. The explosion may have been nothing more than an accident, but frankly, it is the first event which could be interpreted as a test of some sort of a weapons delivery system. We are obviously following up to learn what we can about this event, and will be checking with our people on the ground in Iran."

"Wait a minute," Commissioner Waters exclaimed, "9/11 was a petroleum fire. They used recently fueled jumbo jet aircraft. Is there any new information on licensing or training of foreign pilots? Are we looking at a repeat performance?"

"Not likely," Director Crenshaw responded. "There is no way that terrorists could commandeer the number of aircraft it would take to cripple us as a nation. We would have noticed that from the beginning and we are much better prepared to respond. Aircraft may be included in their plan, but I doubt seriously whether it is commercial aircraft. I am much more concerned about private aircraft, although again gaining control of a large number of private aircraft seems unlikely. We have found nothing unusual in pilot training schools. That does not seem to be the threat."

"What have we learned about unusual activities that require state or federal licenses?" Commissioner Peters asked.

"Nothing really," answered Chairman Knight, "except for some acquisitions of businesses that hold state or federal licenses."

"Do any of the acquiring entities have ties to the Middle East?"

"None of the acquisitions have direct and obvious ties to the Middle East beyond government purchases that are public and involve federal clearance."

"Well, the terrorists may be crazy but they are not stupid," answered Attorney General Rodriquez, "particularly this new group of white collar leaders. There will be no direct ties. Have we sought to go beyond the obvious to seek the real persons in interest?"

"No, but that investigation is now underway," Chairman Knight answered. "The problem we have is isolating what industries can be used to launch attacks. If we knew the weapon then we could narrow the search."

"Airplanes can obviously be used. Have we checked private aircraft services with fleets of planes?" Commissioner Waters asked.

"No, but you have a point," Chairman Knight had to admit. "If the terrorists owned the planes they would not have to be concerned about taking control of air crafts and they would have absolute control for timing and coordination of a major attack. Director Hollister, can you get in touch with the FBI and see what you can learn about acquisitions of private aircraft firms? Also, put a group together to consider other delivery systems that could be purchased in the country."

"Will do," Hollister responded.

"We have encountered opposition in our attempts to voluntarily obtain detailed airline information and information on foreign students from colleges. The president has asked Attorney General Rodriguez to have the Justice Department weigh in and obtain national security sub-poenas confidentially. We got some informal cooperation from the air-lines to the extent that they confirmed unusual heavy and early airline reservations out of the country near Memorial Day. That ties down the meaning of MD and emphasizes the importance of getting names."

"The president's call to the public to be watchful and to report sus-picious activity has produced tens of thousands of leads. Each is being farmed out to the locale of which it was reported unless it has obvious national implications. We expect that as we sift through the reports, the location of the operatives will begin to be revealed. In this one at least, time is on our side. They cannot stay hidden forever. We are also hopeful that the leads will enable us to determine something about their plans."

"We expect to have to fight legal challenges over this, but the courts cannot control private activities of civilians seeking to protect themselves and their country from the threats they see right before their face. We have to guard against abuse, but a vigilant citizenry is our best hope of discovery within the country. Those who are acting within the law have nothing to fear. If there is abuse, it will be dealt with speedily and openly."

"Change of subject," Knight announced. "David and Director Crenshaw, what news have we learned from Iran or intercepts?"

"The Iranian information is frankly alarming," Director Crenshaw reported. "Earlier this week, the Iranian president hosted two key Russian officials to discuss how to neutralize our nuclear response capabilities after MD so that others it may recruit can move on Israel. Setting aside the obvious, this is clear evidence that the Iranians believe MD can succeed. We have further been advised that the Iranian government has somehow come into possession of the MD plan, which is the source of their con-fidence. I believe that we need to recommend to the president that it is time to involve Israel."

"Agreed," Chairman Knight commented. "Eric, this will be yours. We will get in touch with the president later today."

"Should we recommend that the president confronts Russia and Iran?" Commissioner Peters asked.

"You need to leave that to the president," National Security Advisor Steed responded.

"There is much involved here. It is not that simple. They would deny the meeting even occurred and they know we are not going to war with them over a meeting. All we know is that two former Russian officials had a meeting with Iranian officials. We don't know whether Russia has signed on to Iran's request."

"Absolutely, and please don't forget that we lose our intelligence if the Iranians find out how much we know about their activities," Barnes added. "They would kill our operatives immediately. We cannot move until we know what we are facing and how to respond to stop the attacks. If we are able to move on the terrorists first, the Iranian plan fails without much effort. We need to find the detailed information on the plan that they now have. If we approach Iran, we should act ignorant and ask for their help. They know we have some knowledge of their plan, why not 'fish' for help, offering a newly open relationship. It would be a way out for them in the real world where America the super power survives."

"What new thing have we learned about the plan?" Chairman Knight asked.

"The news from intercepts includes location and a question on timing. Darrell Reed has been able to confirm the leader coded J-14 posts from a computer located in Cambridge, Massachusetts. We have a new post from a leader coded as J-1 in Pakistan. We assume that to be the big man himself. We have tried to track a phone call from Cambridge to Williams that was the subject of an earlier message, but have been unable to identify either phone.

"This morning there were two new postings which seemingly relate to the timing for MD. The first was '00. MD down 1. J-14.' This seemingly produced a response from Pakistan soon after it was posted. The second message was '00. Never MD. J-1'. We have not been able to conclude the exact meaning of the messages, but I believe that they are significant both in whom they appear to have been sent to and in the affirmation from Pakistan.

"I believe the '00' is not an address of a leader in a single place. I think it is a way of communicating with all leaders deployed worldwide regarding the status of MD. The message seems to mean that MD is being moved up, the opposite of down. The time unit is less clear. I don't know what '1' means. The number 1 is not simply a day, because that is not an opposite. I don't think it is a week, because that is not enough if the problem being addressed is the renegades. Hopefully, our people on the ground in Iran will be able to get us additional detail since the Iranian-sponsored attacks on U.S. forces in the Middle East must be coordinated with MD.

"My best guess at this point — and that is all it is — would be that the number 1 is the opposite of a 30-day month, if a month is the unit of measure. That would mean we have one less month to prepare."

"Could it be in a month rather than moved up a month?" asked Commissioner Roberts.

"That is possible, but would be difficult to coordinate. The truth is, we don't know. If we go back to the airlines and find lots of Memorial Day cancellations followed by lots of bookings either thirty days from now or then, we would know for sure."

"Director Hollister, have Homeland Security check that out," Chairman Knight requested.

"General Hedge, do we have contingency plans in place to protect our forces in the Middle East and be prepared to respond with adequate force anywhere in the continental United States? Can the implementation of these plans be moved up quickly if the message means what David thinks?"

"We are obviously working on it, but that is an impossible assignment without more detail. Respond to what? Where? When? We are planning in a vacuum. It's like the Alpha Force in Chicago right now. What are they there to prevent or contest? We don't have a clue. We need more intelligence. This might be right in our face like 9/11 was, and we could miss it again. You want me to make plans on taking out Iran; even a nuclear exchange with Russia. I can do that. But to fight a shadow is impossible."

"General, we all understand and share your frustration, but we have to be prepared," responded National Security Advisor Steed. "The president needs options and he needs them in a timely manner. Let us begin detailed contingency planning by Tuesday. That plan will deal with the threat to Israel, our forces in the Middle East, and in the continental U.S. Do the best you can with what information we have. At least by Tuesday, whatever is going to happen in Williams should have happened and maybe we will know more."

"People, the old man in Williams may seem to many to be a fool, but

I believe he is right," Chairman Knight continued. "Like the Jewish King Jehoshaphat, we need God's help to find and defeat this enemy, and this is not the first time. I have been doing some reading on public statement and actions during World War II, and was amazed at the open calls from President Roosevelt and other political leaders for prayer, as well as the number of times churches and businesses, towns and communities gathered to pray and cry out to God for protection and deliverance for our nation and troops. You will find everything if you dig the archives. In this day of 'freedom from religion,' you have to dig.

"Walk down to the World War II Memorial Mall and you will see a great example of history rewritten. On the Pacific side of the memorial are the words President Roosevelt used to announce the attack on Pearl Harbor. It reads: …

> *Yesterday, December 7, 1941 – a date which will live*
> *in infamy — the United States of America was suddenly*
> *and deliberately attacked…. With confidence in our*
> *armed forces, with the un-bounding determination of our*
> *people, we will gain the inevitable triumph.*

"Great words, but incomplete. They left out the end of the quote. They left out the most important part. Roosevelt ended by saying, 'So help us, God.' That was not an accidental exclusion. If we seek to leave out God now, I fear for the future of this republic. It may be getting redundant to hear that you should keep on praying, but please pray and follow your heart on this one. I sense that our answer is out there. We have just not seen it yet. Those who wish to stay and pray, please do."

America & Israel — A Continuing Partnership

"Mr. Prime Minister, this is President Strong. It is good to hear your voice, old friend."

"And yours, Mr. President," Prime Minister Zimri responded.

"I will get right to the point. I have two purposes for making this call. First, I want to apologize for what was said by the majority party leadership at their recent press conference regarding America's relationship with Israel. They may be able to get the microphone temporarily, but as long as

I am president, there will be no change in policy regarding your nation. America will remain Israel's most trusted ally."

"Thank you, Mr. President. I was alarmed at what I heard but took comfort in knowing that you were a man of your word, and consequently America would keep its commitments and stand with Israel."

"Mr. Prime Minister, we have once again come to a time when we need each other to address mutual threats in the Middle East. I want to send to you Senator Eric Besserman as my special representative. Senator Besserman is a great friend of Israel. We have information about a possible plot by Iran to attack Israel, possibly with Russia's support, following terrorist attacks on America that are intended to make us incapable of responding militarily in your defense. I know this sounds radical, but we have been following it carefully for some time now and believe that the plot is real and the plan is advanced. We want to provide you with the intelligence we have and coordinate a response."

"You are obviously speaking of MD and Iran's intention to take advantage of it, as evidenced by the recent visit of Nicholas Vandenburg and Joseph Krenski to the Iranian president," Prime Minister Zimri responded. "Your call beat mine, but had you not contacted me today, I would have called you tomorrow. We have also intercepted intelligence on the plan against America and Israel. Send my trusted friend Eric quickly and we will exchange information and consider a joint response."

"He will fly out tonight, and may God be with us."

"Indeed. Barukh ata Adonai Eloheinu melekh ha'olam shehakol niyah bidvaro."

The Real Question

The surroundings were familiar as the interview went live. It differed from the surroundings earlier in the week when the broadcast was a dual picture live from New York and from Williams simultaneously.

"Mr. White, since the Wednesday night broadcast, ITN's website has been deluged with requests that you consent to another live interview, this time where the people of America ask you questions. Along with that request, one question has been sent repeatedly. The number of requests on that question and the intensity of the messages accompanying the requests made us want to get your answer on air as quickly as possible. Thank you for being willing to take the time to address America's concerns."

"It is my privilege," the Bookseller said, "I only hope that God will use me to provide some light on the issue, whatever it may be."

"Mr. White, America's question is this, 'Do you believe that God has turned against America and that this is why we face terrorist threats?'"

"You ask the wrong question, Mr. Murrow. Let me direct your attention to the leader of the people of Israel as he stood on the site of what was to be a great battleground. As he walked the area contemplating what to do, he suddenly saw a man standing in front of him with a drawn sword in His hand. The Bible tells us that Joshua approached this man with the same question as your viewers are asking, 'Are you for us or for our enemies?' The man answered him, 'Neither, but as commander of the army of the Lord, I have now come.'[51]

"You see, the correct question is not whose side God is on, but rather if we are on God's side? God comes, but He takes only His side. Whether we are His enemy or part of His army is a choice every individual as well as the nation as a whole must make. Joshua's response was the correct response. Scripture records that he bowed with his face to the ground in worship and asked the question which anyone who makes the right choice will ask. The question he asked was, 'What message does my Lord have for His servant?' However, even that was not enough to be identified as being on God's side. Joshua was instructed to remove his sandals for the place where he stood was holy. Joshua complied and only then he heard what he needed to know regarding what he was to do so that the enemy would be defeated.[52]

"To those who have asked whether God is on America's side, I would respond by asking, whose side are we on? Does America bow its knee before the Lord, seeking to hear His command and intending to obey what He says so that America's enemy may be defeated? On a personal level, have you bowed your knee and sought the Lord's command with an intention to obey? The answer to those questions will tell you whether you individually and America as a nation is part of God's plan for the future or an obstacle which must ultimately be removed or defeated."

What followed was a moment of uncomfortable silence as the truth of what had been said sank in. The camera shot faded from the Williams warehouse and the newscast ended nervously as violent screams were heard in the darkness and joyous celebration exploded among those in the great cloud of witnesses.

CHAPTER 10

FINALLY, A STRATEGY

Friday, February 8 — MD minus 77 days

THE RESPONSE TO the Bookseller's answer was extreme in both the visible and invisible worlds. What he had said changed the focus of the inquiry from where God stood to where the hearer stood regarding God.

That blunt truth left no place for the hearer to be a "fence sitter" — a choice was required. Either you were on God's side and subject to His will, or you were an obstacle to God's will which made you His enemy.[53] The reality that God would not support a nation that was not on His side was something most Americans and others throughout the earth who heard the broadcast had never considered.

Many again grabbed their Bibles to find the reference for the events the Bookseller had shared. Wisely, before leaving the William's warehouse, the local producer had asked for the reference and had been told to read Joshua 5:13-6:5.

Soon, the transcript for the question and answer session was posted on ITN's website, along with the reference. Searchers everywhere went to the website to study the response and find the reference. Millions paused to consider what had been said and were alarmed at what the Holy Spirit revealed.

In Washington, another television set made the ultimate sacrifice as former President Cox again lost it. The majority party leadership was enraged and immediately set about figuring out how to punish ITN and keep the old man off the air. "If we only had the White House," Chairman Crow mourned, "we could turn the IRS loose on that network and its executives. They would pay dearly for their public proselytizing. At a time when religious fervor must be quelled, they feed the beast. We need to get that amendment to the Hate Crimes Act passed now!"

"What are you complaining about?" Majority Leader Howard interrupted. "You have the opportunity to strike out against this foolishness quickly. The old man is scheduled to appear next week before your committee. I would assume that all the networks will broadcast the hearings because of the controversy he has generated. That is your chance. Cut him to pieces. This isn't about religion, it's about politics. This is nothing more than the religious right attacking our policies. We can destroy him."

"True," Chairman Crow responded. "We will get our best people on this to prepare a set of talking points and circulate suggested questions. We will be ready for him."

"Sorry about the TV," former President Cox replied, this time actually embarrassed. "I'll pay for that one. I can't stand that religious nut. Who gives him the right to criticize our policy and the America we have created? To use stories of events in the Middle East that occurred, if they occurred, thousands of years ago to tell us what we should do or how we should live is ludicrous. People change and societies mature. We are not barbarians living in tents ruled by fear of some unknown god who will strike us dead if we don't follow his rules. I truly hate that man and all he stands for.

"Having said that, I have to warn you to be careful and don't take him lightly or he will have you for lunch. Go back through the original broadcast and find the pastors who disagreed with him. Find religious leaders with as much public visibility as you can that disagree with his view of God. Find religious historians who support the concept of an evolving society in a changing world. Stage the hearings to be part of the war on hate. If necessary, I will testify. The people will still listen to me."

"Slow yourself down," Majority Leader Howard interrupted, "you don't want to be under oath subject to cross-examination by minority party Senators on the committee. If you testify, the hearings will be about you and our opposition would come well-prepared to attack you and our policies. Your suggestions are good but you watch from home — your home. Two television sets are enough. As it is, Capitol housekeeping may leak their continued clean-up projects and then we will appear really foolish. You need to get that anger under control."

"You're right, of course," Cox answered, "I don't know what it is, but I can't control it against that man. Damn those well-intended politicians who passed the Twenty-second Amendment after Franklin Roosevelt's death. But for that, I could run again and take all of these to the American people on a daily basis as part of my campaign — and I would win. Then we could rule with control of the White House and Congress."

"Too true," Chairman Crow agreed, feeding the former president's ego, "but for now, let's find some religious leaders to go public attacking the Bookseller."

"That will be no problem," Cox added, "those hypocrites are always looking for a microphone and an opportunity to have their picture taken with you. Call them by their first name in public and they will say anything you want."

A Candid Conversation

Down the street, President Strong and Janet were together in their residence. As he placed his Bible down and sighed deeply, the president said, "The Bookseller has done it again. In two minutes, that man can take biblical truth and cut my heart out. He is absolutely correct. The question is, whose side is America on? I am afraid I don't like what may be the answer to that question."

"Yes, but you are not America," Janet responded, candidly as always. "You do not control America or the heart of its people. You are the president, but in reality, you can't just change policy or the attitudes of the people. You are a man, not God. Only God can change hearts. All you can do is seek to be faithful to God in what you do as the president. The people must choose for themselves."

"You're right," he answered. "I wish I had the power or ability to somehow cause the people to walk in such a way that America would remain under God's protection, but I don't. All I can do is choose for myself and govern accordingly as best I can."

"Joshua, I have to be really honest with you. I have a sense that like Esther, you have been raised up for a time like this. There is no one else who will lead by following God. It is meant for you to do."

"I wish you were wrong, but why else would God have allowed me to become president? I feel so insufficient to lead the nation through these times."

"Good," Janet answered. "In God's eyes, that qualifies you. A leader who knows his weakness always seeks God's guidance and does not simply rely on himself. Do you realize that you have gone back to the Bookseller's first counsel? Remember? It was the prayer of Jehoshaphat, 'We do not know what to do, but our eyes are on You.' Keep your eyes on God and you will be shown how to lead these people according to His will."

"As always, good counsel from my Proverbs 31 wife," the president responded gratefully, kissing her cheek. "Before the battle begins again downstairs, let's pray." President Strong and his wife prayed together with one heart to hear God speak and to obey whatever He said. They had made their choice to be on God's side.

Darkness Responds

"This man cannot be tolerated!" Alexander shrieked into the darkness to all who would listen. "The Bookseller must be silenced."

"Great analysis," Molech responded with disdain. "You forget that the Dark Master himself just sought his death and it was denied by the Enemy who thwarted our dual attempts to kill him. I would cease that agenda if I were you, as it is why your predecessor now carries messages as a mere wisp on the other side of the earth.

"We have tried all the obvious means of attacks within the limits set by the Enemy. We have tempted the old man with pride, hurt his feelings, and even made him depressed. We have challenged his faith and caused him to be attacked and rejected by those to whom he was sent to minister. We have attacked his means of outside support, causing him to be cheated and forced into great debt. We have attacked him and his wife within the limits set by the Enemy. We have tried deception, false miracles, even spiritual manifestations, and phony revival experiences. Nothing has worked. He remains faithful to the Enemy despite everything… which is why we have been unable to overcome him."

"If we cannot defeat him by attacking him directly because of his faith, we can defeat his effectiveness by attacking him through our servants and perverting his message," Alexander responded. "We have not been defeated by this man's feeble words. Remember how we negated the effectiveness of Paul the so-called Apostle in various locations where he sought to minister — by motivating our servants to attack him because his message was destroying the business of the silversmiths who made idols. His message claimed that idols were not gods, so people stopped buying idols. When the idol makers began to lose sales and feared for their source of wealth, they responded by initiating riots against Paul.[54] A committed group even pursued him from city to city seeking to destroy him and his message.

"This should be a much easier attack than that because the old man's message endangers so many more groups. Multiple businesses and industries make their money by either promoting or facilitating conduct the Enemy's Book labels as 'sin.' These people are not prepared to surrender their business or income. They will do whatever it takes to shut the mouth of the Bookseller if they believe his words could hurt their livelihood. They control most of the media and are the opinion-makers in America. They can directly attack this man in public, viciously and effectively. They have the resources to recruit help in this effort.

"Also, don't forget the politicians whose party advances the very issues the Bookseller has challenged. They cater to these groups and their positions of power and influence depend on keeping those groups satisfied so they will vote for them and contribute to their campaigns. They are just like the old Jewish Sanhedrin. Remember what they did after word got out that Jesus had raised Lazarus from the dead? They did not care whether this Jesus might be the Messiah who spoke truth since he could raise the dead; all they cared about was that the people might follow Him and the Romans would take away their positions of power and influence. It was an easy sell. They had Jesus arrested and gathered false witnesses so He would be condemned to death."[55]

"I remember," Molech smiled. "That was great amusement and the victory would have been ours eternally if we could have kept Jesus in the grave. Fortunately, we are not dealing with one like Him. The old man is nothing but a man and Chemosh already has an effort ongoing in Washington to destroy him. That Leonard Cox is a lot like the High Priest Caiaphas. He is prepared to sacrifice anything and anyone to retain his place of power and influence."

"True, as long as that sacrifice does not involve him," Alexander responded. "But don't forget that other useful crowd of so-called 'religious' leaders we have sponsored for years. Their positions, income, and book sales are endangered by the old man's words, which are driving people back to reading the Enemy's Book. We have helped them build their little kingdoms by ignoring what the Enemy's Book says and substituting what the people want it to say. If the people find out it is all a lie, they will leave and seek others to follow who will teach them what it really says. It will be easy to find many so-called 'religious' leaders wanting to be exalted so they can attack the Bookseller and protect their place and pocketbook."

"Yes," Molech added, "but the largest group of all is the millions of Americans who don't want to live accountable to anyone but themselves. They already hate the Bookseller. They can be used to divide families, friends, and businesses over what the old man says. This is getting exciting! It is going to be much easier than I had thought. We don't have to kill him to destroy him."

The Instruments of Darkness Prepare

Elsewhere in Williams, Abdul Farsi was rehearsing the plan for the coming day with the chosen six who would launch the attack on College Church. The disguises were cumbersome, but in light of the push for public involvement, they were necessary. Farsi was increasingly angry at the arrogance of the infidels as expressed publicly by the old man and by the president. He felt a new compulsion to push the attacks hard and fast to strike the infidels, thus diverting the authorities' attention so that MD might succeed. He found his desires shifting from one who led from afar to one willing to be a sacrificial lamb if that was what it took to facilitate MD. He felt deeply the responsibility of leading the first attack and wanted to take advantage of the opportunity to extract information from

Tom Campy at the Security Fair that night to be sure there was no added risk from the Citizens Militia.

As he contemplated his role in the night's events, two others were also planning what they intended. Downstairs in the same rental house, Alharad Doeg was completing his own plans for the Security Fair and was making preparations for his death as part of his attack on the Citizens Militia. These people, he thought, must not be allowed to feel safe anywhere. He had two automatic pistols which should allow him to get a massive number of rounds before anyone could get him. His coat, like those worn by all because of the cold, would easily hide the weapons until he was inside and ready to launch his attack. He had dressed like a college student to avoid attention and quietly slipped out of the house to walk to the high school gym where the Security Fair was being held.

Susan had been surprised at how quickly she had passed the police background check and completed her training to become a member of the Citizens Militia. There she stood before her mirror, a red jacket, identity badge and everything else, prepared for her first assignment. She, the shooter who had caused all this, had been assigned to patrol the Security Fair. She was amazed at her good fortune and excited as she got in her car and it slipped silently out of the garage.

Farsi departed for the gym as well, alarmed that Doeg was not in the safe house. Perhaps, he thought, he was going to have to execute him like the others. No one can be allowed to risk the operation. If Doeg is a rogue, we have already been instructed what to do. A compulsion to deal with Doeg filled his mind as Alexander smiled. The pieces of the puzzle were in place, just as the forces of darkness had intended for that night.

Forgot Something

As Paul prepared to go to the nightly prayer meeting at the Williams College Chapel, he struggled with what had gone wrong in his conversation with Samantha. He had been so sure that she would hear him and believe him. Therefore, he was dumbfounded when she rejected what he said in anger.

"That's your opinion," Samantha had said, "and the opinion of that troublemaker. That is not the only opinion out there. Remember what Pastor Elkhorn said? He at least referred to the Bible when he spoke, and he assured us both that we were saved when we prayed that prayer and were baptized. We did exactly what he told us to do. I do not see thousands lining up to affirm what the Bookseller told you, and that is not all. Yesterday, two men came to my door with what looked like a Bible and other materials and they told me something totally different. I have been watching programs on a so-called 'Christian' network, and different speakers have different views. If it is only about opinions, mine is every bit as good as yours."

In the moments of panic that followed, Paul was given the words to answer. "Samantha, you're right. It's not about my opinion, yours, Mr. White's, Pastor Elkhorn's or anyone else's. It is about what the Bible says. I am so sorry to have come over here without the biblical backup for what I said. No wonder you are confused and angry. Please forgive me and let us start over. We need to get together with the Bookseller and ask him to walk us through the Bible so we can see the authority for what he shared with me. If scripture cannot back it up, then it's a lie sent to confuse and deceive. Let us test him and see if he can back up what he says with scripture. If not, we need to start the search all over again."

"Won't that anger him, Paul?" Samantha asked, concerned. "After all, you will be challenging him as a spokesman for God."

"Sam, if Mr. White is speaking the truth, everything he says about God will be confirmed in the Bible. If he is who he claims to be, he will welcome the opportunity to open the Bible with us and show us the verses which support his message. If not, he is a fraud. It is that simple. I don't doubt him, but I am perfectly prepared to test him."

"Thank you, Paul, for not simply dismissing me as one who cannot hear like those in your dream. I want to get this right. See if we can meet with him tomorrow after church, and by the way, where shall we go?"

"If you agree, I would like to go to that little church that meets in a rented high school auditorium. Remember, the pastor of that church, Pastor Wilson, was the one who in the broadcast analyzed biblically what Mr. White had said that first time.

"He is part of a group headquartered in Africa. I would like to hear him and be a part of their services. Chaplain Forrest introduced me to him on the day of the shooting. He sometimes attends our prayer meetings and I know that he leads one in his own church in response to the Bookseller's call."

"Sounds like a plan," Samantha agreed reluctantly. She was still willing to search, but unsure of who to trust and what was really the truth. "Who could know for sure," she thought.

Ahmad Habid Prepares

In Iran, Ahmad Habib received El-Ahab in contempt. Habid met with him only because of his affiliation with the Sheik. If the message was from the Sheik, he wanted to hear and obey out of reverence for the true spiritual leader of the Jihad. The Sheik had proven himself worthy and was being hunted as an animal. Habid prided himself on hunting the hunters.

"Brother, greetings from the Sheik," El-Ahab began. "I bring you his respect and thanks for your faithfulness in the Jihad."

"What message from the master?" was Habid's only response.

"The plan to assault the American mainland has been advanced thirty days to ensure its success. If events require, the attacks will be moved up more. The Sheik asks that you be prepared with coordinated attacks on American forces and interests in the Middle East in two weeks' time. Plan for it to be in the middle of April, but be prepared for any time within two weeks from today."

"I have already prepared a plan and have coordinated with my operatives in the field," Habid answered. "Tell the Sheik we will be prepared to spill much American blood when ordered."

Even El-Ahab was struck at the level of hate and glee in Habid's voice. He really enjoyed killing Americans or anyone else who stood in the way of complete control over all nations in the Middle East and throughout the earth.

In the darkness, they all agreed and rejoiced over Legion's work. None could inspire death and murder like him. "The day will yet be ours!" Dagon declared.

Finally, Some Clarity

The mood was glum in the White House Situation Room as the Joint Chiefs and their staffs sought to prepare the detailed contingency plan the president had ordered. "This is impossible," Admiral Bird declared. "Give me a real target and a real enemy and we will destroy it. We do not know what we are fighting and have no idea where or how or in what strength they will strike. I don't like sitting around and planning for another December 8th scenario."

"Fine," answered General Hedge, "then show me how to stop today's Pearl Harbor attack. Think December 6th. No one likes the assignment, but the threat is real and we must be prepared to respond if we cannot stop it. The potential Russian and Iranian threats are easy compared to the threat to the homeland. Let's focus there for now."

"A suggestion, gentlemen," added Troy Steed, the president's national security advisor, "Let's reverse positions and think like the terrorists. How would we render America helpless and unable to respond militarily to an attack on Israel? Rather than focusing on how it could be done in weapons or personnel analysis, let us focus on what would have to be done to neutralize America. I think the place of the beginning has to be targets rather than weapons."

"Yes, absolutely," General Hedge agreed. "If we can determine the targets required to render us helpless, then we can approach how those targets could be successfully attacked."

"And if we have the targets," Admiral Bird continued, "we have something we can plan to protect. That is the December 6th scenario we have been looking for."

The mood changed in the Situation Room in that instant. It was as if a black cloud of discouragement and depression had been lifted so that the participants could begin to think and see clearly. In truth, that is exactly what had happened in response to the president and Janet's prayers along with the increasing number of believers worldwide that were praying for the leaders of America to have wisdom and discernment after they had asked God to reveal what in their lives offended Him, and they subsequently changed their ways.

Barnabas rejoiced as he saw the Holy Spirit at work among those gathered in the Situation Room, but he knew that a good beginning did not ensure a happy ending. There was much yet to be done. The forces of darkness must continue to be confronted and overcome and many hard hearts and wrong desires changed if America was to survive the threat.

CHAPTER 11

THE SECURITY FAIR

Saturday, February 9 — MD minus 76 days

REPARATIONS FOR THE Security Fair were complete. The high school gym was decked out like a combination pep rally and state fair, complete with a stage and event set-ups throughout the building. Circumstances had changed the initial concept. In light of the known threat, the police had set up a table for citizens to report suspicious or unusual activities in their neighborhoods. Another table was set up where people could register to join the Citizens Militia and Neighborhood Watch program. There were also booths where local firearms dealers were allowed to sell guns and ammunition. Present were police officers equipped with computers linked to the databases in HQ, making it possible to do immediate background checks on anyone who desired to purchase a firearm.

In the center of the booths and tables, on a continuous video feed, the president's statement on the nature of the threat America faced was being played. As they entered the gym, people were confronted by what they had already seen or heard. The president's statement and his call for citizen's involvement were the main themes of the event.

Above the stage, a large banner with white lettering on a red background had been hung. It read, "PROTECT WILLIAMS — PROTECT AMERICA." In the corner of the gym was the most controversial of the booths. After much debate and disagreement, it was decided that Chaplain Forrest and Pastor Wilson's request would be granted and there was a second continuous video feed playing for all to see and hear. This one showed clips from the original press conference, the Williams special, and the recent newscast interview in which the Bookseller called on believers to stand before the Lord and pray for deliverance and wisdom to know why God had allowed the attacks on America, confronting everyone with the issue of whether they were on God's side.

Pastor Wilson and Chaplain Forrest were seeking to recruit a different kind of army, one that would stand together before the Lord in prayer and repentance, seeking God's intervention against the shooter and the terrorists before it was too late for America.

The new organization was internet-based and had been named Together We Pray. They too had a banner, smaller but readable from anywhere in the gym. People from across the world were being invited to gather and pray via the internet. They already had thousands signed up from as far as Iran. For that night, Chaplain Forrest skipped the Williams College Chapel prayer meeting and left it in the capable hands of a young believer, Paul Phillips. Forrest sensed that what God had begun in gathering His people together worldwide was vastly more important that night than the chapel prayer meeting.

For families attending, there was food, entertainment, games, and exhibits. The intention was to clothe a serious purpose with a joyful atmosphere. The event would be a subtle victory celebration as the people gathered together against the common threat. It was to be a public declaration that the citizens of this community had had enough of living in fear and terror. For them, it was about what the future might bring. Together they would ultimately overcome. In their own way, these people were living through a revolution in which they would no longer simply depend on the government for their security or wellbeing. It was clear to them that government alone was not enough. They needed to be involved, and to many, the understanding was dawning that they would fail without God's direct intervention. This new awareness created new searchers for God, which was the cause of great celebrations among the forces of light. To the forces of darkness, there was renewed determination and commitment to launch a reign of terror and fear.

Tom Campy and Sally Johnson gathered the Citizens Militia security force, assigned for the night, before the stage for final instructions, before the doors of the gym were opened to the public. It was a strange looking gathering of men and women of all ages, ethnicity, and economic backgrounds. Present that night at Tom Campy's invitation were two new members for whom that was their first assignment. One, Abdul Farsi, was seen as a symbol of moderate Arab Muslims in the United States who opposed terrorism. The other, Susan Stafford, was a young woman graduate student from Williams College who was seen as a good symbol for encouraging student involvement. The training team had advised Tom that she was amazing in her proficiency with firearms.

"Tonight is an important day to the community and nation as it offers a great opportunity to recruit and fill our ranks," Tom began. "We are already a symbol that the citizens of this community can stand together against violence. We want the people to feel safe. To accomplish that we will need to recruit and train large numbers of new volunteers to meet the massive requests for patrols that we have already received.

"Tonight, we are not expecting trouble, but we are fully prepared for any difficulty. Obviously, the recent incident where a terrorist attempted to kill the Bookseller with an explosive vest is a concern. There has been no information of which we are aware of that would make this gathering a terrorist target. However, there is always the possibility of an attack. Additionally, we are still dealing with the shooter. It is unlikely that he would dare confront us here by trying to kill someone at this event. Public confrontation has not been his pattern — that is why he has not yet been caught — but we cannot take a chance.

"Accordingly, we will deploy into three groups. A third of us will patrol the parking areas to keep the shooter from picking up someone with impunity as he has done many times before. A third of us will patrol both outside and inside the gym and control the doors. You all have the training on how to identify a person equipped with an explosive vest. If you see such a person, direct the police to intervene immediately.

"The final third of us will stand with our backs to the stage to observe the crowd and respond to any threat to those on the stage. The standing rules of engagement limit our response. The police will be with us and they have the principal responsibility to respond with an appropriate level of force to any threat.

"Most of you know our police liaison, Officer Sally Johnson. She has some additional instructions. Please listen closely. Sally?"

"Thank you, Tom. This is a great day for the citizens of Williams as we stand together to confront the shooter and whatever terrorist threats exist among us, as the president has warned. The eyes of the nation are on Williams this night. An ITN camera crew is here filming the event. I have been told that among the reporters assigned to cover the event is George Murphy of the *Times Daily*. Even Homeland Security has a representative here who has been discussing with us about duplicating the Citizen's Militia and Neighborhood Watch programs across the country. It is our job to ensure that the event does not offer our enemies a platform for making a statement.

"You need to be aware of additional precautions that are being taken in light of the events of the past week and the president's warning. Because Williams has been so high profile nationally, and in light of the terrorist attempt on the Bookseller's life, the president has ordered additional forces deployed to assist us. What I am about to share with you has not even been told to the leadership of the Citizens Militia. The only people who have been made aware of the additional precautions are law enforcement and appropriate governmental authorities. Do not share this information with others particularly with the press.

"Taking positions outside the doors will also be a team from the U.S. Military with bomb-sniffing dogs trained to detect explosives and other devices that could be smuggled into the building. If they react to any individual, you are to assist law enforcement to keep that individual segregated from the crowd and outside the building. Bomb experts on site will deal with any explosive device that may be found.

"I assume you have seen the temporary concrete barriers which were installed to prevent a car bomber from crashing a vehicle into the gym and detonating an explosive device. You will see an Army team in plain clothes assigned to protect the entrance. They are near two parked vehicles which contain weapons capable of stopping any speeding car seeking to crash through the barriers. You are being advised of these additional forces so that you will be able to distinguish between friend and foe. When you are released to your assigned position, identify these forces that are already in place so you will not react against them if they move on a perceived threat."

"Why weren't we told about this?" Campy interrupted emotionally. "I thought the police and the Citizens Militia were a team?"

"Tom, the decisions were not made by the police in Williams. They came from Washington and included specific instructions not to share this information with the Citizens Militia until absolutely necessary. What we are doing is new to law enforcement, and until we can prove that citizen participation works, there will be some limits. I can't change that but if we were not a team, I would not have just informed you of the overall plan."

"Sorry Sally," Tom responded. "We have worked very hard to get to this place and we don't want to be taken for granted. I do understand. What we are doing is in its own way revolutionary, but who better than citizens to stand for themselves?"

"Listen, people, we only have a few minutes before we open the doors," Sally continued. "One risk is ours alone to deal with. We made the decision not to go with metal detectors. As a result, the uncovered risk is an individual or group of individuals who are able to enter with hidden firearms. The weather mandates coats and coats can conceal weapons. The team assigned to look out at the audience from the base of the stage must be prepared to respond immediately to anyone who produces a firearm before the person shoots. The drill is to immediately shout 'firearm' and then to respond. Shoot to wound, not to kill. I repeat, shoot to wound, not to kill. We want to take any shooter alive for questioning the purpose. If the shooting is part of a terrorist effort as the president has warned, we might be able to obtain significant information on the overall plan against America. Do not shoot unless you clearly identify a firearm and again, do not shoot to kill. Are there any questions?"

"If not," Tom added, "Let me pray for us before we report to our assigned posts."

There were mixed responses to Tom's prayer. The new role of prayer was becoming more generally accepted. Believers rejoiced and actively joined in seeking God's help and protection. Most unbelievers either accepted this new movement with some curiosity and hope, or like the soldier in the foxhole during a war, were glad for any help they could get from God if there was a God. A small number of people were angered at what they believed to be an invasion of their right not to be confronted by religion, but they remained silent for they were clearly in the minority.

Two among the crowd had uniquely different perspectives. Susan Stafford understood clearly that her inability to kill the Bookseller was the subject of much of the prayers. She wondered how this God, to whom they prayed, would answer their prayer. Already, this God had not punished her for attempting to kill the Bookseller and the boy. Why, she thought, when she so obviously deserved death?

She was deeply burdened with an intense desire to do something, even in a small way, to make up for her crimes. She knew that there would come a time in the present life when she would have to pay for her sins, but that was not what she feared. She feared the second death. Thoughts of judgment and her eternal condemnation continued to frighten her. She remembered the man in the park and wondered if there was any way the God to whom they prayed could forgive one as evil as her. She could not see how that would be possible, but if she could contribute now, she thought, at least there would be something positive to weigh against the entirety of her sins.

The fact that infidels referenced God angered Farsi. However, he did not forget that he was among them by choice and for an important purpose — gathering information and establishing a cover. Already the decision to join had paid off with intelligence beyond anything he had hoped for. Obviously, the U.S. government was onto something or they would have never deployed military assets to a meeting in a high school gym in Williams, Illinois. Fortunately, their efforts were directed at preventing different kinds of attacks than those planned for MD or the execution squads. If tactics or deployments do not change, they would be of little threat to future plans. He had to be sure, however, that they would not face armed members of the Citizens Militia tomorrow morning when the Jihadists were going to hit the church.

As he completed his prayer, Tom announced, "We have two new members who are with us tonight for the first time. Abdul Farsi is a local junior high school teacher and Susan Stafford is a graduate student at Williams College. Because this is their first deployment, I want Mr. Farsi to team up with me, Ms. Stafford, and Officer Johnson. The rest of you, team up with someone close and go to your assigned posts. Good luck."

Doeg's Attack

The gym filled quickly when the doors were opened. The people had come together for a special evening. There was a sense of expectation in the air. The high school band was on the stage playing patriotic songs as the people walked among the exhibits and booths. Many paused to listen to the president's warning and to the Booksellers' call for prayer and introspection. As they passed these two exhibits, people became momentarily sober as individual decisions and commitments were made. Many signed up to become part of Together We Pray. Most joined either the Neighborhood Watch program or the Citizens Militia while others stopped to report activities that seemed suspicious to them. Sales of firearms were brisk.

The program was scheduled to begin at 8:00 PM with speeches from the mayor, the police chief, and Representative Townsen. Sam Will was to speak as head of the Citizens Militia. Sally Johnson, the police coordinator, was to speak for both the Citizen's Militia and the Neighborhood Watch program. Even Josh Douglas, the high school football coach, had been allotted a few minutes. The program was to end with a prayer by Pastor Fredrick Scribes of College Church. The scene was reminiscent of many pep rallies held in that same gym.

Alexander and Areopagus were joined by Molech as they prepared to turn the celebration of security into an evening of death and fear after which a servant of the forces of darkness would be crowned a 'hero' and hopefully given access to more intelligence that would advance the Dark Master's agenda against America.

Also present were Barnabas and many others of the forces of light calmly awaiting instructions and wondering what God would allow that night.

Unknown to all but the forces of darkness, as the mayor began to speak, Doeg had entered the gym unchallenged, concealing two automatic pistols under his heavy coat. The snow, he thought, was an ally. Looking around, most had heavy coats, although they were unbuttoned. He began to sweat lightly as he began to feel the effects of the indoor heating system.

Working his way slowly through the booths, he saw a mass of red-jacketed targets that surrounded the stage. As he deliberately unbuttoned his coat and placed his hands on the weapons, he only wished he had brought more ammunition clips. There were many more targets than he had anticipated.

After considering the task before him, he decided to launch his attack when the leader of the Citizens Militia stood to speak. It would be him first, followed by as many red-jacketed infidels as he could kill before someone killed him. It was a simple plan, one he had trained for many times over the years in Afghanistan. He had no fear.

He listened to the speeches of the mayor and the chief of police. After those speeches, the federal representative and the football coach were to speak next, after which he would strike the initial target. "Won't these people ever shut up?" he said to himself.

Alexander moved quickly to cause Farsi's Keeper to make him aware of Doeg's presence. Alarmed, Farsi struggled with what to do. He could not be identified with Doeg and he could not shoot without cause. One thing for sure was that he could not allow Doeg to be captured alive and risk all their future plans. He began to sweat and looked for an opportunity. His hand dropped to his weapon. He had to be ready without appearing to be ready.

Doeg momentarily saw Farsi in his red jacket and considered shooting him immediately, but he smiled darkly at him deciding that personal issues had to wait. The success that night would be measured by the number of the dead. He could not waste ammunition on a fool. He did not concern himself with Farsi for he believed these college boy leaders were incapable of action. They had become lazy and fearful like the Americans. They would never risk their own blood.

Doeg turned away from Farsi and moved slowly closer to the front of the crowd as Representative Townsen concluded his remarks and introduced Coach Douglas. The target was next. As he waited patiently, Doeg's Keeper flooded his mind with hatred for those who were bragging about a victory that would never be, and those in the red jackets who symbolized the people rising up in their defense. He noted the ITN camera crew filming at his left and prepared to give them something to show to the rest of America. It was to be his hour of glory as he entered into his reward.

Coach Douglas concluded his remarks saying, "And now it is my pleasure to introduce my good friend and fellow member of the Citizens Militia, our founder, and leader, Mr. Sam Will." As the people applauded, Sam stood smiling and approached the podium. Doeg's hands came out of his coat when suddenly his eyes caught sight of two women directly below Will. One wore the red jacket of the Citizen's Militia and the other was a black police officer. His anger immediately flared at these women who, by their dress and conduct, ridiculed men and defiled the teachings of his religion.

Instantaneously he turned and fired two shots to kill them as his body was simultaneously riddled with a full clip from the gun of Farsi who had drawn his weapon to fire the moment Doeg's hands had come out of his jacket. There had been no cry of "firearm" and no shooting to wound. Farsi ran toward Doeg, loading another clip to continue firing. He was stopped by the cries of Tom Campy who almost tackled him from behind.

"I'm sorry, I'm sorry" Farsi blurted out, "I saw him draw his weapon and I had to stop him. He would have killed all of you. Did you see the hatred in his eyes?"

Doeg's two shots were diverted as he was struck by Farsi's assault. One passed loudly but harmlessly just above the head of Officer Sally Johnson. The other had hit Susan Stafford in her shoulder and she lay on the floor in obvious pain, bleeding while being cared for by Sally. Doctor Ed Miller, who was in attendance with his family, pushed his way through the crowd to help care for Susan as police dispatch called for an ambulance. It was obvious that no amount of medical aid could help Doeg.

Panic rose and guns appeared throughout the gym as both professionals and amateurs looked for others present that might be part of a coordinated assault. Sam Will, now standing at the podium, called for calm. "People, hear me! It's over. The attacker is dead. Now calm down and clear the way so that we can get medical attention to our sister."

Stepping up to the podium, Pastor Scribes stood beside Sam Will and asked loudly for all to hear, "Can we pray right now?" As Will backed away respectfully, Pastor Scribes began.

"Father, we come before you now in thanksgiving for your protection from this one who came to kill and injure. Lord, we do not understand the hate that drives a man like this, but we remember that when You died on the cross it was to open the opportunity for all to come to You, including this one. We forgive him as You forgave those who crucified You, and we ask that You teach us how to reach out in Your love to those who seek to destroy us.

"We ask that Your healing hand rest on our injured sister and your wisdom on those who seek to care for her. Calm our hearts and give us peace in these moments. Restore to us the joy of life and give us a thankful spirit. Cause fear to be far away from Your people. Give us hearts to join together and stand before You and pray.

"May America as a nation and Americans individually choose to be on Your side. In Jesus Name, Amen."

The prayer had its intended effect on earth and in Heaven. God heard and answered. Susan stabilized, the bleeding was brought under control and the people gathered in the gym that night were no longer afraid. It was as if a cloud of darkness had been lifted, which it had, and light illuminated to the hearts of God's people. Everyone present knew that they had experienced the protection of God.

Even Farsi wondered about the words of the prayer to forgive and show love to those who sought to kill them. Perhaps, he thought, he did not understand real Christians. An enemy willing to love and forgive was not an enemy that could be destroyed by death. They could kill the body but even in death, these people would live. Tomorrow would tell whether this pastor was one among many or whether they were all like him. Tomorrow would show if they really died.

CHAPTER 12

WHO IS THE HERO?

Saturday, February 9 — MD minus 76 days

IN NEW YORK, Jim Hunt and Carl Stern rejoiced. "I cannot believe it — another exclusive from Williams," Stern declared. "The local producer tells me they caught everything from the opening of the doors until the injured woman was wheeled out on a gurney for the trip to the hospital while the terrorist's body was being removed from the gym. What a story, and we are the only network that will be able to tell it. There is a hero, a dead villain, and a survivor. The Citizens Militia worked under fire and the hero was a moderate Muslim. It was a storybook, almost too easy."

It seemed too easy because it was too easy. Alexander and Molech were also rejoicing for their instrument was now the hero and would be able to know the Citizens Militia deployment plans and could work the attacks around them. The execution squads could proceed and that should divert attention from MD. That was good news, but it wasn't the only news. Doeg's attack had failed and then there was that terrible prayer. "We never seem to have a clear and final victory," Alexander complained.

"Tomorrow, remember, there is tomorrow," Molech responded. "This fight is day-to-day and year-to-year until the end. Do not judge success or failure by a day, a year, or even a century. The Enemy never quits and neither do we."

Their incomplete victory was obvious to Barnabas as the forces of light gathered above the Williams high school gym that night. They had waited patiently and responded in obedience immediately after the Holy Spirit spoke. They never knew what to do or what would happen until the Spirit spoke. They never questioned what He said or delayed their obedience after He spoke, and often they did not understand what their obedience accomplished until much later. Faith to them was to listen, obey, and leave the rest to God. That they knew was the perfect formula for success for man and angel alike.

"I am always amazed at God's judgments against a human whose heart is captured by evil desires, whether saved or lost," Barnabas observed. "For me, I believe God's worst judgment is often to give that person what they desire, but they receive what they want with the consequences of their wrong choice. Take the terrorist Doeg, for example. At his core, he hated women, desiring only to use and humiliate them, so God gave him over completely to that hate and desire at that critical moment so that the consequence was what changed his target at the cost of his life and mission. He was able to express his hate, but he failed at everything he had hoped to accomplish."

"Absolutely true," Lucius added. "Humans always consider what they want but never the consequences of getting what they want. I have watched God often use that judgment to teach believers to trust Him, as well as to thwart the plans of the Dark Master."

"I am glad we don't know the future but serve the One who holds it in His hand," Niger declared with great reverence and respect. "Did you notice how much God left open by what He did and allowed tonight? Clearly, he is not finished with Sam Will or Susan Stafford. Others were spared for purposes only God knows."

"Did you hear the children's angels crying out before the Father for their safety and protection?" Manaen asked. "They always see His face and He always hears them."[56]

"Yes, and He answered," Lucas replied. "None of the children were hurt and most did not even know what had happened, for their eyes were blinded to the threat and their parents were given the wisdom to shield them immediately."

"Did you see the work of the Spirit in Pastor Scribes? His actions and prayer showed real growth within and the message he delivered in his prayer was God's message. I wonder if it is in God's plan for him to survive tomorrow."

"I wonder too," Barnabas answered. "Not all will be protected. The blood of the faithful will be shed as it has been the case over the centuries, but only when and as God allows for His purposes. They must not be afraid or love their physical lives more than they love the Lord."

"I don't think Pastor Scribes is afraid anymore," Manaen observed. "In recent years he has not been useful because he feared what men think about him. I believe that was overcome tonight. I believe that he will again be useful to advance the Father's purposes, even at the cost of his life."

"I hope you are right," Barnabas replied. "Tomorrow may provide that answer for the Light!" And with that, he left, awaiting his next assignment.

The President Responds

The phone rang in the White House, the president received it, and he was informed in detail about what had occurred in Williams. It was first-hand information from Saul Greenfield, the Homeland Security official sent to observe and make recommendations regarding the Citizens Militia and Neighborhood Watch programs.

"Mr. President, it was amazing. The terrorist pulled two semi-automatic pistols with an obvious intention to kill as many people as possible and just as he fired his first shots, he was struck with a barrage of fire from a member of the Citizens Militia who emptied his whole clip onto him. The most amazing thing about it was that this Citizens Militia member was a local Muslim junior high school teacher. Perhaps this is the break in the moderate Muslim community we have been looking for."

"How is the injured Citizen Militia member?" the president asked.

"We don't know for sure but another amazing thing was that after all the commotion, this pastor stepped up to the podium and prayed and she stabilized. It had appeared for a time that she would bleed to death. All I know right now is that she has been taken to a local hospital."

"I wish that the current 'hero' had not overreacted so we could have had a wounded terrorist rather than another body," the president said grimly. "We missed an opportunity here that we may not get again. What were the rules of engagement?"

"Respectfully, Mr. President, the man overreacted. The rules of engagement were to call out 'firearm' and then to shoot to wound. There was nothing wrong with the rules of engagement; it was simply an emotional overreaction to the threat."

"Perhaps, but emptying a full clip into a suspect is not the way to wound someone and he didn't call out 'firearm.' Thank you for the report. Please follow up on the injured citizen and let me know when she will be able to receive a call from me."

"Yes, Mr. President," Greenfield answered, but he was troubled by the suspicious nature of the president's conclusions. Why not simply take advantage of a Muslim hero and use it to encourage others?

The president immediately asked the White House Operator to locate Troy Steed, the national security advisor. In a few minutes, the connection was made. "Troy, have you heard what happened in Williams tonight?"

"Yes, Mr. President, I just got the report."

"I want you to contact both General Hedge and the commander of the Alpha Force on the ground in Chicago," the president directed. "Tell General Hedge to keep his focus on MD. I do not believe this is anything more than another rogue incident, although it may be a precursor to what we will face tomorrow. Tell the commander on the ground to be ready to respond tomorrow to some kind of mass shooting incident. I have a strong suspicion they are going to try and divert us from the real risk which is MD. Keep the Joint Chiefs working on an operational plan to respond to MD."

"Yes, Mr. President."

Again, to the White House Operator, "Please get me, Tom Knight," and in a moment, he was on the line. "Tom, I assume that you have been called about the latest Williams incident."

"Yes, Mr. President, I just got that call a few moments ago."

"Tom, I don't know how you view this, but I don't see it as the attack David Barnes was warning us about."

"I agree," Knight responded, "There is no way this was the event explained in the communications David translated. I wish it was. If a solo shooter was all we faced, this would not be a military concern. It would be a local law enforcement issue."

"Keep the commission focused on MD," the president directed. "Do not let them get diverted from that future attack which, if David is correct, is being moved up by at least a month. I hope to know more about timing when we get Israel's report from Besserman."

"Tom, call George Murphy of the *Times Daily*. Clue him that he may not want to overplay the events of tonight when he writes his report. Let him know we expect something else tomorrow and that none of this is tied to MD apart from attempts to divert our attention. Then, call the ITN producers and request a copy of their tape of tonight's events. Ask for all of it — not simply the edited version. Get it to David Barnes and tell him to study it and that I will want his conclusions tomorrow. If you have trouble with ITN, let me know and I will call them and make a personal request to Jim Hunt or Carl Stern. They have always been fair to us. I think they understand the risk America faces."

"Yes, Mr. President."

Meanwhile, across America and around the world, the major news networks broadcasted the events that happened in Williams. Again, ITN had the advantage because they were the only ones who had filmed the raw footage. As they had done before, ITN left out the prayer of Pastor Scribes which quickly created as much controversy as the shooting itself. Besides the disdain for anything religious, the team at ITN considered the call for people to forgive and love the killer as an unnatural response to violence and hate. Then, there was the cry again for people and for America to choose to be on God's side. How could God be on the terrorist's side? Perhaps this is another opportunity to bring in the Bookseller for some clarification," thought Jim Hunt.

Tom & Sally Plan for Tomorrow

Tom Campy was troubled by the two calls he had just received and did not know what to do about the dread he sensed in his heart. Farsi's call was confusing. There was the continued apology for his overreaction to the terrorist, but the questions he asked were what troubled Campy. There seemed a false sincerity about him. It just did not ring true, but Tom had no idea why it didn't. Farsi was the hero who might have saved Sally Johnson's life. How could he doubt him?

Campy remembered the conversation. Farsi had said, "Mr. Campy, I am only available full-time on the weekend because of my work as a school teacher. Are there other deployments tomorrow I can be involved with? Can I help more with planning or leadership? I want to devote my free time to stopping this slander of my faith by these evil people who pervert the true teachings of Islam."

Campy had responded, "There are no current deployments for tomorrow. You have done enough. Rest tomorrow and we can discuss future assignments next week. If you want, you had said you would attend church with me sometime. I will be going to College Church tomorrow and would be happy to take you as my guest. That might be a good way of appreciating our differing beliefs. The pastor of College Church is the man who prayed at the security fair."

The tone of Farsi's answer troubled Tom. He replied with an unusual emotion bordering on shock or fear, "No, not tomorrow. I can't do tomorrow," and then he seemed to collect himself and the tone changed. "I promise we will do that on another Sunday and you can join me for Friday night prayers."

Even as he had sought to digest that call, the phone rang and it was an obviously concerned Sally Johnson. "Tom, we have to talk. I told you I was concerned about that Farsi fellow. I know he is tonight's hero, but I have issues with what he did and the way he did it. We need to talk." The tone of her voice did not leave room for a negative answer.

"Sally," Tom responded, "I have had enough for one night. How about after church tomorrow over lunch? I am going to College Church. You would be welcome to join me. I want to hear what Pastor Scribes says after tonight. Did you hear his prayer? It was amazing. Something has happened to him. He seems different."

"I thought the same thing," Sally answered. "I'll join you and then we talk. What service are you going to?"

"I tend to be an early bird. Let us meet for coffee at Restoration and then go to the first service. It begins at 8:00 AM on the dot, so I will meet you at 7:15 AM. No discussion of Farsi until later. OK?"

"OK."

"Sally, I just want you to know I have been thanking God that He spared you tonight."

"Thank you for your prayers, Tom. Tonight was sobering. There are obviously more of these terrorists out there and we will hear from them again unless we find them first. Maybe we can invest a little of our time before church praying together."

"Agreed, let's make it 7:00 AM at Restoration. Have you checked on Susan Stafford? How is she doing?"

"The hospital reports that she is stable and will recover," Sally answered, "but she has likely permanently lost the use of her left arm."

"That's sad. I really don't know her at all," Tom said, "We need to devote some attention to her as she recovers. Did anyone follow up on her car? She must have driven to the gym. Someone needs to get her keys and drop it off at her house."

"Sounds like another good project for us after church," Sally answered. "Let's go see her after lunch and get the keys."

The call ended there, but Tom could not dismiss the sense of dread he felt. Before sleep, Tom paused again to pray, and as he prayed, he drifted into a deep and restful sleep.

Farsi Confronts the Remaining Nine

Farsi was careful to ensure no one was following him as he made his way to the old rent house off Bell and 17th. He was met at the door by Kalab Sawori, a man on a mission. "What the hell happened? The television reports say Doeg showed up and you killed him! You better have a good explanation or you are going to be found tomorrow in a garbage can like the others."

"Back off Sawori, the rules of the game are simple. No rogues. We work together on the bigger plan. Doeg went out on his own and he placed everything and everyone at risk. I had to kill him to keep him from being captured. As it is, between the first seven and Demetrius who tried to kill the old man with an explosive vest, the authorities know we are here. Doeg affirmed it again tonight. Stupid, stupid, stupid! The man was too dumb to live."

"He may have been foolish, but he was faithful. He is responsible for many American deaths in Iraq and Afghanistan. He deserves respect for what he meant to the cause," Sawori declared.

By this time, the remaining group had gathered around the two and were listening intently. "It wouldn't have mattered what he did in Afghanistan and Iraq if he had been captured and interrogated," Farsi answered. "Forget Doeg. He is dead and tomorrow we have the opportunity to send a message to those cowardly infidels responsible for his death. I did not kill Doeg, they did, and all the rest of our brothers who have died for jihad. Take it out on them tomorrow; pave the streets with their blood."

"All of you, listen to me. I cannot stay here because I am now known. Tomorrow, drop the disguises; they won't help. Everyone knows we are here, so wear the black hoods, which strike terror in the hearts of the American cowards. We will let them know who we are and who we serve.

"Stay with the plan. Kill and get out of there. I have confirmed that there will be no Citizens Militia deployment there tomorrow. The church has never had a security guard before, so the risk of any opposition should be minimal. However, understand this: should something go wrong, and someone is wounded, if they can't be moved without risking the rest of the force, you must kill them or kill yourself if you are the injured one. That sacrifice is necessary to protect the ultimate mission. No one will be surrendered into their hands alive."

With that, he left quickly to get as far away from that place as possible until the deed was done. "I need an alibi tomorrow," he thought. "I think I will go to church, just not College Church."

A Different Gift of Tongues

Hiram Urbay was astonished as he was browsing the web from his modest home in the eastern part of Tehran. He had been searching for ways to be more involved with other Christians without bringing attention to himself or risking his job as a computer technician with the State Security Force (SSF). He knew better than others that it was a risky affair because the leadership of the SSF was on a campaign to find and neutralize all Christians. They were using torture, threats, and deception to identify Christians. It was the deception which concerned him the most. In Iran, you could never be sure that a person claiming to be a Christian was actually a Christian and not an operative for the SSF. For that reason, Urbay had been very cautious. It was a lonely affair and he felt incomplete and disconnected from other believers. It felt unnatural.

Urbay's new discovery emboldened him. He called to his believing wife, Sasha, "Come, you must see this. It is a gift from God."

Sasha knew nothing about computers or Urbay's work beyond the fact that working for the SSF was a dangerous affair. She knew that he usually browsed the internet regularly to find out what was happening around the world, but was frustrated by not knowing English very well. There were very few websites in Persian that he could trust. She came quickly for he was rarely this excited.

"See, look," Urbay said. "It is American and it is Christian, but it is in our language. I found it while searching for the keyword 'prayer.' It is an organization called Together We Pray and it is all in our language."

"Impossible. How could these American Christians know our language?" was her response, but there it was in front of her on the screen in their language. "How can this be?"

"You haven't seen the whole of it," Urbay said excitedly. "Watch this," he said as he clicked on an icon above a picture of an old man. Immediately, a video began to play of the Bookseller's various statements, all in a voice clearly speaking their language. They sat together in amazement as they heard the Bookseller's call for believers to gather in prayer and to make the choice to be on God's side. With tears in their eyes, they committed to praying together and to find a group of believers for group prayers.

Not far away, in a neighborhood station of the State Security Forces, investigators were surfing the web looking for evidence of conduct, which endangered the government. One of their specific assignments was to find web pages available in the country that advanced Christian teachings or perspectives. They were to identify the offending site and then technicians based in the main SSF headquarters would block it. Because of what they had seen on satellite TV concerning the events in Williams, they were searching for the Together We Pray website to see whether it was a risk. Watching at the same exact moment Hiram and Sasha were viewing the website, they saw nothing but English gibberish. "This is nothing," Akin said and went on with his search.

High above Teheran, members of the forces of light gathered in celebration. "Praise be to God most high. The Father has poured out the gift of tongues. Remember on Pentecost when the 120 had gathered in prayer when they received the gift of tongues and people heard what they said in their own language.[57] Now, God is speaking to Iranian believers through a website. God's message is being seen by his chosen people in their own language."

"Yes, but this is different. God's message is only seen outside the English-speaking world by those with the light inside."

"God is protecting His children in places of persecution and gathering them to pray."

CHAPTER 13

SEEKING HELP AND ANSWERS

Saturday, February 9 — MD minus 76 days

ISRAEL'S USUALLY BLUNT Prime Minister was even more blunt than usual: "Senator, the survival of Israel is at substantial risk as we speak. America must understand that we will not be bullied or threatened, and we will not accept an attack on our soil. We will not accept a nuclear Iran or Syria and we have and will again strike preemptively to block the development of such a weapon by our enemies. We will use nuclear weapons defensively and preemptively to protect our nation. We intend to survive or take our enemies down with us, and that applies to Russia if they choose to join with our enemies. We have weapons that can reach their major cities. We will act alone if we must, and we will not allow even our friends to stand in the way of what must be done to protect ourselves from this threat."

Senator Besserman sat quietly, waiting until Prime Minister Zimri had said all he wished to say. After some time, the Prime Minister indicated with a gesture that the floor was now his.

"Mr. Prime Minister, I believe you know that while President Strong is still in office, Israel will never have to act alone to protect its legitimate security needs. America remains your friend and ally, but America needs your help too. This is not simply a threat to Israel; it is a threat that flows to

Israel only after America has been dealt a fatal blow which is intended to render it impossible for our nation to come to your aid. In that vacuum, Israel would be alone to face Iran and all the Arab nations it could gather and lead. Russia could move traitorously against Israel and America to fill the vacuum left when America is neutralized. In that reality, America's defense against the planned terrorist attack is Israel's first line of defense. To survive, we must face this threat together."

"That will not be easy for your president with the opposition he faces from the majority party's new peace initiative. In all my years in politics, living in a land surrounded by enemies, I have never had to face surrender masked as peace from an opposition party. Our people hate conflict and want to be at peace with our neighbors. However, they understand what is at stake. They know that hate cannot be ignored or eliminated by waving a white flag under the guise of a peace initiative. I have great respect for President Strong. His name mirrors his character. I know that he draws deeply from his faith, which I candidly do not understand, but I appreciate what it does for him. He will need strength and wisdom from his God in the coming days.

"Senator, do you understand what is planned for America? Have you an idea of how little time there is to stop the terrorists?"

"Mr. Prime Minister, I am here so that we share the information we both have so that we can coordinate a preemptive response in future. We know that the date for what is called MD has been moved up and could be moved up further. We have found a way to intercept what we believe to be communications among the leaders of the terrorist organizations. We have operatives in Iraq who provide us information and through whom we can communicate with moderate elements in the country. The president is prepared to move forcefully and diplomatically as required, but we are still in the dark on the details of what we face.

"The president proposes a coordinated operational group. This group will work on effectively addressing the terrorist threats that our nations face. Following the example of President Kennedy's handling of the Cuban Missile Crisis, President Strong has put together what we call the Survival Commission to investigate options and to prepare alternatives.

"Our kind request is for you, Mr. Prime Minister, to designate military and intelligence leaders to join us. I am prepared to take those men and women back with me to Washington today. The president has also asked that you designate a personal representative like me to ensure that your wishes are made known to him at all times. He wants a direct interface with you and he will be available to you at any time, but neither of you can manage this crisis effectively. I have a phone number to a secured line for you, to which the president will have access to 24 hours a day. Use it anytime you wish."

Handing him a card with the number, Senator Besserman said, "Mr. Prime Minister, all we ask is that you give the security of the United States the same priority as you give your country's security. We will do likewise, and together we can defeat this threat and hopefully open a new relationship with friends throughout the Middle East. Not every Arab leader wishes Israel harm, and there are legitimate concerns of Arabs that could also be addressed in a different environment."

"You Americans are always looking to the future with optimism. That is what has made your country distinct among the nations. However, right now, we better focus on whether there is even a future. We can then discuss how it might be crafted into new relationships in the Middle East. I do not oppose a change in relationships, but a change must be a change and not merely a declaration of change — and it must be mutual.

"I want you to get in touch with my intelligence people and exchange briefings while I discuss with the cabinet your president's request. After I get their approval, I will designate those I wish to return with you as part of the joint Survival Commission, along with my personal representative. Please remember that for both of our protection, this must be done in absolute secrecy."

"I understand, Mr. Prime Minister. Thank you."

The Flag is Up

As Ittai drove toward the hotel, he felt a real sense of dread. Legion had been hard at work in the Middle East, doing what he does best. However, even in the midst of Ittai's discernment of the increased demonic activities, there was a quiet peace and resolute firmness originating from the light within him.

Ittai understood that coming events were crucial, and he prayed for wisdom to know what to say and ask. He also prayed for protection as he had heard of recent instances in which the SSF had discovered covert house prayer meetings and killed those present or dragged them away to prison where they were tortured. He had been praying that God would protect fellow believers and worried that someday the flag would be gone.

Hushai climbed into the back seat and they sped away like any other cab driver who appeared to be on a mission to go wherever he was asked to go: as quickly as possible.

"Ittai, my brother, the news is not good. A representative of the Sheik came and advised Ahmad Habid that the date for MD had been moved up by at least a month and that he needed to be ready to strike in two weeks' notice. The time is getting short and I have no further information concerning the possible terrorist attack on American soil. I have tried, but I simply cannot penetrate the upper echelons of government."

"The Americans aren't sleeping, Hushai. The president and his intelligence agencies are making the necessary plans and chasing every lead while also dealing with terrorist attacks caused by lone wolf terrorists in the country. Clearly, there will be more violence, but the focus remains on MD."

"MD is becoming a large nightmare because of the perceived opportunity for settling old scores. The attacks on American forces by Habid's group will now be accompanied by formal military action from Iran and Syria at least. The extent of the effort is not yet clear. However, expect the skies to be filled with missiles aimed at American military personnel in the Middle East."

"These people are either crazy or MD is beyond anything we have ever imagined," Ittai responded.

"I don't know which of the two is the reality and I don't want to find out, but the plans are real plans and they are not just directed at American forces and Israel. They have also targeted Arab governments friendly to America including Pakistan, Saudi Arabia, and Egypt. The plan calls for assassinations to overthrow those governments and it does not stop there. There are also terrorist cells in Europe. Thus, it is likely that they will attempt a coordinated series of bombings to divert public attention in Europe away from what is happening in America and the Middle East. It is ambitious, and with Russia involved, the face of the world could change in a day."

"Hushai, I simply cannot comprehend how some people believe they can neutralize the United States."

"Again, my brother, you miss the point. The terrorists want to destroy you or force you out of the Middle East forever. The Iranian leadership wants to bring forth the Hidden Imam and does not really care about the United States or Israel firing nuclear weapons at them. They honestly believe that the devastation of a nuclear assault would bring about his immediate return, so they can't lose."

"You told me that before, but I didn't believe it. They have to be crazy. No end-time scenario involves mass suicide to bring back a religious leader. How can we stop that kind of blind foolishness?" Ittai asked.

"Most Iranians want to live in peace and they are not tied to this fundamentalist regime," Hushai responded. "Unfortunately, they are not in power. When you think of Iran, you must distinguish between the people and the government. Destroying a nation because of its leadership would be the wrong thing."

"History doesn't necessarily support that conclusion," Ittai answered. "Remember Germany? Hitler led the whole world into a holocaust, and when defeated, the nation of Germany was left in ruins. Can we work with the moderates and overthrow the crazies?"

"Maybe over time," Hushai said with conviction, "However, this crisis will not be resolved by overthrowing the current regime. The only hope is to find out the details of MD, stop it and capture its leaders openly and publicly. The current leadership of Iran will not have the support of other nations to move against Israel or the United States if MD fails. As part of that, the United States and Israel must seek to destroy the nuclear capacity of Iran. Once the reality of what they had tried to do becomes known and Iran is humiliated before the world, this leadership would be history."

"Hushai, how do we get the details of the plan? That is the real issue."

"Brother, I know it is out there," Hushai answered. "The message from the old man confirmed that in my heart. We have to join with other believers and continue to pray for God to reveal where it is. That is all I know to do. My people in the government simply do not have the details and do not know where to get them, but God does."

After a long pause, Hushai continued. "Ittai, I want to ask a favor."

"Anything I can do," he answered immediately.

"Have your CIA messenger deliver this message to Mr. White in America. I sense that it is really important," and he handed Ittai a note which simply read:

My brother, Mr. White: it is critical now.

Ezekiel 22:30-31.

Soberly, Ittai folded the note and placed it in the secure pouch he had under his seat. He knew exactly what the message meant and his heart affirmed the need to send it quickly.

"Drop me at this address," Hushai directed, handing him another note. "I am meeting tonight with some brothers to pray. This is a risky affair, so please destroy this note after you drop me."

"Are you sure you should do this?" Ittai asked. "Particularly with the SSF on such a campaign against Christians?"

"Do not fear for me, my brother. God is sovereign. He reigns over all of this. He will protect us if that is His plan, or He will gather us home to be with Him. His will be done. All I know is that we need to gather and pray. Remember Gabriel's word from the Father? We cannot value our lives more than our obedience."

"Then I'll stay too. I need to pray with other believers just as much as you," Ittai said.

"No, my brother, it is too much of a risk for both of us to be found together. If something happens to one of us, the other needs to go on and seek the answer. I sense that we should not be together this night. Go in peace and God be with you."

Ittai dropped Hushai several blocks from his true destination and Hushai walked to that place of prayer where they had earlier encountered Gabriel. He poured out a prayer from a tired and frustrated heart filled with sadness and a sense of impending doom.

Another Discovery — Another Opportunity

"Hey David, geek here. Sorry for being so slow."

"You? Slow?" David responded, "You should see me. I have been watching the ITN video of tonight's events in Williams trying to determine what really happened and who was involved. I think I have memorized the footage of the moments before the shooting, frame by frame. My eyes are completely bloodshot. Please rescue me with some good news."

"Well, you don't ask for much," Reed responded. "I have a new posting and I found the computer of the J-14 fellow."

"Wow! Lay it on me," David shouted into the phone. "Did you hack into the computer? Have you got the MD plan?"

"Tone down the volume and the excitement for a minute," Reed answered with unusual seriousness. "The computer is one of many in a computer lab located in the Harkins Graduate School of Education. Our boy must be either a Professor, Administrator, student or on the custodial staff."

"You've got to be kidding."

"I may not be the brightest bulb in the box, but I am right on this one," Reed responded.

"Whoever is the American leader of MD is using a PC in a computer lab to communicate with the website — which is both foolish and clever at the same time."

"What do you mean by that?"

"I mean he is clever to use a common computer so there is nothing material to hack into, but it's foolish because there has to be a way to watch the computer when he is making web postings. Maybe there is a security camera in the computer lab, and if there is, we can get the film for the days and times we know he has been posting."

"Darrell, tell me quick about the new message and then I will call Tom Knight so we can follow up and maybe catch this guy."

"The new one is from the big guy himself again. It says '00. Enemy late. J-1.'"

"Well that one is a no-brainer," Barnes said. "The opposite of 'enemy' is friend or ally, obviously an important friend or ally. The opposite of 'late' is early or on time. Their friend or ally in MD is, or will be, prepared on time or early. It has to mean that someone who will help with MD is on board with the new schedule and probably could be prepared to move that schedule up even more."

"That is good news," Reed answered and he paused in quiet reflection, feeling overwhelmed at the need to find these people quickly and stop their plan. "I only hope that friend or ally isn't Russian."

"Sorry David, but I haven't been sleeping much chasing the computer the J-14 guy has been using. I have got to get some sleep. I hope you guys can find the over-educated killer, but somehow I don't think it will be as easy as it sounds. While it seems stupid to use a public PC in a computer lab, somehow they pulled off 9/11 with evidence left everywhere for people with eyes to see. We simply were not looking for it. I hope we've learned something and can stop this one."

"Me too, Darrell, we have to find that guy quickly. Thanks, hero, sleep well," and he hung up and dialed Tom Knight's secure phone to pass on the new information.

"Oh please Lord, let there have been security cameras," he prayed, even though it was unlikely that Harkins College would have security cameras in a graduate school computer lab.

CHAPTER 14

COLLEGE CHURCH ASSAULT

Sunday, February 10 — MD minus 75 days

T HEY MOVED WITH mechanical precision; six human killing machines pleased to finally have an opportunity to do what they had been trained for and had waited to do for months. Each knew exactly what they were to do in those early morning hours of preparation. Everything had been carefully rehearsed numerous times. No verbal commands were necessary.

The driver from Doeg's old team had already left to steal the high school van previously identified for use for transportation. The plan was to use the van and then dispose of it. Breaking into the van and hotwiring it had all been part of the training; it would be easy. The school was careless, and that helped. The van was left over the weekend, parked in an unsecured parking lot. All that was required would be to remember the likelihood of a security camera in the area so the black hood would be worn in the parking lot. The driver carried a backpack with the necessary tools and his automatic weapons. No one would be allowed to interfere with the mission and live.

The team would be taken with their weapons to a rendezvous point just outside of town to meet the driver with the van at exactly 8:00 AM. The meeting place had been carefully selected to be one with no possibility of security cameras in the area, and little likelihood of people to witness the transfer. Timing was everything and they had to move on schedule so that they hit the church at exactly 8:15 AM. They had chosen that time because the service would have begun at 8:00 AM and the late comers should, for the most part, be in the auditorium. There would be fewer witnesses outside of the building, and fewer people to have to kill to break into the auditorium. The surprise would make it easy.

According to Farsi, there should be no opposition from the Citizens Militia or others, and they would have time to execute the plan before the police could arrive. They should be finished and on their way before 8:30 AM. That would make them avoid the traffic resulting from people coming for the second service.

Even as their preparations were ongoing, Tom Campy was up and getting ready to meet with Sally Johnson at Restoration, a breakfast place within blocks of College Church. He had gotten up with the sun, as was his practice to have time to read the Bible and pray before his day began. The sense of dread had not left him, and he had been directed to the 23rd Psalm, which he was familiar with from his childhood. His mother had quoted that to him often and had helped him memorize it as a boy. There was peace in that passage, even though it spoke of walking through "the valley of the shadow of death" and of being "in the presence of my enemies." The peace was in the promise that Jesus, the one who declared Himself to be the Shepherd, would be with him and that in God's presence there is nothing to fear.

He needed a reminder of that promise that morning, and for that reason, the light within had directed him there and had affirmed the promise as personal to him. It was as if God had rewritten the Bible and inserted his name in that passage so that it began, "Tom, I am your shepherd." The heaviness was lifted, but he still sensed danger and made a decision to do something that he had never done before. He had a concealed weapons permit as a member of the Citizen's Militia because they were now an official auxiliary of the police department. He decided to always be carrying his weapon everywhere he went. The terrorists were clearly in the Williams area and were not finished with what they had been sent to do. He felt compelled to be prepared for anything, at any time.

He was looking forward to some time with Sally. She seemed so wise and mature for her years and was a real encouragement and strength to him in his faith. Her concern about Farsi troubled him. Either Farsi was a great unselfish hero — which is what he wanted to believe — or he was a deceiver and an evil person. Could he have been that stupid to trust him? That would be the subject for their post-church lunch. He was glad that the morning meeting with Sally would be an opportunity to pray and share together. There was something inexplicably supernatural about believers getting together to pray. He was reminded of another promise from the Bible from Jesus that says, "Again, I tell you that if two of you on earth agree about anything you ask for, it will be done by My Father in Heaven. For where two or three come together in My Name, there am I with them."[58]

It was the promise of the Shepherd's presence. "That is the message for Tom this morning," Barnabas said to the forces of light gathered to be available to the Holy Spirit as events would unfold in Williams. "I hope he holds onto that in the midst of whatever the Father may allow. He will be in great danger soon; as will all who are called to College Church this morning."

"Yes, I can already hear the cry of the children's angels," Lucius answered. "They always sense danger and seek the Father's deliverance that the children may grow up and have the opportunity to choose. One of the greatest surprises believers learn when they are called home is on how many occasions as a child or young person they were spared or protected by the Father when their angel cried out for their protection. They lived to choose because of their angel's prayers, and for the fortunate, the prayers of a relative, friend or praying church.

"Do you remember how Jesus displayed the love of the Father for children? I cannot forget the look in His eye, the tone of His voice, the gentleness with which He
looked into each pair of little eyes, and the blessings He gave."

"No one who saw that could forget," Niger added. "It was when Jesus rebuked the twelve for trying to keep the children away from him. Even the Apostles were reminded when they wrote the Gospels of the sting of Jesus' rebuke and the emotion He obviously felt. They wrote that Jesus was indignant, and that He received the children and 'took them in His arms, put His hands on them and blessed them.'[59]

"God loves children in a very special way, and His heart breaks with every broken marriage and over every child who is kept away from Him by the action of parents or schools or government or society or anyone. He remains indignant at those responsible and will not sit and watch forever. The day will come when He will act in judgment against those who keep the children away from Him."

"Without question," Barnabas agreed, "but this day does not appear to be that day, for the Father continues to seek to give all people the chance to choose including those who draw the children away, and even those who seek this day to harm or kill children. The way into the Kingdom yet remains open for a time."

"Yes, Barnabas, but when that door closes on an individual or a nation, it is over. When that happens, all that is left is physical death, judgment, and the second death; for their choice will have been made for all of the eternity."

Passionate Intervention

Long before dawn, the light within had awakened the Bookseller, Chaplain Forrest, Pastor Wilson, and Paul Phillips with an incredible burden to pray for the safety of believers here and around the world. The call had been individual and unknown to each other, but it was the same. It was what was on the Father's heart for them. All four clearly understood the message and immediately commenced praying.

For Paul, the burden was greater because of his dream. The Curtain had again opened briefly for him, and he had heard the cry of the children's angels. He did not know what it was he had heard, but the intensity of the anguish alarmed him deeply.

The Bookseller understood that he was sensing the heart of God, and that like Moses and Elijah on the mount of transformation, or Peter, James and John in the garden of Gethsemane, he was being invited to share God's anguish but not to experience His pain.[60] All he knew to pray was like Christ had prayed and so he cried out, "Father if it can be within Your will for this cup to pass, let it pass. Yet, not my will, but Your will be done."[61] He thought about what happened after that prayer was prayed by the Lord. It was only moments later that the crowd of soldiers came, and with a kiss the traitor Judas betrayed Him and the pain began.[62]

The old man felt tears begin to stream down his face as the reality of what that day might bring became clear. He changed his prayer to be that only believers would die that day and that those called to die would die faithful as witnesses to the truth of the gospel. It is only a person who understood the second death and all it means for eternity that could pray for unbelievers to die and Christians to be spared. It was only the Christians who were prepared to die.

Pastor Wilson jumped from his bed and quickly posted an emergency call for immediate prayers on the Together We Pray website. It read simply, "pray now for the safety of believers here in Williams and around the world. Pray that we do not compromise to preserve our freedom or our physical lives." Throughout the earth, believers that were directed by God to that site in that moment read the message in their own language and began to pray fervently. The message was clear and alarming. Some were being called to die or suffer imprisonment, and that may be only the beginning.

One of the many who had been directed to the Together We Pray website at that moment was Joshua Strong, who in his residence fell immediately to his knees crying out to the Lord. For some time he had sensed that the execution type attacks would come not as random killings, but directed against Christians and Jews. What he had been shown by the light inside was affirmed by the website posting. He felt so helpless, which was not simply arbitrary — it was how God wanted him to feel.

In a hospital still recovering from the anesthesia given for the surgery, Susan Stafford also felt the call to pray. She knew there would be more shootings, and she cried out to God that she be delivered from this hospital to have an opportunity to somehow make a difference. "What a foolish prayer," she thought, "me, the killer of scores wanting a chance to protect others." Her eyes closed and she saw what seemed to be the arms of Jesus outstretched to her. I have to live and get out of here, she thought. I have to find that old man and ask him if there is yet a way for me. I have wasted my life, but perhaps I do not have to waste my death.

Pastor Scribes Preparation

Pastor Scribes had been up before the sun rose, as was his practice on Sundays. This morning the message God had laid on his heart was about the prayer he had been given Saturday night after the shooting at the Security Fair. He had struggled with the source of hate and the need for believers to stand against hate and evil, but to stand in love, willing to forgive anything; even as Jesus had set the example and the Bible commanded. But, he had also been shown that it was also time for believers to be bold and public with God's message. For too long, Christians in America and he, in particular, had surrendered the stage to those who opposed the teachings of the Bible and wanted all Christians to be silenced. It was as if the louder society screamed, advocating what the Bible called sin, the more believers hid their faith and were silent. "Enough of that," he thought. "Sin is sin and should be declared publicly to be sin," he said to his wife Tami. "People may choose to sin as long as their conduct does not violate existing law, but they don't have the right to sin or the right to call their conduct something other than sin."

As he was making final revisions in that week's message he had titled, "Forgiveness in Love," and made notes on next week's message he had tentatively titled, "Love is Not Silent," he wondered at the new sense of boldness he felt. It was as if the teachings of the Bible so burned within his heart that he could not be silent, whatever the cost. For the first time in his ministry, he felt like God's messenger. This was true, for that was the first time he was willing to deliver God's message whatever the cost; exactly as God wanted it delivered.

In His sovereignty, God had not chosen to burden Pastor Scribes to pray that day as he had burdened others. Pastor Scribes had different tasks for which he was being prepared for.

A Day to Just Be a Girl

Sally loved Sunday mornings. She was up early to prepare her heart for church and to pray for wisdom regarding her time with Tom Campy. He was a precious man with good intentions, but in her heart, she knew he was wrong about Farsi. There was something not right about Farsi, regardless of what the police background investigation had revealed or the parents of his students said about him. "In truth, I think in that Tom is troubled too," she thought.

Getting dressed, she delighted in the fact that she got to be a girl that Sunday — a woman. No pants, gun, handcuffs, or radios. Just a skirt, a blouse, and the accessories that made her feel feminine. Sunday was the one day that she always tried to schedule as her free day, a day totally away from the demands of being a police officer. That Sunday, with the exception of the conversation with Tom Campy, she was a civilian going to church like any other civilian. She even got to go in her car, not the patrol car. It was for her truly what Sundays were meant to be — a day of rest and a time to go to church and worship the Lord.

She too had not been awakened to pray, for God had other purposes for her that day. She had not forgotten the warnings of Homeland Security regarding the threats on Williams, but she dismissed those and left them to the Lord. She was excited to be able to hear Pastor Scribes after hearing his prayer the preceding night. God had something to say through that man, and she wanted to hear.

In Chicago, the Alpha Force was deployed and ready by the time the sun came up. They had received no additional information on the nature of the threat beyond what had happened the night before in Williams. All major public events were being covered, and a mobile strike force was ready with vehicles and helicopters to respond to attacks anywhere in the city or surrounding communities. All they could do now was sit and wait for the enemy to strike. Major Luther Hedges hated being in defensive mode. "We have to find those people and attack before they strike," he thought, but attack who and where? They had no clue, so they waited in frustration, hoping they could respond before the damage was severe.

Tom & Sally Meet

Sally arrived earlier than Tom at Restoration, so she got a quiet corner table and ordered coffee for two. Tom came in looking for police officer Sally Johnson and did not immediately recognize her in civilian attire. When he did, he was surprised at her softness and beauty, but the eyes were still the eyes of steel he had come to respect and they were focused on his concealed weapon. "What is this? Are we going to church armed?" she asked.

"After last night, I'm going everywhere armed, except to bed," Tom answered firmly. "You know I have a concealed weapons permit, so it's legal. I am not going to allow people in my presence to be defenseless if there is another terrorist attack. Two here is enough for me. I have an overwhelming sense of dread that something bad is coming, and I am prepared to stand against it. I'm sorry if it offends you."

"Sit down for a minute and let's talk," Sally responded. "I am not offended, I am just surprised. I hope you are wrong, but you could be right. Do you believe the services this morning are at risk?"

"I don't know, but if I had my way I would have Citizens Militia people at every church this morning."

"Well, you are definitely right that this is not over," Sally continued. "I have problems with your friend Farsi, but I will wait until this afternoon to discuss that subject."

"When we talk about him, remind me to mention his cell phone. I have that number and there is something a little strange about it," Tom revealed.

"I want to know," Sally added, "but for now let's finish our coffee and go across the street to the park and pray. The best way of addressing your sense of dread is to pray, and His peace will come."

"Perhaps, unless God has a purpose for the dread," Tom said as he finished his coffee. They got up, and together they left for the park.

Death to the Infidels

At exactly 7:45 AM, the organ began playing quiet music to welcome the worshipers into the service and to prepare them for a time together before the Lord. People came in and the seats were filled quickly. The whole community had seen or heard about what happened last night, and there was a sense of anticipation at what Pastor Scribes would say in light of his prayer. Sally and Tom took seats in the middle section near the back of the auditorium. Tom wanted to be able to view the whole facility and be able to respond anywhere if needed. It was strange to feel this way in church, but he could not ignore what he felt. Sally could only watch in amazement and pray that Tom was wrong.

When the clock showed 8:00 AM straight up, the organ stopped and Pastor Scribes rose to open the service with prayer. At that exact moment, Kalab Sawori's team met the van driver at the rendezvous point, loaded themselves and their weapons into the van, pulled their black hoods down over their faces and the van departed for College Church — right on schedule to arrive at 8:15 AM.

The choir had just begun singing a special as the van pulled up and the five designated shooters rushed in an orderly fashion toward the entrance of the building with automatic weapons at the ready, initial targets already identified. Inside the auditorium, the sounds of the choir and orchestra muted the initial shots fired as Sawori's team approached the outer doors. Kyle Turner, the head greeter, heard the shots and saw the six college students fall as the shooters rushed towards the doors. Standing to block the doors, he was felled by a blast from Sawori.

Now in control of the outer doors, the two designated to clear the atrium began to fire at the remaining ushers and those waiting to enter the auditorium. Panic and chaos reigned as people ran for their lives and parents covered their children, seeking to protect them from the killers.

Inside the auditorium, Tom Campy knew exactly what was happening the minute he heard the doors shatter. Standing and drawing his weapon he shouted, "Citizens Militia, everyone on the floor. Someone call 9-1-1!" Even as he yelled, the two doors into the auditorium burst open as the two assigned there forced entrance and began to spray the stage with automatic weapons fire. Turning to his right and pushing Sally Johnson out of his way, Tom fired two shots at the shooter in that aisle, dropping him immediately. Spinning to the left to confront the other shooter, he was struck in the chest and arm, falling backward onto Sally Johnson. His gun hit the floor, landing near his face.

Grasping for the gun, Sally saw the shooter seeking to reload as Pastor Scribes stood and ran down the aisle toward the shooter shouting, "Shoot me. I am the pastor. Leave my people alone." A new magazine in place, the shooter sought to accommodate Pastor Scribes when he was struck in the leg and side by shots fired from the floor by Sally Johnson, now covered in Tom's blood. The shooter's gun dropped onto the aisle as he limped into the atrium and fell. Sally screamed for a doctor and pushed her way into the aisle to pursue the killers.

Not knowing the extent of the force he would face from the auditorium, Sawori yelled, "Now!" and the two remaining shooters covered each other as they made for the door. Sawori turned and emptied the remaining rounds in his clip into his injured team member and ran for the door. Already the 9-1-1 call had engendered a response as teams of police were on their way and the Alpha Force strike team and medical team were in helicopters on the way to the site.

Down the street, the two police officers providing security for the Bookseller heard the call on their radios and raced to the church, arriving just as the three remaining shooters were through the doors and running for the van. In the shooting that followed, one of the officers was killed and the other wounded. Their pistols were no match for automatic weapons in an open field. However, they killed another shooter and wounded Sawori.

Arriving at the van, the sole uninjured shooter threw Sawori into the van and they raced off seeking their escape. The injured police officer radioed a description of the van and the direction in which it had departed. That information was immediately forwarded to the Alpha Force strike team, which was now over the city and altered their course seeking to intercept the terrorists as the medical teams were on their way to the church.

Inside the church, as people tried to attend to the injured as best they could, Sally Johnson had returned to the auditorium and was laboring over Tom, trying to stop the bleeding, crying, praying, and shouting at him, "Don't you dare die! We are not finished with this yet. There is still too much to do. We need you," and then she quietly added, "I need you. Please God, preserve his life."

Pastor Scribes stood over the scene, now back on the stage, and began to pray loudly. Helicopters carrying the medical teams landed on the outside lawn and immediately began treating the wounded as ambulances arrived to evacuate the most severely injured. Police cars with armed officers also arrived, searching for any remaining shooters. For the medics who had experience in Iraq and Afghanistan, the scene was all too familiar. It appeared to be just like the aftermath of an ambush, only the victims were civilians on American soil.

Above the city, the Alpha Force identified the fleeing van and was in pursuit. They radioed the location to the police officers on the ground, who immediately joined in the chase. Soon every available police vehicle in the region was headed to intercept the killers.

The commander of the strike force radioed Major Hedges, seeking authority to take out the van, but was instead ordered to try to disable the vehicle and capture the surviving terrorists. Recognizing the hopelessness of their situation, Sawori ordered the driver to crash the van into a grocery store they were passing to kill as many as possible and then to commit suicide. "We cannot allow ourselves to be captured," he said loudly. The van altered course and crashed through the glass exterior of the supermarket, striking numerous early morning shoppers until it came to a halt at the back of the store and three shots were heard. It was over.

CHAPTER 15

IDENTIFYING FRIENDS AND ENEMIES

Sunday, February 10 — MD minus 75 days

IT HAD BEEN many hours since they entered and began to pray. Hushai rejoiced at the opportunity to gather with other Christians, and had been unusually candid in the times he prayed out loud. All present in the room understood that they lived in dangerous times, literally behind enemy lines. All knew of instances where meetings such as this were invaded and the participants either killed or dragged away to prison or worse — tortured. No place was safe in Iran as a Christian committed to living his or her faith, and there was no way to know for sure whether someone who claimed to be a Christian was actually a Christian. But Gabriel's message had been clear, "Stand together and pray." So Hushai determined to obey, and left the results of that obedience in God's hands.

Suddenly the door crashed open from the force of two men who ran into the room with automatic weapons at the ready yelling, "State Security Force. Everyone against the south wall — now!" They pushed and forced anyone who delayed, even momentarily. Fear like thick, overwhelming fog descended throughout the room as the seventeen who were present lined the wall, expecting death.

"Everyone who is not a Christian, leave now!" the SSF leader ordered. "The rest will die."

Decisions were made quickly in groups. The first group of seven ran from the room in fear of death, thinking only of their survival. The second group paused, but soon four more joined the previous seven, fleeing for their lives and afraid of what would happen to their families after their death. They knew that the SSF would discover their identities and would kill or imprison their families — even the children.

The third group encountered Legion's deception at its best. The temptation so often used was simple logic, "I am worth more to God alive than dead. I will run now, but only to boldly serve Him later. If none are left alive, who will share the message?" The hidden truth, covered by the lie, was that when nothing is worth dying for, nothing is worth living for. Three more raced from the room and out into the darkness of the night. Now it was Hushai and two left against the wall.

"One last chance, leave now and live. Turn your back on this false teaching about this Jesus and embrace Allah, the faith of Iran. No one will know you were here and nothing will be done to you or your families. Decide now."

There was an unexpected peace surrounding the three who remained. They had made their decision before they had come to the prayer meeting. There was nothing for them to decide. Jesus had taught that if you deny Him before men, He would deny you before the Father in Heaven.[63] They understood that Christianity had spread throughout history by the blood of the martyrs, and if they had been called to die for their faith, they would.

"Down on your knees now!" was the command. Placing down the automatic weapon and drawing a pistol, the SSF leader approached Hushai, the first one kneeling. Placing the gun on the back of his head he said, "I know who you are and what you do for our government. I do not want to kill you. Leave now with your friends and this will be forgotten."

Remembering what he had studied about the martyrs of the past, Hushai modified the answer given by Polycarp when he was offered the opportunity to recant his faith before being burned to death. He said, "For twenty-seven years I have been Christ's servant and he has never done me wrong. How can I blaspheme my King who saved me?"

And with that, he closed his eyes and began to pray the Lord's Prayer out loud and was quickly joined by the other two kneeling on his left.

"Our Father in Heaven, hallowed be Your name, Your Kingdom come, Your will be done on earth as it is in Heaven …"[64]

He got no further when his head was struck, not by a bullet, but by tears as the SSF leader dropped his gun to his side and said, "My brothers, please forgive us. We too wanted to join with believers in prayer, but we had to be sure that you were indeed believers because of the position in which God has placed us as members of the SSF."

There were tears of rejoicing everywhere in the room as the five embraced and praised God loudly together. The cloud of protection which had surrounded Ittai's car when they prayed together now surrounded this house as angels rejoiced in anticipation of what the Father was preparing to do.

An Unnecessary Conflict

Hours before giving the speech, the president had placed a call to Dr. Harold Bristol, the president of Harkins College. "Dr. Bristol, this is the president. I apologize for calling you at home on a Sunday afternoon, but it is a matter of national security. We need your help."

"Yes, of course, Mr. President. How can we help?"

"I expect you have seen the news reports on what happened this morning in Williams, Illinois," the president answered.

"I have, but what does that have to do with this call?"

"Dr. Bristol, our intelligence has confirmed that the stateside leader for the Jihadists who were involved with this attack has been using the computer lab at the Harkins Graduate School of Education to communicate with operatives in the field and with their ultimate leader in Pakistan. We have traced communications from a computer in the lab — through a link to Williams — regarding this very attack. We need Harkins' cooperation to catch this man quickly so we can prevent a catastrophic attack planned for the next several months."

"What are you asking us to do, specifically?"

"We need to know whether there are security cameras in the computer lab, and if so, we need tapes for specific days and times to identify this leader," the president asked. "If not, we need your consent to install cameras so we can catch this leader as he makes transmissions to operatives. We need a list of Arab students enrolled in the Graduate School of Education over the past five years, and any information you may have on their current location. We believe that this plot against America was launched at Harkins by possibly one or more graduate students, or even a professor. Therefore, we also need information on all Arab-born faculty at the Graduate School of Education, so they can be checked out confidentially. Our purpose is not to harm any innocent person, but we must quickly find that leader and identify his operatives."

"Mr. President, with all due respect, do you realize what you are saying? Do you honestly believe that Harkins University is a 'hotbed' of terrorist activity? Do you think we would surrender the privacy rights of our students and professors to what is nothing more than racial profiling? There is no way we can voluntarily cooperate with a witch hunt against our faculty and students and Harkins' good name."

"Dr. Bristol, I would rethink that position if I were you," the president responded bluntly. "Take a good look at the carnage in Williams, which before this day ends will be broadcasted on every American television. That carnage may have been initiated on your campus by a student or professor, and you are not going to help us find the people responsible and to prevent future attacks? Take that position and we will pursue whatever is required legally to get that information, and in the meantime, the blood of every American killed by these cowards from this day forward is on your hands. Someday the truth about this will be written and Harkins' refusal to stand for other Americans will be known. I guarantee that."

"Are you threatening me, Mr. President?"

"No Dr. Bristol, this is not a threat. This is a promise. I am not going to allow anyone or any institution to stand in the way of protecting Americans from these cold-blooded killers. If you want to aid terrorism that is your choice, but when you choose to do so, you become an enemy of America — as guilty of the killings as the one who pulls the trigger."

"You are unbalanced. I don't know how you ever got elected," Dr. Bristol responded angrily. "Perhaps it is you who better rethink your position. Do you really want to take action against this institution that has stood for generations? Rather than taking away the rights of Arabs living in America, why not grow up and address the real cause of all of this? If you did, it would end. The problem is America's interference in the

Middle East and its continued support of the repressive state of Israel that crushes the life out of its Arab neighbors. Deal with that, and the terrorists will leave us alone. Goodbye Mr. President." He slammed the phone down so he could clear the line to call the Senate majority leader.

Turning to Attorney General Rodriquez, who had heard the whole conversation, the president said, "I probably shouldn't have wasted my time. Now the majority party leaders will know more than I wanted them to."

"Sometimes, Mr. President, you trust too much," Rodriquez smiled. "Those who have been your political enemies will not suddenly become patriotic Americans willing to help the government they are trying to discredit and replace, especially in the midst of an election cycle. They have a different agenda."

"Fine," the president responded. "Felix, do whatever it takes legally. Get that information out of Harkins as quickly as you can. I am going to instruct Homeland Security and the FBI to get someone undercover in that computer lab to watch for the leader. If there are security cameras and they destroy video, that would be obstruction of justice, wouldn't it?"

"It would certainly be something that a grand jury would consider," Rodriquez answered.

"Respectfully, Mr. President, a warning: in effect, you have declared war on a group that has enormous power and influence in this country. Be careful how far you push this. Working against the majority party can hurt you."

"Perhaps," the president answered. "But, Felix, this is too important to be careful with, and we have the advantage anyway. I don't care about the political repercussions of this fight. All I care about is defending America. I trust the American people to make right decision if they know the truth — and we are going to tell them the truth. They will decide who gets hurt, and if it's me, but the country avoids MD, I don't care. Have you ever read John Kennedy's book, *Profiles in Courage*?"

"No sir, I've heard of it but never read it."

"You should," the president continued thoughtfully. "It is brilliant and insightful, telling the story of eight US senators who stood against their times for the good of the nation and willingly paid the price for being right when the majority was wrong. America is a better place because of their courage. They thought of the future and not of themselves. Most people today know nothing of what they did, and yet history has affirmed that they were right and the majority was wrong. We must be like them and do what is right, regardless of the cost. The future depends on it."

"Mr. President, do you ever wonder how our country could drift from leaders like you describe to the self-serving 'care only about the next election' bunch we have now?"

"Felix, the politicians have changed because the people have changed. America is not like it used to be, and don't get me wrong, I'm not longing for the good old days. The truth is, we are different and that difference is not an improvement, for the most part. The heart of the differences is really apparent if you look at the inaugural address of President Kennedy," he said, reaching behind his desk for a well-worn bound copy. "I keep this close by to read whenever my head begins to swell," he said, laughing.

"I just want to read you a few statements I have highlighted. Remember this is 1961. Think about that pre-Vietnam America compared to today. Are these statements true for today's America?"

The world is very different now… and yet the same revolutionary beliefs for which our forebears fought are still an issue around the globe — the belief that the rights of man come not from the generosity of the state but from the hand of God.

Let every nation know whether it wishes us well or ill that we shall pay any price, bear any burden, meet any hardship, support any friend, oppose any foe, in order to assure the survival and success of liberty.

To those old allies whose cultural and spiritual origins we share, we pledge the loyalty of faithful friends.

And so my fellow Americans, ask not what your country can do for you — ask what you can do for your country.

With a good conscience our only sure reward, with history the final judge of our deeds, let us go forth to lead this land we love, asking His blessing and His help but knowing that here on earth God's work must truly be our own.

Pausing and remembering, the attorney general shook his head. "Not even close. Today, Kennedy's speech would be as foreign as Patrick Henry's, 'give me liberty or give me death.' Unfortunately, America has changed and certainly not for the better."

Combined Political/Judicial Attack

Surprised, Majority Leader Howard took the call. Their years together as students at Harkins and their continued cooperation on the majority party's political ideas had created a special bond. Dr. Bristol had always been available over the years to initiate whatever study he wanted, draw whatever conclusions Howard needed, or to provide expert testimony to advance a political agenda. Returning the favor when needed was expected.

"Dr. Bristol, to what do I owe the honor of your call, and on a Sunday afternoon at that?"

"This president has gone off the deep end over this terrorism thing. He claims that Harkins is where today's killers allegedly made their plans, and from where they received their orders. I am not going to sit by while he drags our good name through the mud. He must be stopped."

"Slow down Dr. Bristol, this is a hard day for all of us. What exactly did he say to you?"

For the succeeding fifteen minutes, Harold Bristol unleashed a torrent of anger as he retold the conversation with President Strong, adding numerous expletives for effect.

"How dare that man threaten me and Harkins College? I am far too mad to be rational. How can we hurt him and stop his investigation?"

"That's easy," Senator Howard responded cunningly, "you strike first and we will investigate him. Both of us will go public. We'll hoist him on his own petard."

"Sounds great, but how do we do that?" Dr. Bristol asked.

"Get Larry Trice, your extraordinary constitutional law professor, to file suit tomorrow morning in both state and federal court alleging invasion of privacy and violation of civil rights by racial profiling and anything else his brilliant mind can come up with. He will tell you whether Harkins can be the plaintiff or if it needs to be one of your students acting to protect a class of students. If you file first, we can shape the issues in court and in the press.

"We have to be careful because of the Williams attack, but this will give us a basis in our response to standing for individual rights and against blanket governmental intervention after the president's speech. When you file and go public, that gives us the opportunity to launch a congressional investigation into racial abuse, which would be good politically and should slow the increasing popularity of this president."

"Trice wants a Supreme Court nomination from the next president. He will jump at the opportunity for a stage and a chance to attack. Maybe we can sue the president individually because he made the call. I like this," Dr. Bristol responded. "We need to make an example of this little man so no one will again dare to attack Harkins."

"Who cares about Harkins," the majority leader thought to himself as he hung up, "let's just win the White House and then we control everything. At that point, it won't even matter what the people think. We will rule."

The Truth About Farsi

David Barnes made his way up from his White House basement office to respond to the president's call. He had the video of the Security Fair shooting, but that seemed insignificant after the massacre at College Church. Still red eyed and exhausted, he entered the Oval Office to report.

"Mr. President, I have been through the ITN video a hundred times and found nothing, but I got a call earlier today after the church shooting from Jim Hunt who said they had obtained a home video made by one of the parents of a kid in the choir who was filming at the fair from a different angle. I believe the parent caught something significant. Sir, give me a minute to set this up on the VCR and I will show you.

"I know you are still working on your speech, so I only want to go from the part where we can follow the terrorist as he makes his way through the crowd and then begins his attack. Look right there," Barnes said stopping the video, "that is the terrorist scoping out the stage and the Citizens Militia people in front of it. Now, when I start again, watch carefully as he moves through the crowd toward the front to launch his attack. There," he said, stopping the video again. "See? The terrorist and the Citizens Militia member who later shoots him see each other. Watch, the militia member's hand immediately drops to his weapon and the terrorist smiles directly at him and then goes on. I can't read minds, but it looks to me as if these two were acquainted and the terrorist wasn't supposed to be there that night. The militiaman was surprised.

"Now, watch how the militia member keeps one hand near his weapon and his eyes directly on the terrorist the whole time. The minute the terrorist brings his weapons out of his coat, the Citizens Militia member draws his weapon and empties his clip into the terrorist, making sure he was dead. I don't think our 'hero' is much of a hero as he's thought to be."

"David, I think you're right," the president responded. "Have some copies made and let's get them to the FBI. I think Mr. Hero may need to explain himself."

"Praise God, maybe we finally have a break."

CHAPTER 16

HISTORY REVISITED

Sunday, February 10 — MD minus 75 days

"THREE, TWO, ONE — cue the president now," the producer said pointing to the off-screen announcer.

"Ladies and gentlemen, the President of the United States."

"Good evening my fellow Americans. I come to you tonight both thankful and with a heavy heart. You will remember my recent statement on the threat America faced from those who have entered our country illegally to organize attacks against us within our own borders. I asked for citizen involvement to help find those here illegally whose sole purpose was to do us harm and warned that the day would come when they would launch their hate-filled attacks against innocents on our soil. That day came today in Williams, Illinois, as these cowards struck against men, women, and children who rose early this morning to attend the first service at College Church directly across from the Williams College campus.

"Six young Arab men wearing black hoods, five of whom were armed with sophisticated automatic weapons, sought to launch a killing spree against a totally defenseless crowd of our citizens whose only crime was to join together on a Sunday morning to sing, worship, and hear the Bible taught by their pastor, Fredrick Scribes. Within minutes, 32 were dead and 17 more were wounded, 5 critically. Soon thereafter, at a supermarket four miles away, a stolen van attempting an escape suddenly careened into another innocent crowd where 11 were hurt, but miraculously, none were killed. Three shots were heard as the surviving terrorists committed suicide. All six were killed, three during the church attack and three at their own hands when escape became impossible.

"I am thankful today because as bad as it was, it could have been so much worse. Williams has been unique among us in preparing to face violence as a result of their response to a shooter who terrorized their community for months. They have organized and banded together to establish a Citizens Militia that — in cooperation with the police department — is a visible shield to protect their citizens. Since this group began its patrols, there have been no more shootings of civilians by the sniper; but, that is only the beginnings of their success thus far. Last night, it was a Citizens Militia member that acted to protect a crowd from a single terrorist attack. Today, it was the leadership and direction of another member who with an off-duty police officer confronted the killers and caused them to flee.

"This morning before church, Tom Campy, a member of the Williams Citizens Militia, told his friend Sally Johnson, a Williams' police officer, that he sensed danger and felt compelled to take his firearm to church with him this morning. Having a concealed weapons permit and authorized by the Williams' police department to be part of the Citizens Militia, Tom had every legal right to carry a weapon — and thank God he did. He told Sally that he believed the threat was real and that he had to be prepared to stand against this evil to protect unarmed innocents.

"Tom Campy sat in the back of the church auditorium to be able to see the whole crowd before him and respond to anything that might happen. When the terrorists began their killing spree, he stood and shouted instructions to protect the crowd and prepared to face the terrorists. As they entered, spraying the stage with gunfire, he shot and killed one and was then shot by the other. Sally Johnson's police training took over and she grabbed the pistol from the floor where he had fallen and shot another terrorist, which caused the remaining to flee. They ran immediately when confronted by armed opposition.

"Outside, the killers encountered two Williams police officers, and in the ensuing gun battle another terrorist died, but it was at the cost of

Police Officer Carl Burns life. The terrorists' escape attempt was not successful, as the government — in cooperation with state and local governments — was working together to be prepared to address the threat. Within minutes of the shooting, a military team was airborne to intercept the fleeing terrorists. Another was dispatched with medical teams to assist in meeting the medical needs of the survivors. The crash into the supermarket and the suicides were the terrorists' response to the reality that they could not escape the combined efforts of the military and local police working together. Rather than be captured, they killed themselves.

"This evening, the report on Tom Campy is not encouraging. The hospital statement merely reads, 'He still clings to life.' He and four others are in critical condition. So much more are wounded or injured. I ask you to pray for Tom and the others, and particularly for the family and friends of those who were killed. It is a dark hour for America, but it could have been so much worse. I am afraid of thinking of what would have happened if there had been no one to stand against the killers.

"My friends, please hear me. We can defeat these killers who have invaded us and live in secret among us if we join together to find them and stand against them. Your government is aggressively pursuing these terrorists here and abroad, and in cooperation with state and local governments, is preparing to respond to any attack. That was evident today as a military response was launched within minutes of the first shot being fired. But, that is not enough for we were unable to prevent these attacks because no one among the citizens of Williams came forward with information about where these six terrorists were hiding in the months before the attacks. Had we known where they were, there would have been no attack. We must do a better job together.

"Here is what I am asking of you. First, follow the Williams model and consider establishing your own Citizens Militia and Neighborhood Watch Program. The best offense is always a good defense, and the terrorists must know that there is no place in America where they are safe to either launch an attack or hide. If you have information on suspicious activities or people, call your local police immediately after the end of this broadcast so that all leads may be investigated. Our enemies are careless. If we are diligent and observant, we will find them.

"I am not asking for people to go on a witch hunt. Arab people are not our enemy; as was shown last night when a young Arab man acted against a terrorist. It is the terrorists that are our enemy. Please understand that not all Arabs are terrorists. However, these recent terror attempts have been conducted by Jihadist operatives, so it is imperative that if you see suspicious activity by Arabs or anyone else of any ethnicity, please report it so it can be investigated. If it is nothing, the police will dismiss it. If it is real, you might be the one to prevent another massacre.

"Secondly, I implore Congress to wake up and secure our borders! We are being left vulnerable to those who want to enter our country illegally to kill us. There are many other issues relating to relationships between our friends that border us on the north and south, but now is the time to address security first and then the other issues will follow. If we cannot protect our nation, the rest will not matter.

"Thirdly, I want to assure those Americans who attend our places of worship that they will be safe. I have instructed the secretary of defense and chairman of Homeland Security to work with the governors of all fifty states to either provide active duty military personnel or call up National Guard forces as necessary so that every place of worship that desires protection will be protected during their services. It is my hope that communities will follow the Williams example — that all cities will deploy their Citizens Militia in coordination with local police so that our armed forces can be fully available for other duties. We will do whatever it takes to ensure our people can go to their houses of worship without fear.

"Finally, I want you to walk with me through history and hear from several of our presidents. I share with you what they said because their words are true and the time has long since passed to hear them again. All were spoken during or after a great crisis which endangered the future of our nation.

"Listen to the declarations of our first president on Thanksgiving Day, 1789, shared from the city of New York when it was our capital:

It is the duty of all nations to acknowledge the providence of Almighty God, to obey His will, to be grateful for His benefits, and humbly to implore His protection and favor...

"Our second president, John Adams from Philadelphia in 1798 wrote:

The safety and prosperity of nations ultimately and essentially depend on the protection and the blessing of Almighty God, and the national acknowledgment of this truth is not only an indispensable duty which the people owe to Him, but a duty whose natural influence is favorable to the promotion of that morality and piety without which social happiness cannot exist nor the blessings of a free government be enjoyed…

"From Washington DC on August 12, 1861, Abraham Lincoln, wrote:

It is fit and becoming for all people, at all times, to acknowledge and revere the supreme government of God; to bow down in humble submission to His chastisements; to confess and deplore their sins and transgressions in the full conviction that the fear of the Lord is the beginning of wisdom; and to pray, with all fervency and contrition, for the pardon of past offenses, and for a blessing upon their present and prospective action…

"Three years later in the midst of the darkness of the Civil War, from Washington DC on March 30, 1863, Abraham Lincoln wrote:

It is the duty of nations as well as of men, to owe their own dependence upon the overruling power of God, to confess their sins and transgressions in humble sorrow, yet with assured hope that genuine repentance will lead to mercy and pardon; and to recognize the sublime truth, announced in the Holy Scriptures and proven by all history, that those nations only are blessed whose God is the Lord.

"We have heard similar words in these days from an unlikely source, an old man from Williams, Illinois, who many simply call the Bookseller. Mr. White's recent statements have not been his own any more than the words I quote herein were the original thoughts of Washington, Adams or Lincoln. These are truths which you can accept or reject; but your acceptance or rejection does not change the fact that they are true.

"My final request is modeled on the March 30, 1863 proclamation of Abraham Lincoln in which he observed:

It behooves us then to humble ourselves before the offended Power, to confess our national sins, and to pray for clemency and forgiveness.

"As he did, I do by this proclamation, designate, and set apart next Friday as a day of national humility, fasting, and prayer. I asked that all Americans everywhere abstain from their secular pursuits and join together at their places of public worship or in their respective homes for that purpose."

Pausing to sign the formal proclamation, the president then continued.

"Good night, and may these truths which have carried our nation through its first two centuries again be embraced as our hope for the future."

The Bookseller Answers

Even before the pool camera crew had left the Oval Office, the networks and politicians had begun to try to spin what the president had said to support their political agendas, but it was different that time. The White House was not spinning or even commenting on the president's speech to the nation. He had said all there was to say, exactly as he wanted to say it. The only reporter who would get more was George Murphy at the *Times Daily*, who had been promised an exclusive. He had been briefed in detail before the president's speech, and had already posted an article on the *Times Daily* website — which would be the next day's front-page lead, with facts and insights no one else knew that had been made available to him by the president.

"This man," he thought, "can be trusted. He did exactly what he said he would do, and his intelligence on the Williams attack was right on. Perhaps I need to reconsider and use my position as a reporter for a national daily to help prepare the nation for the potential larger attacks that are part of this thing called MD. Maybe he is right and together we can find these people and stop this. We have to."

Barnabas smiled as he watched Murphy's heart being changed, something only God could do. It excited him because it meant that there was still hope for America.

George Murphy's heart was not the only heart affected by the president's speech as the commentators, politicians, and networks soon discovered. The American people weren't listening to the criticism and spin. They were coming to trust this man as more than their president. He was their friend who cared about them. He had warned them before the

Williams attack, and the military had been ready to address the assault. They heard his call to join together to find those among them who were there to do harm, and for a day of national humility, fasting and prayer.

The vast majority had never heard the declarations of the former presidents regarding God and many wanted copies of the speech. ITN had already posted the speech in video and in print. Millions from around the world sought copies, crashing the website once again. By agreement with ITN, the Together We Pray website had downloaded both and now believers around the world could see and hear what the president had said in their own language as the gift of tongues continued to be manifest so God's message could be heard and understood.

ITN continued to hold the audience that night, for they had the Bookseller willing to answer some additional questions live from the warehouse. People tuned in because they wanted to hear what this apparent representative of God had to say. The president's comments regarding him increased people's desire to hear from him.

As the ITN news team reviewed the president's speech and commented carefully, Samuel Evans White sat quietly praying while waiting for the broadcast to shift to his location. He reviewed in his prayer the events of the day and the two messages he had received that afternoon.

That morning, as soon as he had realized what had happened, he walked the two blocks to College Church and ministered as best he could to the grieving, the injured, and the dying. His heart was broken at the carnage and he cried out to the Lord for the hurt and the injury suffered that day — which went far beyond the flesh. He thought of his friend, Tom Campy, whose call inviting him to the press conference had started all of this, and he prayed that God would be merciful and would preserve Tom's life. He knew that was really a selfish prayer for Tom, a believer, would be much better off in the Lord's presence, but he sensed that the purposes for Tom's life had not yet been completed.

The messages he received throughout the day humbled and frightened him. The first came from the female member of the Citizens Militia who had been shot last night, asking if he could come see her in the hospital tomorrow. She had questions and needed answers. There was something desperate in the message, which affirmed in his heart that he needed to go.

The other message was from his two friends in Iran, delivered again by Carl Varvel. It read simply, "My brother Mr. White, it is critical now. Ezekiel 22:30-31." He knew that passage instantly and that is what frightened him. The passage read:

> *I looked for a man among them who would build up the wall and stand before Me in the gap on behalf of the land, so I would not have to destroy it, but I found none. So I will pour out my wrath on them and consume them with my fiery anger, bringing down on their own heads all they have done, declared the Sovereign Lord.*

He shared the message with Margaret and then penned this short reply, "Unworthy, but willing if this is God's call. 1 Timothy 1:15." As he had arrived, Carl Varvel left again to make the journey to Iran, wondering why the CIA was facilitating this communication.

The timing and opportunity had to be of the Lord, the Bookseller thought. The president has just called for a day of national humiliation, fasting, and prayer and he would be asked about it. It was high time to stand in the gap for America and be sure the people understood the significance of what had been placed before them. He prayed quickly for wisdom and for the words to share as he saw the light on the camera go red and heard the voice of Walter Murrow.

"Mr. White, College Church is two blocks from where you sit at this moment. Today, six men sought to kill hundreds there. Last night, the pastor of College Church prayed after the shooting at the Security Fair. He prayed what in many occasions is considered a strange prayer, particularly so now in light of what happened at his church today. We have received thousands of questions about that prayer and wanted to ask some of them to you. Thank you for making yourself available."

"I hope I can help," the Bookseller responded. "What about Pastor Scribes' prayer was strange?" he asked, not waiting for a question.

"Well," Murrow began, "after thanking God for protection, he forgave the killer and asked God to teach us," and he paused to search for his exact words. "Yes, here it is, he said, 'Teach us how to reach out in Your love to those who seek to destroy us.' Mr. White, how can we seriously be expected to forgive these people and why would we want to reach out to them in love? Most Americans would want to retaliate and kill their leaders immediately if we knew where they were and who to kill."

"Mr. Murrow, Pastor Scribes' prayer only seems strange because we have fallen so far from our biblical roots. Forgiveness is never an option for a Christian. Jesus commanded that we forgive if we want to be forgiven by God.[65] That settles the issue and there is nothing strange about it if you believe that Jesus suffered and died for all sinners. If He paid the price for sin, what right do you have to refuse to forgive and demand more? In doing so, you are saying that the cross was not enough. No believer should say that. We forgive as commanded and leave final judgment to God.

"As to your other question, it is never strange for a Christian to love the unlovable. We are commanded to love as Christ loved even to love our enemies,[66] and that is certainly how He loved. If He had only loved those who loved Him, He would have loved no one most of the time. To share Christ's love does not mean we refuse to defend ourselves or simply accept violence. Rather, it means that we pray for our enemies as commanded,[67] and we mourn that a child can be raised in hate to kill as these men obviously were raised. They were not created to kill. They were created to give and receive God's love. Pastor Scribes' prayer was that God helps us to teach them by words and example so they might become what they were created to be. There is nothing strange about that prayer other than it is not prayed often enough."

Murrow breathed deeply, pausing to consider what to ask, understanding that he had just heard profound truth and would need time to digest it. "Mr. White," he said without thinking, completely abandoning the list of questions he had prepared. "You people are just different. It's not natural to think like that."

"It may not be natural," the Bookseller answered, "But it is Christian, and God enables us to love and forgive as He commanded. He always gives the power to obey what He commands because His commands are always unnatural to a sinful human nature.[68] He will do the same for you if you ask."

Murrow began to feel really uncomfortable with what he was hearing because he knew it was true.

"And if I could say just one last thing about the importance of what the president said tonight," the Bookseller continued now soberly. "It is a defining moment in history for any nation when its leader stands before his people and calls for a time for the nation to stand together before God humbly to do what President Lincoln called for in his mid-civil war proclamation, 'to confess our national sins, and to pray for clemency and forgiveness.' Now that the call has been given, America and Americans will be accountable before God for how we respond.[69] Will we humble ourselves and seek to know what God considers to be our national sins? Once our sins are made clear, will we confess them in prayer for clemency and forgiveness and then turn from them? If America is unwilling to bow its knee before God as has been called for by our president, then America should not expect to live under God's blessing or protection."

Standing in the gap for America, the Bookseller pleaded, "I urge every American to join together next Friday humbly before the Lord — exactly as the president has asked — that God's anger may turn from our nation and we may become a nation whose God is the Lord."

Recognizing that Murrow was now speechless, Producer Hunt cut the microphones and morphed the picture into a live feed from County Hospital in Williams where hundreds had gathered spontaneously with candles to sing and pray for the injured and dying. In the surgical intensive care waiting room where Sally Johnson sobbed and prayed and waited, they could hear the singing.

There were screams in the dark as multiple dark wisps were sent to gather the Council of Darkness before the Dark Master to deal with this increasing threat to his plans. Things had not worked in Washington or in Williams as they desired. It seemed the harder they pressed to defeat the forces of light, the more it was turned to a witness of the light. Now they had to deal with the American president's call to prayer and repentance. "How I hate America," Legion thought. "When it is finally destroyed, how we will celebrate," and he left to join the others in the plot to bring about that destruction.

CHAPTER 17

THE MAJORITY PARTY STRIKES BACK

Sunday, February 10 – MD minus 75 days

KNOWING WHAT WAS planned for the morning, the majority party's response was carefully orchestrated to set the stage — to change the subject from the acts of the terrorists to the threat from this government and advance the theme of a war against hate. They selected the only Muslim member of Congress to deliver their response, and the focus was on healing the differences that give rise to hate and violence while warning against social injustice against the innocent. The words sounded good and were certainly not all false. Half-truths have always been the most effective tools since the beginning. Keepers throughout America sought to embed the roots of deception deep into the minds of those under their influence.

"Tonight, we grieve with the citizens of Williams," he began. "We have suffered another senseless act of violence in which scores have been killed or injured. But as we seek to bind up the injured and comfort those who have lost loved ones, we need to be careful to keep our focus on the real enemy who has caused this mayhem and destruction. There is a real danger we may target the wrong enemy.

"I stand before you tonight as a Muslim member of Congress. Am I responsible for what happened in Williams? Was I the one who heartlessly launched the attack on a group of people whose only intention was to go to church on a Sunday morning?

"No. I am one of the several millions of other Muslims living legally in America, and want nothing to do with these attacks or any of the others we have witnessed over the years. Muslims are not the enemy and neither are Arabs. The enemy who has engendered this violence is HATE, and the cause of that hate must be America's target if America is to win this conflict. The hearts of those who hate must be changed, and that is only possible if the causes of that hate are addressed.

"The president asks us to spy on one another and assures us that the government is doing everything it can to find and destroy those responsible for the violence. He tells us we need to live in fear of future attacks that could destroy America. The implied agenda does not differ much from how our government dealt with Japanese Americans after Pearl Harbor. In one of the darkest chapters in American history, tens of thousands of innocent, law-abiding American citizens of Japanese heritage were wrongfully taken from their homes and interned in camps throughout the country. Is this the president's plan? Are all Muslims and Arabs now America's enemy?

"History is our teacher and if anything can be learned from history, it is that a people who are oppressed often make wrong decisions and follow wrong leaders who take the world into strife and conflict. There are two responses to this reality. You can fight the fight until someone is hurt so badly that they can no longer stand and fight back, or you can deal with the oppression and remove the reason for the fight. Our president has chosen the first path, which guarantees future conflict and risks the personal freedoms which we as Americans hold to be our heritage. The rejected path is the path to reason in which we seek to address the causes of hate and make a friend rather than kill an enemy.

"Our party has chosen the second path, and in the coming days we will continue to present to America an alternative which will end this violence by attacking the root cause of the violence. We grieve over the Williams' massacre, but our focus must not be on continuing down a path which will only lead to more grief, death, and sadness.

"My fellow Americans, we fear what this division among us advocated by this president will produce. Neighbor against neighbor. Suspecting everyone who is a Muslim or Arab is not a formula for peace. It is rather a formula for an increasingly authoritarian government to take away our freedoms by convincing us we need more surveillance and that the government needs to be able to invade our privacy secretly to find the so-called 'evil ones' among us.

"You will be asked to sacrifice, but be warned that whatever you voluntarily relinquish will never be returned to you. This is a dangerous time and we are all angry at those who committed these atrocities, but remember that the same Bible this president quotes so often also warns against going to bed with your anger.[70] There is real danger in overreacting to the tragedy in Williams.

"Consider the facts that we now know about the attacks in Williams. Six men attacked a church meeting. All six men were killed or killed themselves. They will not be hurting anyone in the future and their example will not realistically excite anyone to repeat what they have done — unless those actions are motivated by hate. Even if the president is right and there are thousands among us illegally who will seek to kill us, how do we stop them? Law enforcement can deal with random acts of violence as it always has but who sent them here and why? That is the issue this president refuses to address, and until he does, there will be no end to the violence.

"We offer an alternative, a new and improved 'contract with America' — a new world where the emphasis will be on making friends, not killing enemies. I hope you listened to our plan when it was recently laid out for you. If not, we have a website that details the agenda of peace which is part of our war against hate. The website is simply waragainsthate.com. Please go there tonight and learn how to stand with us for an end to this violence by attacking the root cause of the hate which motivates the violence.

"Together we can win this conflict by changing the focus. Don't let this president turn us against one another while taking our freedoms away. Stand with us for a real and lasting end to the violence and hate.

"Good night, and may the gift of peace be yours."

Besserman Makes His Choice

"Well Mr. President, it looks like you have a three-front war on your hands," Senator Besserman observed as the majority party response ended. "You are going to have to fight the killers that are loose in America, MD, and my party. I am astounded that there is no room for unity or cooperation in their agenda. This really is a battle for the future of the world, but at least we will not have to fight it standing alone. My meetings with Prime Minister Zimri went better than expected. Their intelligence confirms ours and they are totally on board for a joint response."

"We will need that, and I want to get specific as soon as we can," the president responded. "The timetable on MD is fluid. We may find ourselves facing this attack much sooner than originally thought; particularly if we are able to pierce their forces here. We may have a lead that could open lots of doors quickly."

Changing the subject for the moment and getting personal, the president continued. "Eric, the majority party has declared a political war and it will not be pretty. We can expect congressional investigations, sorry legislation, issue ads, lawsuits, and a passel of personal attacks on me and on you if you stay with us. I am going to confront them up front before the American people. We will duck nothing. If you want to get out now, I would understand. This is your last chance to change your mind before it is too late. You could really get hurt politically, and I am a short-timer so I can't offer you anything more than a chance to stand for your country while dodging political attacks and character assassination."

"That's enough for me, Mr. President. You are right about all of this," Besserman replied. "Nothing is being done here domestically that wouldn't be done in any major criminal investigation. They are sounding an alarm for a fire that isn't burning. The American people will see the truth if you continue, to be frank, and honest with them. I sincerely believe when America understands where this so-called 'war against hate' will lead, they will junk it and its advocates."

"I hope you're right," the president answered. "Let's shoot back now." Picking up the phone to reach the White House operator, that always pleasant voice on the phone, he said, "Please get me George Murphy at the *Times Daily*."

Legal Reality

In Cambridge, Massachusetts, the reaction to the majority party's response was a little different, to say the least. In a conference room of the law school, some of its best and brightest rejoiced as they put the final touches on the two lawsuits set to be filed in the morning. Professor Trice had done a quick recruiting job and the place was packed with law students eager to take on the president and protect Harkins. He felt good that he could accomplish what he wanted now that President Bristol had given him the required affidavit.

"Listen up gang. Great work, but a teaching moment please," Professor Trice said, addressing the gathered crowd. "In your enthusiasm, a touch of reality is needed. As a lawyer, you start with a goal and then figure out how to get there. The goal has to be realistic as the law does not always allow what you want, but that is only the starting point. The law offers other ways to get what you want by using the process and the natural fall-out from the process. What then is our goal?"

"To crush the Neanderthal," one student responded, immediately referencing the president.

"To protect Harkins," another added.

"To stop racial profiling and protect the innocent from an unlawful invasion of their privacy," a third said with equal passion.

"Hurray, finally there is a lawyer among us," Trice continued. "The trick is to use the legal strategy Mr. Tucker has proposed to accomplish the former goals of Mr. James and Mr. Ball because ultimately we will lose the lawsuit. But that doesn't matter."

It got very quiet as the gathered students began to wonder why they had worked so hard if a loss would be the result.

"The reality is that the government in a criminal investigation can use a grand jury or national security measures to do what the president has asked to be done voluntarily, but not as quickly as they like — and they cannot easily share the information they obtain. That does not mean we don't send a shot across the bow to slow them down or make this public and personal; which hurts the president and protects Harkins by giving any idiot wrongfully using the computer a warning before they get caught and Harkins looks stupid."

"So, here is what we are doing. First, we file before they have time to do anything of substance. Second, when we file we seek 'ex parte' relief. Anyone know what that is?"

"Yes sir," Tucker answered. "It means you seek temporary emergency relief from a judge without having to give the other side notice of what you are doing. You make your case with affidavits and get an order which temporarily stops the other side from doing what you don't want to be done."

"Absolutely right," Professor Trice continued, "and then we make sure that the suit is not just to stop the government action, we also sue the president individually, which gives us the basis for a personal attack politically and the argument to try and get his deposition. Finally, and most important of all, when we file, we release a press statement. That gives us the first shot at spinning this properly and notifies any bozo to get away from the computer lab. That protects Harkins and puts the administration on the defensive in the public relations war. Don't get me wrong, I don't believe the 'terrorist at Harkins' idea. These people think there is a terrorist under every bed.

"We have picked our judges carefully, so we have a good chance of winning at the trial court level which will slow them down while they appeal. By the time we lose, we will have already won. See the beauty of the law?" he said smiling to a very appreciative audience.

Inconsistency Answered

It was late but Paul and Samantha had waited patiently. Margaret had invited them in and they had watched with her from the couch as the Bookseller answered Walter Murrow's questions following the president's speech. Then they had watched the majority party's response and Paul saw clearly the clash between the physical world, what man was seeking to do on his own, and the real issues preeminent in the invisible world.

Both the president and Mr. White had laid out the real issue for anyone with eyes to see or ears to hear. For those who had neither and remained blind to truth, the majority party had carefully crafted a presentation to appeal to the head and heart — logic and emotion, the greatest weapons of deception. The reality was that man needed God because man was unable to resolve the persisting issues apart from God. Man's alternative focused on the ability of man to resolve the issues — man caused it, and thus, man could solve it. There was no need for God's help and no desire for His perceived interference.

Still, without the light inside, Samantha was confused. In her heart she sensed that what the president had called for and the Bookseller had cautioned were correct. America had fallen from God's standard as it was laid out in the red-letter books. She knew that God had issues with her too, but what the Muslim senator had said appealed to her. Obviously, it was better to make a friend than killing an enemy. Without question, the Arabs had legitimate complaints about some of Israel's policies toward them and must resent the United States interference in their part of the world. There are always two sides to every coin.

Then there was the teaching regarding forgiveness. Forgive killers that had butchered men, women, and children who did nothing more than go to church? That was illogical and something she didn't want to do. She was angry watching the grieving families. Before they went to the warehouse, they had walked by College Church and saw the blood-stained grass where many had been shot outside the building. It was an ugly reminder of the reality of what had happened there a mere few hours before. She didn't want to forgive anybody. She was glad the killers were dead and secretly wished they had suffered mightily before they died. She was glad that they would suffer the second death — if it existed. They deserved it. "What a surprise for them when they look for their collection of virgins to enjoy," she thought.

Yet in the midst of the confusion, she still felt the urge to know and understand God. She wanted to be at peace with Him, and was confused about how to accomplish that. Paul had told her what he thought was true, but that was his opinion and there were lots of other opinions. What was the truth? Her head was in a fog as her emotions were spinning out of control.

"Sobering day," the Bookseller said. "How mightily God has moved and how fearful the consequences may be."

"What do you mean?" Samantha asked. "It appears to me that God abandoned us for the day, just like He did on 9/11."

"Oh no, had God not intervened on 9/11 there would have been 50,000 killed in New York City and United flight 93 would have crashed into the White House or Congress or whatever was its intended target. Everything about 9/11 showed God's mercy and restraint, even in judgment. The same was true today. Consider what would have happened had God not directed Tom Campy to be in church, prepared to stand against the killers or if He had not directed Sally Johnson to go to church with her friend Tom and be there to fight back when Tom fell. God again showed mercy in judgment.

"Did you hear about the change in Pastor Scribes, running up the aisle toward the terrorist, screaming for the terrorist to shoot him and not his people, declaring that he was their pastor as others laid on the floor in fear? Only God could make him bold like that, and then only God could protect him as He did. It was absolutely amazing."

"What concerns you then, Mr. White?" Paul asked. "God has been good and gracious just like you said. The president has called the whole country to a time before God. That is the greatest miracle of all."

"You are exactly right," the Bookseller continued, "but that call requires a choice to be made by America and all Americans. I tried to make that clear in the end of my comments to Mr. Murrow. When the president declared a day of national humility, fasting, and prayer to confess our nation's sins and to pray for clemency and forgiveness, he crossed the line of accountability. All of us now must make a choice. We must decide whether we will honor that request or reject God's call. The consequences of rejecting that call are what I fear. I truly don't know what America will do, but the Bible is clear on what God will do if America rejects Him. If America rejects God, God will reject America."[71]

"I am really confused about all of this," Samantha said almost pleading. "The God you describe does not sound like the one Pastor Elkhorn preached to us about and we accepted. It doesn't sound like Jesus. It sounds like the one described in the Old Testament that threatened to kill everybody if they didn't do exactly what He wanted. I frankly don't see a lot of difference between the God you describe and the terrorists. You are scaring me."

"Samantha!" Paul exclaimed, only to be cut off by the Bookseller.

"No, Paul, she said nothing wrong. She spoke honestly about what is in her heart. God is never offended by an honest searcher, and she raised good questions for which there are real answers in the Bible.

"Samantha, listen. The issues of God's love, mercy, and compassion were settled on the cross. You know that. John 3:16 says it best, 'For God so loved the world that He gave His one and only Son so that whoever believes in Him shall not perish but have eternal life.' You know what Jesus was given to do. You have read the gospel books. He was given to the cross where in turn He gave His body for us, His blood shed for us to establish the new covenant which provided the opportunity for forgiveness of sin.[72] That is what we remember when we celebrate the Lord's Supper.[73]

"You say that Jesus is not like the God I described, but in fact, Jesus is the God I described. The night before He went to the cross, one of His followers asked Jesus to show them the Father and He answered, 'If you have seen Me, you have seen the Father.'[74] On multiple occasions in the gospels, Jesus declared, 'I and the Father are one.'[75] If you want to know anything about God, all you have to do is study Jesus. He is God."

"I still don't understand. How can you say that Jesus is one with the Old Testament God of anger and judgment?" Samantha responded.

"I didn't say it, Jesus did; the God of the Old Testament is not a God of anger and judgment. The God of the Old Testament is the God of the New Testament without the cross. Think about that, and I believe you will come to understand. Jesus pictured it perfectly when He entered Jerusalem that last time, and amid all the celebration, He cried. He cried because God's people had rejected Him and thus, in the future, the nation would be destroyed by an invading Roman army.[76] That was the consequence of their sin of rejecting God among them.

"In that moment, you can see God's heart is totally consistent in New Testament and Old. If God is rejected, then He must reject and there is no forgiveness of sin. In the absence of forgiveness of sin, the sinner must bear the full consequences of their sin, but that is never what God wants and so Jesus cried with a broken heart.

"However, those tears did not prevent the consequences of their rejection because God is holy, and a holy God must punish all sin and rebellion. In A.D. 70, Jerusalem was totally destroyed and the nation of Israel ceased to exist until 1948. A person or nation who rejects Jesus will ultimately receive the full punishment their sin deserves because they rejected the one who offered to take that punishment for them on the cross. What was true in Jerusalem in Jesus' days on earth is true in America in our days on earth, and that is what I fear. Will we reject God even as they did?"

The Absent Farsi

The phone rang and rang and there was no answer. The recorded message began, "Hi, this is Abdul Farsi. If you are getting this message, I am either out or temporarily unavailable. If you will leave a message, I will return your call as promptly as possible. Thank you for calling."

"My, he sure is a polite one," she thought. "Mr. Farsi, this is Dr. Janice Girds, vice president of the American Teachers Society. I know you are registered for our annual convention in Phoenix next week. I just wanted to give you a heads up that our board met in special session today and you will be presented a special award on Thursday night at the banquet to honor you for what you did to defend against the terrorist in Williams last week. We are all proud of you as a teacher and as a Muslim. We want to thank you publicly. I look forward to meeting you next week. Goodbye."

They heard the phone ring as they approached the front door. Special Agent Andy Samuels, the agent in charge, had been in the Bureau for thirty-five years, but for him, that was a big one: a chance to catch a terrorist leader and stop a major attack on America. They came prepared, armed with a search warrant and wearing bulletproof vests. They had adequate firepower for an urban war. If Farsi was the leader of the six who had attacked the church, they had the armament for a major firefight. The law required they knock, which he did. "Mr. Farsi, this is the FBI. We need you to open the door."

Not surprising, like the unanswered phone call, there was no response. Samuels gave a silent predetermined sign and the door was forced open by two agents. They all entered the house quickly to establish predetermined fields of fire, covering all possible angles of danger if there were armed persons in the house. Rushing through the dark house to be sure they were alone, Samuels stopped at the kitchen exclaiming, "My God, what happened here?"

What they had found sickened even the crusty old veteran. The floor was drenched in a pool of blood. When they turned on the light, they saw a message on the far wall which read, "Death to all infidels," written in blood. In the corner by the refrigerator was the remnants of a fire obviously set by an accelerant. Papers, a cell phone, and a computer had been burned. They appeared to be too late to recover anything useful. They had everything but a body.

When they turned on the lights throughout the house, they saw the evidence of a major struggle, pieces of bone in the bedroom, and a bloody trail across the living room into the garage where it ended. Catching his breath, Samuels paused and shook his head. "I've seen a lot in my 35 years, but this is beyond my imagination. Looks like this Farsi fellow was relieved of his command by a less than enthusiastic group of followers. So much for this terrorist leader," he said in frustration.

"Lock down the house and complete the search, then we will call the local police. I know that is out of the usual order, but the national security issue trumps the murder investigation."

They found nothing. Every book, paper, video, and picture had been meticulously shredded and burned. The phone message recorder had only that one message from the teachers' organization. There were no stored messages or phone numbers. Someone who knew what they were doing had done this. The house was clean. Whoever did this had stayed a while to be sure nothing of value was left.

"Call the local police and call for forensic backup."

CHAPTER 18

NEW FRONTS, SAME WAR

Monday, February 11 – MD minus 74 days

H E WAITED UNTIL he was sure that the president had time to finish breakfast with Janet before calling. "Good morning Mr. President, Troy Steed with news, and the news is not good."

"That is a terrific opening," the president answered. "And a good morning to you as well."

"We received a report last night from the FBI strike team that was sent to Abdul Farsi's home that he was not there, and the house appeared more like a slaughter house than a home. Everything of intelligence value had been destroyed, and it was apparent that someone had been killed in a terrible act of violence. There was a message in blood on the wall that read, 'Death to all infidels.' This morning, Farsi's decapitated body was found in a dumpster with a single shot through his severed head. These people are really smart. They killed one of their own for whatever reason, but in his death, he becomes a hero and the terrorists have a great victory by making a public threat to kill anyone who stands against them."

There was silence on the phone as the president paused to take it all in. Finally, he spoke, "Troy, call Tom Knight and David Barnes and you three get here as soon as you can. I am going to have others called so we can focus on this quickly. We have to get more aggressive if we are going to stop MD. It is just so frustrating; the terrorists stumble but escape. They always seem to be one step ahead of us, almost by accident. We still have the computer lab at Harkins. Perhaps we can catch the North American leader there."

But the news from Massachusetts was taking a turn for the worse as Professor Trice stepped to a microphone to make his public announcement of the new front in the war on hate.

"Ladies and gentlemen, I have asked for time this morning to announce that Harkins College, its President Dr. Harold Bristol, and several of its students have this morning filed suit to protect the university and its students against a malicious and racially motivated attack on people of Arab origin, and students at Harkins in particular. Because of his personal involvement in the conduct complained of, we have included President Strong as a defendant. Our suit is filed in federal court seeking protection under the United States Constitution and federal civil rights laws. It is one thing for our government to seek to protect our citizens from terrorists, but another to label everyone of Arab descent a terrorist and to seek to invade our privacy such that it is not even safe to use the Harkins Graduate School of Education's computer lab without being watched by federal agents.

"Both courts have agreed and have issued temporary restraining orders that will protect the college and students for ten days until there can be an evidentiary hearing. During that time, we will be seeking depositions and document production, including the deposition of the president because of his involvement. We will not allow the government to negate our constitutional rights. Thank you." He took no questions.

As he left the microphone, Trice was elated. "I love the stage and an opportunity to drive an arrow through the heart of this president. This should advance my appointment to the Supreme Court in the coming administration," he thought.

Harkin's administration followed Trice's advice and closed the Graduate School of Education's computer lab temporarily so that if there really was a terrorist student or professor, at least the fool would not be caught using Harkins facilities and reflect poorly on the school. Someone that stupid would soon be caught anyway, but since there were no security cameras in the computer lab, there should be no other evidence to tie him to Harkins. That should end the threat and the lawsuits should help the majority party take the White House next year.

The news flash was everywhere in Cambridge and Demas Assad got the information. "So much for the computer lab," he thought. "If they have figured that out then they know about the website. It has to be abandoned immediately."

Using his laptop from home, Assad posted this message on FS2.com: "00. Start. J-14."

Realizing that they might be close to identifying him as the leader, Assad made the decision to destroy his computer hard drive and start over. "The whole MD plan is on this," he thought as he took a hammer and pulverized his computer, placing the remains in several plastic garbage bags to be disposed of in different locations.

Within minutes of the posting, David Barnes' secure cell phone rang as he was entering the west wing of the White House in response to the call to meet with the president. "David Geek here. There is trouble in wonderland. The FS2.com website has been taken down. There was a new posting from that J-14 fellow and it crashed within minutes. I happened to be looking for postings or I would have missed it."

The sound of his voice evidenced the discouragement Darrell Reed felt. "What now?"

"What now is we hit it again," Barnes responded. "Put an army on searching the web for a replacement website while you go back through everything. We have to see if we missed anything."

"Will do," Reed said and paused. "It's hard to believe, I thought we were so close."

"We were close, Darrell. I wonder what happened. Why did they take that site down?"

Barnes learned the answer to that question as he was watching with the president and a group assembled in the White House conference room, a video replay of Trice's press statement. "No wonder," David sighed, and explained to the group what had just happened in cyberspace.

For a moment it was like half-time at a football game where the home team was badly behind and the coaches had lost the playbook. There was a sense of panic and depression in the room. The unspoken question lay on the room like a crushing weight — what now? We're blind.

In the invisible, the war in the room raged violently. The battle for the hearts and minds of the men and women in that conference room was intensified as the forces of darkness sought to sow confusion, fear, and helplessness in everyone. Soon, thoughts of blame and retaliation were passing through minds as Chemosh and others of the forces of darkness were working hard to cause an angry emotional reaction to the circumstances. Yet, in the midst of the assault, those with the light inside found a different force pouring peace into their hearts and clearing their minds so they could reject the thoughts sought to be planted by the Dark Master's Keepers and Tempters.

Standing up from his seat at the middle of the table, the president spoke calmly and resolutely, "Ladies and gentlemen, we have lost a battle, perhaps two, but we have not lost the war. Do not lose hope. Rather than focusing on what we have lost, let us focus on what we have to work with and move forward to address this threat. It is hardly a great victory when your local commander is killed by his own people and their national commander barely escapes capture. Remember, they are blind too and must be afraid because they are now aware that we know something of their plans. Our biggest problem is that we are fighting a war with many fronts; some of which have been launched by the people who should be our friends and allies.

"I want to focus on how we turn what seems to be a negative into a positive. We have these negatives to deal with: (1) loss of the website, (2) loss of the immediate opportunity to catch the Williams leader and the national leader, (3) the reality that there are many terrorists still in the country, (4) MD has been advanced and we don't now know what the terrorists' response will be to the loss of their communications, (5) the Majority Party's public relations focus on surrender packaged as a 'war on hate,' and (6) the Harkins College lawsuit. Let us turn this around and get more aggressive. Our enemies are scrambling now, so they are more likely to make a mistake. This is our opportunity to strike back. Don't squander it in doubts and fears or looking for someone to blame."

It was as if a dark cloud was lifted from the room as despair and fear turned to hope. Ugly circumstances were suddenly opportunities, and for those with the light inside, there was the calm assurance of who was ultimately in control of all things. The focus shifted to, "What's next?"

The president excused himself to give the assembled group an opportunity to discuss the issues out of his presence. He returned to the residence to take some time to pray with Janet and get his heart right and his mind cleared for action. He knew this was a critical time and he could not risk separating himself from the only One who had the answers.

Target the Children

And now there were three, and they were angry. "We have been cooped up in a house in our enemy's country for months and the only blood we have spilled is the traitor among us," said Ackmid Hasine, the new leader by default. "We were told to wait and we waited. We were told that Farsi had infiltrated our enemies and would warn us of their preparation. He killed one of our own and told us nothing of the military presence or of the Citizens Militia plant in the church. No one kills a brother and walks free. He was a rat, and rats die. We sent a message to the Citizens Militia that they are not safe in their homes. It is high time to strike their children — even as Doeg the martyr had planned.

"We will let things calm down for a few days and then Thursday we will strike Kingdom Day Care. If we survive that, then Saturday we will strike that Jewish Place. Finally, if we survive that, Sunday we should strike the biggest church we can find. If they have soldiers or Citizens Militia there, we fight to the death and kill as many as possible. If we survive that, we find another target until we are sent to our reward. Our brothers throughout the states will hear of our courage and will follow our example. Blood will flow in every major city."

"Yes," the remaining two agreed, "Death to all infidels! A martyr's glorious death for us all."

The five in whose house they lived were afraid of the three. They had no training in killing and the fire of hate did not burn within. They had tried as much as possible to continue with their routine and not draw attention to themselves or their "guests." They had begun to appreciate life as graduate students in America and wanted to survive this and continue, but how?

Further East, Phygelus Aldar was angry too. His first execution squad had struck successfully, but they had all been killed and now their leader had apparently been killed by the remnant in retaliation. If that wasn't enough, Assad's carelessness had almost gotten him captured and resulted in a total breach of the means of communication with the leaders in the field. It was only by extreme good fortune that the American Teachers Society convention was next week. The leaders would be together one last time before MD. All they could do now was wait until they received further instructions from the Sheik. Much planning had provided for this contingency. The message would come shortly.

Ultimate Deception

"We are winning, Ahmed," the Sheik observed. "The infidels are in complete disarray. They are fighting one another. Already one major political group in America is ready to abandon the fight and abandon Israel. These Americans make me sick. They have great technologies for bloodshed, but they are unwilling to stand and fight and bleed themselves. They are soft. They are no longer great as a people and they do not need to be feared. If we had the time, they would collapse from within, but we cannot leave them with a monopoly on the technology of death."

"But, Exalted One," El-Ahab responded, "They almost captured our leaders in America and have disrupted our means of communication. How can MD proceed?"

"It will proceed as planned only on an accelerated schedule. It must be moved up so that the attacks are launched within 30 days. I will inform our leaders by alternative means and use that same means to feed the division in America and the attacks on their president. He is the only one in that crowd that I fear. Set up the video equipment. I will do this myself to encourage and instruct our people. You will deliver it for broadcast on your way to meet with our Iranian brother Habid to coordinate the attacks against American forces in the Middle East. Now leave while I work through this."

"A great opportunity," Legion smiled. "Now we can counter Strong and the old man," he said, as the Sheik's Keeper dug deep within his skull to deliver the Dark Masters' inspiration for preparing the message.

The Sheik was surprised at how easily the words came and how perfectly they seemed to tie events in America to their agenda. It took some time, but after reviewing it with his key lieutenants, he was prepared to film.

Today I speak to the people of America. You have made yourselves the enemy of Muslims throughout the earth by the policies of your government and its violent intervention in our world. You support our enemies and blaspheme our faith. Yet recently there have arisen voices among your leadership who speak of peace and declaring a war on what caused the declaration of jihad against the West.

I have heard the statement of the brother in your Congress. He speaks with a heart of understanding and offers a real hope for peace. Even your president has called America to a time to confess wrongs and ask your God for forgiveness. Now is a unique time in history, where the opportunity has arisen for you to address wrongs and explore what is necessary for peace. We have no desire to fight you until the death, but we will. We only want to be able to live in peace with the same opportunities for our families as you have. I will not now address the wrongs and sufferings of my brothers which you have supported for so many years. I will rather hold out my hand in an offer of real peace.

I am prepared to meet with an official representative of the America government in an agreed protected nation anytime within the next 30 days. Continued resistance is futile, but together we can find peace by addressing the causes of hate. Must more die before men of good will seek peace?

We will be watching for the public response to our offer.

Watching a replay to be sure that he had gotten it right, the Sheik smiled and turning to his lieutenants said, "Having so many now who live in America with an American education, we know better how to play these people against themselves. We were so crude in the beginning and only united them against us. Now we will divide them and before they are willing to even talk with each other, MD will have come and gone and they will be in a struggle for survival."

"Yes, but what will you do if they accept and want to meet?" Abdul-Aziz asked.

"It does not matter. The message to our people is clear and it will be over before we could meet. It will be fun toying with them, should they accept, but not this President Strong. He will never negotiate with us. He understands well our purpose."

"El-Ahab, be gone," and he went with the video and the new timetable.

A Different Invitation

The phone rang in the residence and it was the White House chief of staff who said, "Mr. President, I think you will want to take this call. It is Pastor Scribes from College Church in Williams."

"Yes, definitely," he responded immediately, and the connection was made.

"Pastor, this is Joshua Strong. I want you to know that my heart is truly broken for you and your people. Such a senseless tragedy; so many people hurt or killed. I wish we could have prevented this attack. We have tried more than you will ever know, but we can't seem to turn the corner and catch these people although we have been so close."

"Mr. President, you have been more helpful than you will ever know by recently calling the country to accountability before God. Unless God moves, you will never be able to not stop these attacks."

"Pastor, I have been living with the cold reality of that fact for some time. Before the Bookseller ever publicly called for the prayer of Jehoshaphat, it had been my prayer. I know that only God can deliver us from the threat we face internally and externally. I don't have the answers. Pardon my candor but I know you understand."

"I do," Pastor Scribes responded. "I understand perfectly and my confidence in our future is in the fact that the leader God has placed over our nation at this time understands. If you do not bend or compromise while seeking God's answer, I know He is faithful and will not allow you to fail."

"Thank you, I needed to hear that," the president answered. "What can we do for you and your people? Believe me, I want to do something if I can."

"Mr. President, we need your presence. Thursday afternoon we are having a service to minister to those who are grieving and suffering and to praise God for His deliverance from what could have happened. This will not be the typical service, but then these are not typical times. We will also pray for our enemies who did this and for their grieving families.

I know that there are political risks for you to be a part of such an event, and there could be physical risks as well. There are obviously still terrorists in the Williams area as the events of this morning prove. We would understand if you or your security people said no."

"Pastor, I will be there. Being president does have some benefits. I can still overrule security and political people. I want to be with those who have suffered this great loss. I am totally on board with what you want to do at the service. I heard your prayer after the shooting at the Security Fair. You are right. That is God's heart. What specifically do you want me to do?"

"Just share whatever God lays on your heart. I believe that you need to be there and to speak. That's all I know."

"It's a much greater burden when you put it that way," the president responded. "Janet and I will pray. Pastor, can I ask you a favor?"

"Certainly, Mr. President. Anything…"

"You know the Bookseller — I would like a few very private minutes with him if he will, and I want to meet Sally Johnson and Tom Campy if he survives."

"The Bookseller is a strange one, Mr. President. He will not meet with you unless he believes that is God's direction and that he can do it in such a way that it does not draw attention to him. He has the stage, but he has never sought the spotlight and guards his heart about the issues of pride. But if it is really to be very private, he will have trouble telling his president who is also a brother, 'No'."

"If you see Tom, you will see Sally," Pastor Scribes continued. "She is camped out at the hospital until the doctors are sure he will recover. The reports today are encouraging. God has heard the prayers of so many for him, and he has improved. It is a miracle."

"Pastor, please keep this confidential. I would like to slip out of Washington secretly without a big press following and without the people there knowing I am coming. That is important for security reasons, but it is also important because I want to come privately as much as possible. I don't want this time to be about me."

"I understand, Mr. President. We won't make any announcements about the program, only the time of the service. Would it trouble you if we allowed the service to be broadcasted? ITN has already asked, and we feel they are almost one of us in all that has happened."

"Pastor, you do what you believe you are being led to do. That is totally your call. Please, just don't tell them or any other press people of my involvement."

"Yes, Mr. President."

"And one more request, Pastor. Before we end, could we pray? There are difficult decisions which I must make today and I need God's wisdom and direction to make the right decisions."

And they prayed.

CHAPTER 19

A LITTLE LIGHT IN A SEA OF DARKNESS

Monday, February 11 – now MD minus 28 days

IT HAD NOT been a good day. Forensics had not turned up anything. The body was a mess. Even the cell phone was a mystery. There was no record with any of the national cell phone companies of an account in the name of Abdul Farsi. "Who was this man?" Agent Samuels wondered as he once again walked through the murder scene looking for anything which could lead to the local terrorist cell that had killed him and still threatened the city. They had made one discovery in a simple computer background search of the name. A man named Abdul Farsi had graduated from the Harkins College Graduate School of Education three years ago. "Of what possible significance could that be?" he thought.

The investigation on the six was a dead end. It was another group of aliens who were inside the US illegally. "How is that possible?" Samuels asked himself. "If we don't do something to secure our border… but then it is probably too late already," he stopped in mid-thought, shaking his head in disbelief.

Across town, another law enforcement group was meeting and their day was not beginning any better.

"Look, Sally, I am sorry for calling you while you are still in the hospital," Detective Samson said, "but we still have the primary responsibility to find the shooter and he is still at large. I know we are dealing with another group of killers, but we can't drop our original investigation until it's closed."

Sally Johnson's mind and heart were elsewhere as she prayed silently for Tom Campy and fumed at being dragged from the hospital waiting room for this. The remaining group of four was silent, waiting for her to speak.

"Sally," Todd Wilson said loudly, trying to get her attention back to room 107 at 1637 Washington where they had been meeting regularly since the shootings began.

"Alright, alright, I'm here now," Sally answered. "Sorry, I have been through a lot recently and this just doesn't seem that relevant in light of all the carnage at College Church and the murder of Farsi. I don't know what has happened, but it seems as if the shooter is on vacation since the shooting at the warehouse. I don't think he is much of a threat anymore."

"How can you say that? He has single-handedly done almost as much damage as the six terrorists did Sunday," Samson answered. "At least you got in the fight and shot someone," he muttered.

"Sometimes I think your brain is perverted," Sally responded. "It is not that difficult to understand. The presence of the Citizens Militia has increased the risk to the shooter. He has always been a coward. He would shoot from hiding and run. He never took a risk. I believe we are finished with him until the emotion dies down and people are not willing to be on the street to protect their neighbors. When people begin to feel safe again and get careless, he will return; or maybe he has had enough. We need to shift gears and go for the terrorists."

"I like that idea," interjected Greg Peterson, a former Army ranger. "The president is right. That is where the real danger is, and after this morning, we know they are still here — at least some of them — and they are not finished. The message on the wall was a notice that more is coming, and I believe that it is coming soon."

"I am on board with that," added Troy Dallas. "We have no clues to follow on the shooter and he isn't a present threat. Let us deal with the real threat."

"Wait a minute," Samson declared loudly. "We haven't been authorized to shift gears and drop the shooter investigation. The feds are dealing with the terrorist threat. We need to finish what is before us."

"Hogwash," Sally responded. "I don't care what our formal mandate is; we have to get the terrorists before we have another College Church incident. If anyone wants to listen, I want to talk about this Abdul Farsi fellow. I strongly believe he was absolutely no hero and is not a victim. He is the leader of the rest of the terrorists."

"What are you talking about?" Wilson asked with keen interest. "Do you know something that isn't public? The press is making this guy out to be a martyr. There is already talk of a memorial at the school where he worked, and they only found his body a few hours ago."

"Abdul Farsi is no martyr. Tom and I were having that debate right before the College Church shooting. Tom knew something that he was going to tell me but obviously, he didn't have that opportunity."

"I was there at the Security Fair. Farsi knew the man he killed. He killed him so he would not be captured and talk. No one empties a full clip into someone in a crowd and then runs reloading to shoot again. Farsi was a public relations plant; literally, a spy. I know it's true but I can't prove it yet."

"You'd better keep that to yourself. You won't find many that agree with that and you seem to have forgotten that he saved your life by shooting that terrorist," Samson responded.

"Your half right Pete, he shot the terrorist."

"I am through with the shooter until something else happens. We have no clues and no time to waste. If anyone is interested, that is what I'm going to devote my time to," Sally said in a tone such that no one doubted either her intent or resolve.

"Rebellion, it's rebellion, but you are right," Samson had to admit. "Let us get the Neighborhood Watch call-in information and see if we can find these people."

"Now, what do we know about Farsi?"

Needed — A Timothy

The Bookseller was sobered by the call from Pastor Scribes, but it affirmed something that had been on his heart for a long time. He needed help to complete what God had put before him and had a deep desire to disciple and prepare a replacement for when he would be called home. Life had changed suddenly. He had not sought the stage, but found himself on it. He no longer had the strength of a young man, for he was not young. Time seemed to be running short.

Because of the exposure he had received from the opportunities to answer questions on television, he had been inundated with invitations to speak throughout the country and also with death threats. He wanted to do whatever God called him to do, but he could not do so physically alone and he needed to be preparing his replacement. His time could be short and he believed he knew who God had called. Picking up the phone, he called Paul Phillips.

"Paul, can you spare a minute? I have something I want you to pray about."

Recognizing the voice immediately, Paul answered, "I always have time for you sir."

"In your studies, have you come across Paul's young friend, Timothy, the one he calls, 'my true son in the faith'?"[77]

"I know something about him, but not much. Why?" he asked.

"The Bible is filled with examples of older believers walking with younger believers to teach and prepare them to replace them. It is the New Testament equivalent of obedience to God's command to Adam and Eve in the garden to be fruitful and increase in number to fill the earth.[78] They were made in God's image and were to fill the earth with people made in God's image.[79] Believers today are to seek to do the same with spiritual children. That is why Paul called his young friend Timothy his true son in the faith.

"There are numerous other examples. Peter calls John Mark, 'my son.'[80] Mark is a perfect example of what I am sensing God may have for you. Mark walked first with Barnabas, then with Peter and was molded into the man of God who ultimately was used to write the Gospel of Mark. I believe that God has a great purpose for your life and that he has called me to help prepare you for that purpose. I want you to pray about being my Timothy. Margaret and I have space in the upstairs of the warehouse for you and a wife, if God puts that in your future. We have a separate apartment there which could be yours. I am asking you to pray about leaving school for a time and walking together with me in whatever way God will lead you. You would travel with me wherever I am sent, and we would have time every day to study and minister together until God calls you back to school or somewhere else."

"I don't know what to say," Paul answered, "my heart leaps at the thought of learning from you, but you have taught me to pray before making decisions and I believe I should."

"While you are praying, I want you to consider joining me in things that I know are coming. Pastor Scribes just called and the president will be attending the memorial service on Thursday. He has asked for a few private minutes with me. I want you to be there, but please, the fact that the president is coming is confidential. You must tell no one.

"Also, I have been asked to appear before a congressional committee looking to make real faith and belief in the Bible illegal by changing the hate crimes law. I want you to come with me. Pray about that and call when you have your answer from the Lord. I will be praying too."

As he hung up the phone, it rang immediately. The caller was Samantha. "Mr. White, I have been thinking about our discussion last night and I need to talk with you. Would you have time this afternoon? My last class ends at 3:00 PM."

"Yes, I will reserve time for you after 3:30," he said.

"God is still at work in her," he thought. "She is still searching and if she does not stop, she will find an answer. What an exciting day," and with that, he left for County Hospital to see Susan Stafford, who had sent him a note yesterday and to check on the progress of his friend Tom Campy.

Significant Tips

Hidden deep in the recesses of one of the older federal buildings in Washington, Kayla Walker sat at her desk perusing a small portion of the mass of contact information phoned to Homeland Security by citizens across the country after the president's request. The tens of thousands of tips regarding suspicious conduct had been processed and divided into geographic divisions and by subject matter. That morning, Kayla drew suspicious tips regarding large trucks. "Not a very inspiring assignment," she thought as she picked up one that had caught her attention and made a call.

"Good afternoon, this is Kayla Walker with the Homeland Security Department. Could I speak with Juan Martinez?"

"Juan is still in school," a concerned Mother answered. "Is he in some kind of trouble?"

"Oh no, Juan called in a tip regarding suspicious activity in the community as the president requested and we are following up. When will he be in?"

"Please call back around 4:00 PM and you will find him. What was his tip?"

"I am sorry, I can't share that with anyone. You will have to ask him. Good-bye."

"Well," she thought as she looked through other tips, "I will try this one."

"Good afternoon, this is Kayla Walker with the Homeland Security Department. Could I speak with Sam Will?"

"This is Sam Will."

"Great. I am following up on the tip submitted to Homeland Security regarding suspicious activity in the trucking industry."

She paused for a moment thinking, "Sam Will, where do I know your name from?"

"You probably have been following events in Williams, Illinois," he answered. "I head the Citizens Militia in Williams."

"Of course, you people have done great things in a short period of time. Mr. Will, would you take me through the tip again to be sure I get all the facts correct?"

"Sure, it's not complicated," Sam began. "I am a retired over-the-road truck driver with lots of friends who are still driving. When they are around, we get together for coffee and chew the fat, you know, talking about changes in the trucker lifestyle and work. It gets in your blood and you miss the road.

"My buddies who drive fuel trucks started talking about a change in their work days. Seemed the whole operation was going to be closed on Memorial Day. That is a great idea, but something that has never been done before. I don't mean that there was anything suspicious about that, but recently I heard that this Memorial Day holiday had become a floating holiday. Out of nowhere, it was moved up 30 days to April 28th. That is no holiday and it just seemed strange to me. The other strange thing was that it doesn't seem to be industry-wide, or even company-wide. It is only truckers who drive the fuel rigs, and the only company I know for sure is doing that business is an outfit called Brothers Trucking. That's all I know, but it sure seemed strange to me."

"Thank you, Mr. Will. I am going to leave you my direct number and if there is any other information you hear on this or any other issue, please call me immediately. This could be important."

"Not a problem, thank you for following up," Mr. Will added. She gave him her cell phone number and said her good-byes.

Kayla knew what Mr. Will had said could be significant. She picked up on the possible MD implications and went back into the pile of tips regarding large trucks to see what else might be there.

What are the Targets?

Down the street, the president began a series of meetings to address the multiple fronts of the war he was facing. In the White House Situation Room, he had gathered the Joint Chiefs to follow up on the MD target inquiry. Their charge had been to put themselves in the terrorist's shoes and find the targets necessary for the destruction of America.

"Before we begin, General Hedge," the president commanded, "I want you to have someone call the commander of the Alpha Force to instruct him to keep his forces in position in Williams through the memorial service, which will be on Thursday. The terrorists have demonstrated that they are still present and intend to strike again. We cannot tolerate another attack on these same people, and we really cannot tolerate it at a media event. Coordinate with local authorities and College Church's pastor to provide whatever level of security may be necessary for that event."

"Yes, Mr. President," he said, turning to an aide who left the room to make the call.

"Now, Troy, where are we on identifying the possible targets of MD?"

"Mr. President, if the MD target is not people or structures of significance, the target would be those things which are required to sustain life. These include air to breathe, water to drink, food to eat, energy to power essential equipment, and communications infrastructure. Any substantial attack on those essentials would create chaos quickly and it would be difficult to recover from the chaos in the short-term. It would paralyze the nation — which is clearly the expressed intent of the terrorists."

"That is certainly much more difficult to prevent than planning a defense against execution squads or people who want to blow up symbols," the president answered with concern. "How would that be possible?"

"Unfortunately, it is not as difficult as you might think," General Hedge added. "If our mission was to paralyze America, we would be able to use the internet to locate the infrastructure that supports the essentials described above. The issue is not so much about identifying targets, for we can do that; the issue is how those targets could be successfully attacked with what is available to our enemies. That is planning we have never done."

"Help me a little with that," the president asked. "Walk me through what would have to be attacked to damage the essentials you identified."

"Let me answer you by going through one of our contingent plans to do the same thing to Iran if we cannot negotiate away their nuclear bomb development program," General Hedges continued. "In our plan, there are two parts to the attack and two goals of the attack. We want to destroy the nuclear facilities and we want to paralyze the country without inflicting massive casualties. The results should be the removal of the threat and removal of the people who caused the threat by their own people. Sound familiar?"

"Setting aside the direct attack on the nuclear installations, how would that second goal be accomplished? How would you paralyze Iran without killing massive numbers of people?"

"It is scary simple. Iran has a single oil refinery and depends on imports for fuel and food. Take out the refinery and blockade the sea lanes into the country and Iran will fall into chaos quickly. Within days, people would not have gas for vehicles, food could not be transported, the military could not use their mobile weapons and essential imports would be in short supply. Other attacks on power generation facilities and communications facilities would cripple the country and strike a blow that would take years to recover from. Action would have to be taken to deal with potential missile strikes, but the elimination of command and control of their military would limit that. Effectively, Iran would cease to be a force in the Middle East or an organized country. The people suffering would rebel against those who provoked the attack.

"Mr. President, that is what we believe the terrorists intend to do to us with MD."

"Ladies and gentlemen, I believe you have it," the president responded. "Now comes the hard part. I need a plan to defend essential facilities and a plan for what to do if the terrorists are successful in whole or in part. I want to know how this could be done with what they have available so that we can hit the source of the weapons and prevent the attacks. I want us to be ready to respond within thirty days.

"General, I need your plan by the end of Wednesday, and in the meantime, draw up orders to put our forces around the world on notice of this threat. The plan has to include how we respond to protect our forces in the Middle East and how to cooperate with Israel to deal with Iran. Coordinate with their military liaisons that are here on special assignment to deal with this threat. We need a plan to deal with Russia, Syria and others who may join Iran against us."

He rose to a chorus of, "Thank you Mr. President" and left for his next meeting with Attorney General Rodriquez who was waiting in the Oval Office with Tom Knight and David Barnes.

Act II — Harkins "Justice"

Further down the street, Senate Majority Leader Howard stepped to a microphone in the Capitol to read a press release prepared the night before.

Ladies and gentlemen, the leadership of Congress views with grave concern the allegations of the eminent Constitutional Law Professor Larry Trice that this government has launched a racially motivated attack on Arab students and faculty members at Harkins College. The suits filed today and the orders entered by the two courts provide clear evidence that Congress must exercise its oversight responsibility to assure that this government acts within constitutional limitations and protects the rights of all people. The allegations of wrongful conduct by President Strong are particularly troubling.

Accordingly, the Senate Judiciary Committee will begin an

investigation into the allegations this week. We call upon this adminis-
tration to rethink how they are dealing with the threat they constantly
tell us we are under. We ask for restraint and call for complete and open
cooperation so that the truth may be revealed to the American pub-
lic quickly. Administration officials should willingly appear and tes-
tify. Relevant documents should be voluntarily provided. Hearings will
commence Friday morning with Professor Tice as the first witness.

After viewing a replay in the Oval Office, the president smiled. "Anyone who thought that the Harkins suits were serious constitutional challenges and not part of the congressional political assault now knows. It appears that the leadership of Congress has decided to ignore my call for a time on Friday to humble ourselves before God, and have chosen instead to provide an alternative 'show' for the American public to direct them away from consideration of whether we have done anything to offend God. 'Great' TV moments, hate crimes and an investigation of me; everything but addressing the real threat to this nation."

"Mr. President, I am really angry about this too," Attorney General Rodriquez added. "That bunch in Cambridge think they can do anything they want, regardless of how it may harm the country. They have earned the title, 'The People's Republic of Cambridge.' Have you seen what they did recently to the Boy Scouts? A local scout troop placed donation boxes at polling places to collect items for care packages to send to American soldiers in Iraq. Cambridge officials stopped it claiming that it was 'political.' What is political is the filing of these suits and the farce on display in Congress."

"Slow down for a minute Felix," the president responded. "You are right and your anger is both justified and shared. The actions of the local authorities in Cambridge are despicable just as the actions of the leadership in Congress. However, we are in an election cycle and we must be careful not to lose sight of our theme. Remember, the theme for us must be how to make the negative a positive. I do not care what they do or say; we know what we must do so we will work with whatever they throw at us to accomplish what must be done, and in the process will educate the American public so they will continue to be a part of the solution. It is they who will end up playing the fool."

"I have to be honest and say that I am deeply concerned by their decision not to stand before God for the country with our people. They have now made their choice, in the words of the Bookseller, not to be on God's side. May they not take the country with them in their latest political folly."

"Enough about them; how shall we proceed?"

"It is really not that difficult Mr. President," the Attorney General said. "We have three approaches available simultaneously. I have already convened a grand jury to investigate the terrorist's leader at Harkins. We will have subpoenas issued for everything they have refused to provide. We have their civil suit in which we can take the deposition of Harkins' president and through which we can fight the political and public relations war. Finally, we have available legal rights to obtain information through the intelligence laws. I suggest we aggressively pursue all the three immediately."

"You have stated your own mandate, proceed with vigor," the president responded.

"Felix, I want you to know how much I appreciate your wisdom and leadership. You are a very important part of this team and I thank you."

"Thank you, Mr. President," and he departed to proceed with vigor.

Turning to the two remaining participants the president said, "Tom, I want you and David to get together with Troy Steed and have him brief you on the status of the military plan. I believe they have isolated the targets and are working on a weapons analysis and response. I want the Survival Commission brought up to date on all of this including the Harkins foolishness and then they need to focus on the diplomatic and foreign response. We need a plan and quickly. I want to be ready to move within thirty days, sooner if possible. We are not going to sit and wait to be attacked."

He sat quietly for a moment, seeking to gather his thoughts. Tom and David said nothing. They understood the man well enough to know what was happening and waited for the president to speak.

"You two and Janet have become my prayer partners. It helps more than you will ever know. I am really troubled by the congressional leadership choosing to ignore the call for prayer and confession of sin. The Bible has a lot to say about God's response when He is rejected. We need to pray for them, no, we have to pray for them because they have chosen to be our enemies. Would you stay for a few minutes and pray with me?"

"Absolutely, Mr. President," Tom responded. "I feel privileged to work for a man who has that kind of a heart."

"It is easy," the president answered, "the secret is — it is not my heart. It is God's heart."

CHAPTER 20

CHOICES AND CHANGES

Monday, February 11 — MD minus 28 days

AS THEY SAT together in his study, the Bookseller puzzled over what he had just experienced. "Margaret," he began, "I just witnessed some kind of incredible spiritual battle over Susan Stafford while I was visiting her at County Hospital. You remember her? She was the Citizens Militia member that was shot at the Security Fair on Saturday."

"I do," Margaret answered, "and I understand what you mean by a spiritual battle. While you were gone, I had a sense that it was important to pray for you — and I did. As I sought to focus my prayers, my mind was flooded with diversions; the phone rang and people even came to the door. It was as if an all-out assault was launched against me being able to pray for you in those moments. I have learned that when that happens it is even more important to dismiss all outside interference and concentrate on prayers."

"I needed every prayer," he continued. "There is something unusual about that woman and I don't know what it is. She had been badly used or abused somehow. She carries scars and an ocean of guilt. I sense that all Hell has been unleashed on her. She couldn't look me in the eye as we began. She spoke in the third person, you know the 'I have a friend who' talk. It was all about evil and 'is there any hope for a person who' in the abstract, but it was her she was talking about. Of that I am sure."

"What do you mean? What kind of evil?" Margaret asked.

"She talked about movies, asking if a mass murderer could be forgiven. She used examples like Charles Whitman, the man who shot all those people from the tower at the University of Texas and those kids at Columbine who went on that shooting rampage in their school in Colorado. She had obviously studied people she considered really evil to make the question about forgiveness as difficult as possible."

"How did you answer her?" Margaret wanted to know.

"I told her the story of King David, how he saw the beauty of Bathsheba, Uriah's wife, and lusted after her. How he used his authority as the king to take her and when she became pregnant, he first tried to deceive Uriah but when every attempt at deception failed, he send a sealed note with Uriah as he returned to the army with instructions that he was to be placed in the front of the battle and when the fighting was the most fierce, those around him were to withdraw so he would be killed. It happened exactly as David ordered. Then he married Bathsheba so the people would view the child as a product of their marriage and he went on with his life thinking he had hidden the murder and the rape but God knew.[81]

"I explained how God sent Nathan the prophet to confront David by telling him a story and ultimately pointed his finger in David's face saying, 'You are the man,' followed by the revelation that God knew all the evil David had sought to hide. David confessed what he had done as a sin against God and was forgiven, but there were awful consequences from which God did not deliver him. They followed him all the rest of the days of his life and the child he had conceived died.[82]

"I told her that was how God would deal with her examples had they lived. They would be confronted with their sin and could be forgiven if they, like King David, acknowledged their sin and turned from it but also like King David, they would not escape the consequences of their sin in this life. However, if they were born again, they would be delivered from the second death."

"Did she understand?" Margaret spoke quickly, wanting to know.

"I think so. I tried to make it really simple. I explained that simply saying you are sorry isn't asking for forgiveness or turning from the sin, even Judas Iscariot was sorry for the consequences of his sin.[83] He was not forgiven.[84] I also told her that asking for forgiveness, really, demanding forgiveness without turning away from the sin, isn't repentance. Biblically, to be forgiven, you have to agree you did the wrong thing and then come to the place where you hate what you did simply because God hates it. You hate it so much that you will do everything you can with God's help to keep yourself from doing it again.[85] That is a heart God can forgive.

"She seemed to really understand. It was amazing. Her whole visage changed. She smiled and peace came over her. She even looked me in the eye. The darkness and depression were lifted and she called the nurses' station and demanded to check out of the hospital and return home. They protested, but she insisted.

"It was the strangest thing, Margaret. She appeared to be almost overcome with a sense of duty, something she had to do. She asked me to wait for her and take her back to the school to pick up her car that was still in the gym parking lot. I left her as she dressed and went to check on Tom Campy in ICU. He is better and we prayed together. He is going to make it, praise God. I had thought all along that God was not through with him yet."

"So, finish the story, Samuel. Did she say anything else on the way to pick up her car?"

"She just thanked me and seemed absorbed in whatever it is that she has to do. She asked me to pray for her when I dropped her off, which I did. The prayer God put on my heart was that He complete in her and through her all He was seeking to do. I had no other leading."

He paused for a moment and then said, "Margaret, we really need to keep her in our prayers. I don't know why but it's important. Like Tom Campy, there is a purpose yet for her life. She has only one working arm but that will be enough for whatever God wants to do with her."

Getting Closer in Williams

"Wait a minute, what's this?" Greg Petersen said as they sifted through a mass of call-in notes at the Williams' police headquarters. "This is from a neighborhood here regarding five supposed Arab students who live in the same rent house off of Bell and 17th. We ought to check that out. They may be tied to our remaining terrorists."

"Slow down, Greg, the initial follow-up notes say the five are all

Williams College exchange students here legally with papers," Detective Samson answered. "No one in this room would rather crush anyone involved with the people who did that over at College Church more than me, but we need to do a little more investigation before we kick down doors simply because they are Arabs. You saw this morning the lawsuits against the president. We don't want to walk into one of those."

"Look," Sally Johnson added, "we have their names. Let's check with Williams College and find out if the five were all in class this morning and what their recent attendance record has been. We can interview some of their professors and see what we can learn. Unlike the Harkins crowd, I think the Williams' administrators will voluntarily cooperate with us in this investigation. They don't want another massacre. There are terrorists still here. This morning proved that. We have to find a reason for a search. If we get one and they were involved, somewhere in the search we will find forensic evidence on Farsi's murder. There was too much blood and mess for them to be able to clean everything up that quickly."

"Fine, you do that and I am going to take a black and white and drive through the neighborhood to go see the woman, Joan Brewer, who called in the suspicious activity," Samson said. "If I observe or find out anything that would justify the issuance of a warrant, we will get one pronto and do a little door kicking. If not, my presence in the black and white may at least get their attention and our tipster will watch them even closer going forward after we talk. Maybe then we will just drop by for an interview."

"Alright Greg," Sally agreed, "you go, but please be careful. Those responsible are indiscriminate killers the likes of which you have never encountered before. They kill with passion and pleasure. Their eyes reveal an unearthly hatred," she said, remembering Sunday morning.

In Iran - Hiram and Sadah Must Choose

Ahmed El-Ahab dropped off the video with their media contacts in Tehran on the way to a prearranged meeting with Ahmad Habid at the training camp in Kerman Province. He still carried the sealed envelope containing the Sheik's message on the new MD date. "By morning in the West," he thought, "the video message will have thrown our enemies into confusion and taken their eye off MD preparations. Our people will know when the attack is coming even as the Americans and their allies fight with one another over the proper response. The Sheik is inspired with wisdom from above."

"Yes," said Legion to an admiring crowd of wisps, Keepers, and Tempters, "inspired."

Across town, there were many more home invasions that night as the State Security Force moved against the Christian infidels. No group meeting anywhere was safe unless that house had been designated, on the master plate, as an official house of the faithful by the SSF authorities, and a coded identifying mark had been placed above the door. The plan was to carpet the city, house by house, until all Christians had been identified and all Bibles and other Christian literature seized. It was a different kind of terrorism, not unlike that exercised by the Roman government against first-century believers. No Christian was safe anywhere in Iran.

The two SSF believers who had crashed into the house where Hushai had joined others to pray were now banging on the door of a suspected Christian couple who they knew. The man, Hiram Urbay, worked with them at the SSF as a computer tech. The light within drew them to this man as one who appeared to be a believer but they had to be sure.

The door was opened in fear and the two raced in, guns raised and they repeated what had been done at the prayer meeting. This time they made it even more difficult because the risk was greater. Pointing their guns at Sadah, Hiram's wife, the leader turned to him and spoke firmly, "Renounce your faith in Jesus or she dies now!"

Before he could speak, Sadah spoke calmly, "Do what you must. We will not renounce our faith in Jesus. I will not deny Him now or ever. Kill me if you will. Kill us both."

"Yes," Hiram agreed, "kill us together that we may come into His presence even as we have lived our lives as one."

Again, there were tears as the SSF leader spoke, "I have not come as an angel of death. We have come to protect those who truly are followers of Jesus but we have to know who they are and not what they pretend to be. Deception is everywhere and the consequences of a single mistake are death or imprisonment."

"Hiram, I am so sorry to have done this, but better us than those who would have killed you or dragged you and Sadah off to prison. We are going to designate your house as an official 'house of the faithful' so that the SSF forces will leave you in peace and your house can be safely used by believers as a place for prayer gatherings. I have only one request; you have seen the US president's call for a time to gather before the Lord to confess sin and seek forgiveness?"

"Yes," Hiram answered, "I have watched it many times on the Together We Pray website. I have a desire to gather with others and pray but don't really know others and there is such danger."

"We want to use your house Friday night, now that it will be designated as an official house of the faithful, to bring together believers we have found in the city who have proven themselves faithful at the risk of their lives, to pray and stand before God together even as the American president has asked."

"Oh yes, please come and bring others," Hiram answered. "It would be the joy of our hearts to gather with others who believe in our home, but how will we know for sure that those who knock on our door are sent by you and not by others in the SSF to identify believers?"

"Do not be afraid. The coded identification mark we are going to place above your door will direct the SSF away. When people come to your door, greet them with, 'He is risen.' If they are part of us, they will respond, 'He is risen indeed.' Then you will know for sure. Expect only us and three or at the most four others." No names were used or given to protect identities from being revealed in torture if someone was discovered to be a Christian in the future.

"Thank you. For our home to be so used for the Lord is a privilege," Hiram responded with emotion. "There is something very important about the American president's call."

After a time of prayer together, the two SSF members placed the coded identifying mark above the door and left to make the appropriate entry on the official plate in a hurry so they could tell the others of the place to gather on Friday night.

For Samantha – No Place to Hide

"Samantha, come in," the Bookseller answered as he opened the door and welcomed her. She appeared troubled, he thought, and had obviously been struggling hard with something. They walked back to the study where Margaret rose to greet her. The Bookseller never met alone with a woman if he could avoid it. He knew that he was but a man and guarded carefully against any possible temptation or false allegation. He represented the Lord and did not ever want to do or even be accused of anything which would bring disgrace on God.

"Mr. White, why haven't I been born again?" she asked bluntly and then like a proverbial broken dam, her thoughts and feelings began flooding out of her.

"I know I am not like Paul now. Sometimes I am shocked by the words that come out of my mouth and the thoughts that race through my mind. I am angry with Paul, but I still love him. I resent him for what he has that I don't and I sometimes say cruel things to him that I know I don't even believe. I am confused by all this religious rhetoric and I have no peace. I can't live like this. I alternate constantly between hating God and hating myself. Can you help me?" And the tears began to flow.

"Oh, my child," Margaret said as she reached over, placing her arm around Samantha and they embraced. Margaret held her silently and let her cry for she sensed that it was cleansing something within her. The Bookseller prayed silently for wisdom, knowing that this was an eternal moment and he needed to speak only God's words.

Around them and over them, the forces of light formed a protective barrier which excluded the Keepers and Tempters who sought to continue their hold on Samantha. This was her time to choose and they would not be allowed to interfere. The light within the Bookseller glowed brightly as his prayer was answered and he turned to Samantha ready to speak.

"Samantha," he asked, "do you believe that you have the 'right' to choose whether to obey what God reveals to you in prayer or in your study of the Bible?"

"I don't understand what you are asking," she answered. "Of course I have the right to choose how to live my life. Everyone has that right."

"Let me ask you another question. Samantha, do you believe that as society changes in what it does or accepts that you should change too and be just like society?"

"Well," Samantha responded, "everyone knows that for sure things change and that's a good thing. Women were once seen as property and slavery used to be legal. I don't want to live like that. We have to change in order to grow."

"Who then has the right to decide what to change and how that change is to affect society?" the Bookseller asked.

"What is this, twenty questions?" Samantha said with obvious increasing frustration and discomfort. "This is America. We have the right to decide things individually. You know, 'the pursuit of happiness.' It is our God-given right. We are to make our decisions in ways that don't hurt other people but we still decide. Society weighs what is happening in its midst and then changes as it finds the individual decisions to be acceptable to the whole. That is America. What's that got to do with God and with being born again?" Samantha asked with a touch of irritation now as her critical decision fast approached.

"You have asked the right question, really, the only question," the Bookseller responded gently and with real affection for her. "It has nothing to do with God. In a society such as you describe, the truth is that you have made yourself a god. What did you just say? You set the rules and make the decisions as you want. It's you and only you."

"Wait a minute," Samantha attempted to interrupt but the Bookseller stayed the course.

"No, you wait a minute," he said firmly, reaching for his Bible on the coffee table by the couch.

"In John 10:27, Jesus said, 'My sheep (a term for His followers) listen to my voice; I know them, and they follow me.' I don't hear anything in the society you describe or in the individual decisions you say you have the 'right' to make, where anyone listens to Jesus' voice and seeks to follow Him."

Samantha was stunned. She had never considered what it might mean to follow Jesus in her world. "Listen and follow," she thought, "but what does that really mean?"

"Or consider this passage," the Bookseller continued, "again in the 14th chapter of John where on three separate occasions, Jesus says, 'If you love Me, you will obey what I command,' and then He says, 'He who does not love Me will not obey My teachings.'[86]

"What does it mean when you say you have the right to decide without even considering Jesus' teachings or seeking His voice in prayer to know what He would have you do in any circumstance? It means that He is not your God – you are. It means you don't love Him. You have chosen to live independent of God."

"I do love Him!" Samantha objected strongly, her voice rising, "I am not living independently of Him. I joined a church, I prayed and was even baptized! I am a Christian. The pastor even said so."

"Are you?" the Bookseller continued. "Do you know what the word 'Christian' means? Do you know where it came from?"

"It means being a church member, a believer in Jesus who accepted by faith what He did on the cross and tries to live like Him," Samantha answered quickly from memory.

"I know where you heard that," the Bookseller responded with obvious disdain, pausing to be sure he had her attention.

"Samantha, listen to yourself. Everything you said was about what you were going to do. There is no God in the world of self-effort even if that effort is done in His name."

While Samantha's head spun as she tried to understand what she had just heard, the Bookseller continued. "The term 'Christian' was originally used to describe Jesus' followers in the city of Antioch soon after His ascension to the Father.[87] It was intended to be a term of insult. It meant, 'little Christ.' These people were not trying to live like Jesus, they had become like Jesus. That is what it means to be born again. God gives you a new Spirit within, His Spirit, and He gives you a new heart which the Bible teaches creates a desire within to know His word and to obey Him. Look, it is right here in the book of the prophet Ezekiel. Read chapter 34, verses 26-27."

Samantha took the Bible and read:

I will give you a new heart and put a new spirit in you; I will remove from you, your heart of stone and give you a heart of flesh. And I will put my Spirit in you and move you to follow My decrees and be careful to keep My laws."

"Has that happened to you?" he asked. "If you don't have that desire within to seek to hear Jesus' voice through His Word and prayer and then to follow Him by obeying what has been revealed, you are not born again and remain your own god. You decide everything because you rule over your life.

"The early followers of Jesus required every person who claimed to be a Christian to publicly declare, 'Jesus is my Lord.'[88] That meant Jesus is my God, my ruler, the one whom I follow and obey. They had given up the 'right' to rule over their lives and had surrendered that right to Jesus which made Him their God. The Bible teaches that no one can say, 'Jesus is Lord' and mean it unless they have the Spirit within which some call the light within and that occurs only when you are born again."

"Show me that," Samantha asked and the Bookseller directed her to Romans 10:9 and 1 Corinthians 12:3. She read the verses carefully to be sure what she had been told was what was actually in the Bible.

"You probably also ought to read what Jesus said in Luke 6:46," which he looked up and handed to her. Samantha read out loud:

Why do you call me, 'Lord, Lord' and do not do what I say?

Samantha was troubled, confronted openly by the conflict between what society taught and what Jesus said. She knew she had to decide one or the other. She looked to Margaret for a way of escape. Margaret smiled lovingly and said, "Samantha, what Samuel says is right. Hand me the Bible, I want to show you one last verse that settled it for me."

Turning to Luke 9:23, Margaret read, "Then He said to them all, 'If anyone would come after Me, he must deny himself and take up his cross daily and follow Me.' It is the daily part that helps me. We have to make a decision every day that Jesus is Lord and I am not. That is what it means to deny yourself. You willingly submit to Jesus as your Lord and give up what you call the 'right' to decide how to live. If you are born again, that will be your heart's desire because you have the new heart and new Spirit. If you don't have that desire, you cannot manufacture it and you know you are not born again."

"I want that desire," Samantha asked almost pleading. "What can I do to be born again?"

"It is not for you to do, it is for God to do," the Bookseller answered. "You need to seek God in prayer asking to be given the new heart and new Spirit. When you come to the place where you are truly seeking God with all your heart, God will answer that prayer and you will be born again. You will know when that happens for you will have been changed from within. You will be what Paul calls in 2 Corinthians 5:17, 'a new creation; the old has gone, the new has come.'"

Handing her the Bible, he said, "Read it for yourself. I didn't make it up."

The Bookseller waited for her to finish reading and then said, "Samantha, we will pray for you as you continue to seek Him."

"Can we pray now?"

"Of course," and they did.

Two Messages

A second messenger sent from the Sheik arrived at the Ministry of Foreign Affairs in Riyadh, Saudi Arabia, looking for Baqir Dawood. He carried an envelope similar to what Ahmed El-Ahab was carrying for Ahmad Habid. It contained the same information on the new MD date.

Finding Dawood, the messenger handed him the sealed envelope and he saw the name, "Demas Assad," and knew immediately what to do. No words were spoken as he placed the envelope in a diplomatic pouch and left for the airport to catch the next diplomatic flight to Washington, DC.

Meanwhile, back in Washington, Kayla Walker made the follow-up call to Juan Martinez who was waiting by the phone. "Mr. Martinez, this is Kayla Walker with Homeland Security. I wanted to talk with you about your report of suspicious activity. Please tell me about it."

"Thanks for calling," he began. "I've been kind of afraid to report what is going on here because I'm just a kid, but when I heard the president talking on the TV, I knew I had to call.

"I ride my bike to school and back every day past the old Craig place. For months now, maybe two or three times a week, one of those big trucks is parked there. I've seen guys get out of the house and into the trucks as passengers. They look foreign. I don't know what it means, but the Craig place is nowhere near the interstate. I can think of no reason for the big trucks to be parked there."

"Where exactly are you located?" she asked.

"I live in Carmen, Arizona, a small town off Interstate 19. It's a straight shot up from the border."

"Did you notice anything unusual about the trucks?"

"All I can tell you is that every truck I've seen has the same name on the side, Brothers Trucking. There are different kinds of trucks but always the same name. That's all I know."

"Thank you, Juan. What you saw could be very important. Please be careful around that house. There could be danger. I am going to recommend that Homeland Security sends someone out to meet with you and check this out. Here is my number, call me if you see anything different and, I will call you when we set up the visit from here."

Hanging up, Kayla took a deep breath, "Brothers Trucking again," she thought. "I wonder what this means" and she sent an email report to her supervisor suggesting a visit to the young man in Carmen, Arizona. Then she left for a private dinner with her fiancé, David Barnes. "Maybe he can shed some light on the subject."

CHAPTER 21

DISCOVERY AND MISTAKE

Tuesday, February 12 – MD minus 27 days

B EFORE AHMED EL-AHAB had delivered the sealed envelope to Ahmad Habid, the video of the Sheik's purported invitation had been shown around the world hundreds of times and was readily available on the internet for any who wished to see. All eyes turned to the American president to see how he would respond, and all inquiries were met with official silence.

In the invisible world, the war between deception and revelation raged person by person and nation by nation. The agendas collided as two critical dates approached. One was the president's call for a time before the Lord on Friday and the other was the date contained in the two envelopes on their way to Habid in Iran and Demas Assad in America. The plan called for Assad's envelope to be delivered in Phoenix later in the week at the American Teachers Society convention when all the coordinators would be together. March 11th, the new date selected by the Sheik for MD, was now less than a month away. The video message was clear to the operatives around the world that the date had been moved up to less than a month away so they could begin final preparations. They knew a courier would deliver the exact date soon and it would be revealed to the coordinators at the ATS convention later in the week.

David Barnes' secure phone rang and he was greeted by a cheery, "Good day, Geek here, have you seen the news?"

"I have," Barnes responded. "I assume you mean the Sheik's invitation."

"Hogwash," Reed answered quickly. "Their website is down. That message is nothing more than a carefully packaged notice to the operatives and their leaders that MD has been moved up. It is now within 30 days and they will strike if we don't stop them. That is all the message means although the president is about to be buried in demands that he respond and send a delegation to meet with the chief killer."

"How can you be so sure?" Barnes asked, expressing his doubt and frustration.

"I just know," was the response, "they have never offered to negotiate with anyone although they will temporarily accept your surrender while they reload for the next attack. Here they are making their final push to render America helpless. Remember their website designation – FS2.com? 'Final solution' doesn't mean 'wait until next year.' These people don't need more time to prepare. They have been at this plan for at least five years. What they need is to divert the enemy, us, from our preparation and then they can kill our country on their schedule.

"Watch the airline reservations, the date will be confirmed as the cowards make arrangements to bail out of the country before the attacks. Remember what we have learned; the leaders are white glove, educated people, apparently living in America with legal status. They are not going to die in this fight. They intend to live and be rewarded after."

"There may be another way to confirm the date," Barnes said, thinking out loud. "I got some information unofficially last night from Homeland Security that would seem to indicate that there is another way. Darrell, what have you found regarding the possible use of trucks as weapons by the terrorists?"

"I haven't looked for that, David, but it has been right before our face all along," Reed responded, feeling stupid. "I've watched the satellite photographs of the training camp regularly since we started investigating this and fuel trucks are all that I have seen there. That would explain the earlier explosion. Maybe it was a test, but fuel trucks alone could never accomplish all they want to do."

"Don't play 'Pentagon planner,' just look and see what you can find?"

"I'll make you a deal," Reed answered. "You make sure the president understands the danger we are in and that this message is a dagger hidden in a charade and I will. If the MD date is within thirty days, we have to be prepared to move within three weeks max. Please, I have no access to the president but I know this is right. I have been studying these people's every move for over four years now. I am right on this one; any other reading is totally inconsistent with their history. Please make sure the president understands and ignores all the political pressure. If we fail to be ready quickly and do not move first, it may be over for us as a nation."

Barnes was surprised at the passion but knew that it was not mere emotional speaking. Reed was a little strange at times, but he was the consummate professional. Something inside told him that Reed was right and he better join in the effort with similar passion or it would be too late. For a moment, fear descended on him as the academic possibility of an attack was made real and he saw the destruction, understanding what the world would be like without an America.

"You have a deal," he answered and hung up so he could call Tom Knight to seek an appointment with the president. Then he called Kayla to bring her up to date and encouraged her to follow up on every lead about big trucks, then left for the White House.

Enter the Vice President

The phone rang on the president's desk right after David Barnes and Tom Knight had brought him up to date on the Sheik's video and Darrell Reeds' interpretation of its real meaning and purpose. Troy Steed was also present and in agreement. "Trucks – how stupid can we be?" the president thought to himself, frustrated that he had not connected the dots earlier. Shaking his head, he picked up the phone as the White House operator announced, "Mr. President, it's the vice president."

"Thank you, put him through please, I will take his call anytime," the president answered.

Vice President Wilburn Marshall was out on the campaign trail visiting the early primary states. It was some twenty-one months until the election but the campaign was already on. Because of his position and experience, Marshall led at this point in the race for the minority party nomination. A former South Carolina governor, he had been instrumental in the election of President Strong by carrying the South and had served faithfully throughout both terms. They were close which is what concerned him now and motivated his call.

"Good morning, Wilburn," the president began. "How goes the good fight?"

"I don't know how good it is, Mr. President, but it is certainly a fight and I need your help."

"What can I do?" the president immediately responded.

"Mr. President, you have kept me completely in the dark on this latest terrorist threat. What I know I have heard from the media just like my opposition, and since you have kept the real story away from the media, I don't know how to play this. I don't know what's going on or how to answer questions because I don't know what you are addressing and now this video calling for some kind of peace conference? I need information. I'm going to be asked today to comment on what you are doing and then asked what would I do differently. I can't answer that with any sense of reality because I don't know what's happening."

The president paused and sighed deeply, thinking and praying about how to answer. After a long moment he finally said, "Wilburn, you know me and know that I am not proceeding for any purpose other than the security and preservation of this nation. I have intentionally removed you from the process because you are out campaigning and will be asked questions regarding what we are doing. I have not wanted you to be in the position of having to decide whether to disclose information that needs to be kept secret or to lie to protect what we are preparing to do from disclosure. Like Truman, who knew nothing about the atomic bomb until he became president after Franklin Roosevelt's death."

"You got that right," the vice president answered, "and I don't like it. I am not comfortable because we have worked together so closely over these years in partnership and I miss that. Also, it is an obstacle and a hindrance on the campaign trail because I don't want to make statements that hurt you or the country, and I don't want to be wrong in what I say and look foolish as events unfold. The attacks on you are merciless and will only get worse. American politics has become nothing more than a combination of attack, insult, and accusations. I am not going to run my campaign that way, but I am running blind and it frightens me."

"Wilburn, here is what I can tell you. You know me and we have stood together for all these years. You need to stand with me now even in your ignorance of the details. If not, you will really seem foolish very soon. I will tell you this off the record. The threat we are addressing is real and endangers America's entire way of life. It will all be over, one way or another, in the next thirty days. As it gets closer, I will call you in for official consultation. Right now, we are still in the discovery stage and in the stage of planning a response. I will not keep you in the dark when we are ready to move, for I have a significant assignment for you and will call you back off the campaign trail. But, for now, you need to stay with 'the danger of terrorism' theme and 'we must support our president in times of real crisis' theme, both of which are true."

"How do I handle the video invitation," the vice president asked.

"Our best intelligence is that the video is actually a message to operatives in the United States and around the world moving the date for a massive attack up to within thirty days. This is not unconfirmed suspicion, this is reality and you need to pray for us even as the old man from Williams said – pray that God reveals what is missing in our analysis. I cannot even begin to tell you what will happen to America if we fail.

"Here is how I am going to handle the video. Publicly our only comment now will be official silence until after the memorial service Thursday, out of respect for those killed and injured in the Williams College Church attacks. Privately, I am going to respond simply, 'My name is not Neville Chamberlain[89] and we do not negotiate with terrorists.' That is my position and it will not change."

"Mr. President, if the danger is as real as you say, I will suspend my campaign and return to Washington immediately to help prepare our response."

"Wilburn, the timing is important. Our enemy is unaware of the extent of our knowledge and we don't want to tip them by your official return. Here is my suggestion: the call for prayer and to stand before the Lord was real and I believe may be determinative of whether God protects us against this terrorist threat. I know your faith and that you understand. Consider joining in my call publicly, suspend your campaign for

Friday and return to Washington where we will hold a time of prayer in the East Room. I am going to ask the old man in Williams to come and lead the prayers. Identify yourself with this movement to return America to its spiritual foundation. The majority party has chosen very publicly to ignore my call. While you are here, I will get you fully briefed because by Friday, we should be close to being ready to respond. However, you should not use what you will learn on Friday, publicly but at least it will make you understand the significance of the threat and you can give us your opinion."

"I will be there Friday, Mr. President, and I will be praying for you."

"Thank you, Wilburn. You have always been one I could trust. If America survives, she would be blessed to have you as its next president." Hanging up, he turned to continue the discussions with Barnes, Knight, and Steed as the vice president tried to fathom what was meant by, "if America survives...."

An Opportunity Seized

"We've got him now!" Majority Leader Howard screamed with delight, "Even the biggest of the bad guys supports our agenda of peace and has fired a fatal shot to the heart of the 'war on terror.' We win! Even this president cannot keep harping on the terrorists' danger when the big guy himself extends the olive branch. The president has to take this and shut up or live with the consequences."

"Anything from the White House yet on what they are going to do with the invitation?"

"Nothing but stone cold silence," responded Chairman Crow. "They are probably all gathered together, hustling with damage control. How do we maximize our advantage?"

"That is easy," former President Cox chimed in, "you need to force the issue, make him commit publicly one way or the other. If he comes out with that, 'we don't negotiate with terrorists' stuff then we will offer to negotiate. I will go and I am willing to make the offer public if the White House won't accept the invitation. I bet they would accept my offer as a former president."

"As usual, you're right on," Howard agreed. "Let's see if he will meet with us and we can make a statement after the meeting one way or another. If he agrees to have someone meet with the Sheik then we will take credit for bringing it about. If he refuses, Leonard can make his offer to go. The president really can't refuse to see us. We've got him now," he said repeating himself with glee and thrusting his arm up with fist clenched.

Picking up the phone, he pressed the button for a direct line to the White House and asked for the president. The phone rang in the Oval Office and the White House operator announced, Majority Leader Howard.

"Yes, Mr. Howard," the president answered. "What may I do for you this morning?"

"Mr. President, we need to meet. This offer from the Sheik is important even historically, and we need to discuss a joint response. This opportunity cannot be missed. This could be the key to a resolution of this whole conflict and a new Middle East policy that eliminates the major causes of the hatred we have been fighting against. A Nobel Peace Prize awaits an acceptance."

Shaking his head in disbelief as he carefully framed his answer, the president finally spoke, "Senator, I understand your reading of this message. We here in the White House have an entirely different reading. Only time will tell who is right, but you seem to have forgotten that the bodies of those killed in Williams in the last terrorist attack have not yet been buried. The memorial service is set for Thursday. I have no intention of entertaining anything to do with this video until that service has ended. Friday, I will be involved the whole day in the prayer meeting we are holding in the East Room. I suggest you consider joining us. If you still want to discuss the video on Saturday, I will be glad to meet with you then but not before on that subject."

"Did I hear you right, Mr. President? You are refusing to meet with the leadership of the majority party on the video invitation before Saturday?" Majority Leader Howard replied with indignation.

"You absolutely heard me right," the president responded firmly. "The people in Williams deserve better than a quick surrender because American blood has been spilled – their loved ones' blood. I will not dishonor the dead by responding to that killer now."

"Understand, Mr. President, we don't intend to let this opportunity pass or for you to hole up in the White House wrapped in your 'more righteous than thou' cloth," Howard spoke with complete disdain. "We will go public and we will seek an alternative means to accomplish what you should be doing immediately. Peace is too important to sit on for a week. This is a colossal mistake you are making. Perhaps even an impeachable offense."

"Do what you think you can, but stay within the law," the president warned.

"Constitutionally, foreign policy is the exclusive prerogative of the Executive branch."

"Are you threatening me?" Howard roared into the phone.

"Why is it always a 'threat' when you are reminded to stay within the law?" the president answered as Howard slammed the phone down.

"Tom, we better put together a press release to put out the fire Howard is about to start. Nothing defensive and nothing about them. All I want the American people to know is that our focus is on caring for the wounded and comforting those who have lost loved ones. I don't want to give that killer the time of day."

"Yes, Mr. President."

Conflicting Press Releases

During the course of the day, three press releases gave the world a snapshot of the two radically different views in competition for the future of America.

THE WHITE HOUSE: The president will have no official comment on the terrorists' video released today. His focus remains on those killed and injured in the most recent terrorist attack in Williams, Illinois, and on the effort to limit or prevent future attacks. He calls upon all Americans to unite in prayer for the recovery of those still injured and for the comfort of those who lost family members, friends, and loved ones. He reminds Americans of his call to gather this Friday, to humble ourselves as a nation before God, to confess our national sins, and to pray for clemency and forgiveness. We must become what we claim to be, one nation under God.

THE UNITED STATES SENATE – OFFICE OF THE MAJORITY LEADER: A historic opportunity has arisen to address the real cause of the hate which has generated the violence we have suffered from terrorist attacks these past years. The president refuses to even discuss accepting the invitation to seek an end to the violence. We in the majority party believe this to be a tragic mistake. Since the president has no interest in seeking peace, we the majority party will. We accept the invitation to meet and address the causes of hate. We have designated former President Leonard Cox as our official representative. This opportunity for a real sustained peace must not be missed. We await further public information on the location and timing for the meeting.

CANDIDATE WILBURN MARSHALL: I fully support the president in his refusal to ignore the dead and wounded in Williams and send a representative to negotiate with the one responsible for the attacks. This is America. We do not surrender when attacked and do not bow our knee to any tyrant in fear of a future attack. I urge all Americans to unite behind the president as he seeks to defend our country and end the violence that threatens us all. I urge you to join with me on Friday in standing before the God who can protect us and on whose side we wish always to be.

Seeking an Iranian Future

In a unique set of circumstances, Ittai and Hushai almost collided on their way to raise the flag, both were in such a hurry to set a meeting. Then, acting as if they did not know each other, they separated temporarily until later at the prearranged time when Ittai drove up in the cab, picked up Hushai, and together they raced off to their special place of prayer. "I have to show you the Bookseller's response," he said, handing Hushai the envelope. "Can you believe his humility? He is an amazing instrument of the Lord."

"Yes, but his usefulness has hopefully only just begun," Hushai responded. "He is needed more now than ever. I assume you have seen the Sheik's latest video message?"

"I have," Ittai answered. "The influence of the Americanized terrorists shows through. He is playing the Americans against themselves while speeding up the attack, at least that is my opinion. The video was nothing more than a ploy to divert attention from MD while telling his people in the US that the timetable was within 30 days. Do you concur?"

"Absolutely, I hope the president is not fooled," Hushai said with concern. "All signs here are for an accelerated schedule. El-Ahab is traveling to the training camp to meet with Habid to notify him of a specific date. We are going to try and get that date but you have to tell the Americans to try other means. I have still not been able to get inside the inner circle. I do know that someone has been sent to apprise the Russians that the schedule will be changed. President Sorboth has yet to buy into the plan but Vandenburg and Krenski have. They are planning to attempt a military overthrow of Sorboth if he appears too weak. I am not optimistic."

"Look, Hushai, here is what I need from you. The president has not been fooled. The response plan is being moved up to address the threat. If we can get the date, we can be sure. There may be other ways than through the Iranian government. We need more detail on the plan and we need to know if you have sufficient contacts among the so-called 'moderates' to allow us to work with them when we move against the Iranian military threat."

"What do you mean?"

"I mean, is there a way we can empower the moderates at the same time as we neutralize the current leadership and its nuclear program? We are looking for real cooperation and suggestions, intelligence if possible. We have to address the immediate threat, but we want to eliminate the threat going forward and find people we can work with now and in the future."

"Let me ponder that one and get back with you. 'I don't know' is the answer right now. You are asking me to find people not only willing to put their life on the line but to help in attacks on their country. That is, as you Americans would say, a tall order," Hushai answered.

"It is, but think about it. It is also a great opportunity for the future of your nation, an opportunity to take back what has been stolen from the people by the hate mongers who are going to bring complete destruction to the nation if they are not stopped," Ittai emphasized.

"You are correct but in a totalitarian regime it is not that easy," Hushai sought to explain. "One mistake and you are dead, along with all who associate with you."

"A change of subject – I believe that I am to send another message to the Bookseller to be sure no one misses the fact that the video is a scam covering new instructions to American operatives and to let the Bookseller know how important God has made him in this process. Please send this note:

> Brother, the days are now much shorter and God's protection is essential to prevent disaster and open eyes to deception. Don't believe what you see in the video. Ezekiel 3:17, Jeremiah 8:11, 15."

Folding the message and putting it in a diplomatic pouch, Ittai said, "It will be delivered."

"Now the good part, and there is a good part," Hushai said with a complete change of tone. There was joy in his speech as he continued, "Friday night, when hopefully people all over the earth will be gathering in response to the president's call, we have a safe place to gather with other believers who have been proven faithful at the risk of their lives. Come, join us, and pray."

"I will," Ittai immediately responded and they agreed on where to meet for the drive over.

SNEAK PEEK

WORLD
AT WAR

THE CURTAIN SERIES

BOOK III

DAVID T. MADDOX

CHAPTER 1

THE FIGHT FOR FRIDAY

Wednesday, February 13 – MD minus 26 days

EVERYTHING ACCELERATED IN the visible and invisible worlds as America careened toward the fast approaching MD date. Powers wrestled over events they could see coming, from the planning for the Thursday attack on Kingdom Day Care to MD now scheduled for March 11th. As important as these events would be, the only day of true significance was Friday when America and Americans would be required to consciously choose whose side they were on. It was D-Day, "Decision Day," and America's future depended on those decisions. Unfortunately, few truly understood what was at stake.

Some had already decided. The president had made his choice and issued the call for America to follow him in prayer and humbly choose God. The Senate majority leadership had made their choice; they would ignore the president's call and continue with business as usual. For them, religion was a "private matter" that should not interfere with their politics. At that moment in history, they saw what they perceived to be a vulnerable president and were circling in for the kill.

Businesses had to decide whether they would allow their employees a day off on Friday- the day for national prayers. Workers had to decide what they were willing to do and at what cost. Churches had to decide whether they wanted to have services on Friday where people were to gather and confess sins. The word "sin" had become the most unpopular word in modern American Christianity. Who could lead such a service since those who called themselves Christians were not in agreement on what was sin? But then, many of them weren't born again so how could they know? Those without the guidance of the light inside argued over what was acceptable, ignoring what the Bible called sin. For them, confession would be impossible because they didn't consider their conduct to be wrong.

The battle in the invisible world centered in America, for the forces of darkness recognized the opportunity to turn America further away from God. The hoard of Keepers and Tempters were released in all directions in an attempt to influence every person in America to reject the president's call as unimportant and inconvenient. He was pictured as a "good man" who was becoming a little fanatical about his religion. After all, hadn't the so-called leader of the enemy offered to meet and discuss peace? There was really no need to call out to God to help America. He obviously was already helping.

Likewise, Guardians and Providers acted to draw every person in America to join with the president or at least make a knowing choice whether to stand before the Lord with some understanding of its importance. The battle raged person by person, dividing homes, families, and friends. It was like oil and water as the two views found no place to compromise. Either it was important to stand before God and seek forgiveness for offenses to God, or it was neither important nor necessary. There was no middle ground.

Turning to Barnabas as they had gathered over Williams with others of the forces of light, Lucius observed, "This is one of those moments of choice which Jesus warned would come when He walked the earth. Do you remember?"

"Yes," Barnabas answered, "these people although made in His image, have never really understood the reality of choice. They have fallen for the Dark Master's deception that Jesus was a man of tolerance, peace, and love and thus they should expect to be able to live as they wish in complete harmony with others who live as they wish, all under the blessing of God. And when they die, so the fable goes, they will all go to 'a better place.'

"They think they don't have to make a choice, that God accepts them where they are and as they are. I have difficulty understanding how they can be so foolish. God would not be God if that were true. The people would be God because they could dictate what was is right and wrong."

"There is nothing worse than the result of people not reading the Bible," Lucius answered. "The deception and half-truths are more dangerous than the lies. The teachings of Jesus are taken out of context and thus He is pictured falsely. Jesus didn't call Himself a man of peace although in Him is peace. What He actually said was that He was God[90] and therefore you must choose who you will follow and obey. He warned that the wrong choice would bring conflict into every part of the life of those who made the wrong choice. He said:

Do not suppose that I have come to bring peace to the earth. I did not come to bring peace but a sword. For I have come to turn a man against his father, a daughter against her mother, a daughter-in-law against her mother-in-law – a man's enemies will be the members of his own household.[91]

"For centuries, nations and societies have sought to hide the sword, the division of choice, in secrecy and increasingly in the modern idea of tolerance and compromise, to maintain 'peace and unity' at any price," Lucius continued soberly. "It is sad what that deception has produced as God's word is ignored and people are encouraged to live their lives in direct rebellion to God's teachings. They have had their way these past decades, but the choice now hangs over America and this time they will not escape making that choice."

Below the celestial gathering in the city proper, a small group met in Chaplain Forrest's office. It was the chaplain, Pastor Wilson, Pastor Scribes, the Bookseller, and Paul Phillips. As they prayed together, the light within each of them burned brightly as the Holy Spirit sought to unite them with the will of the Father. Their eyes had been opened to the significance of Friday's call and they sought God's wisdom to know what they were to do in order to share what they had been shown.

This little band had not been spared the Dark Master's attacks. God had placed limits but within those limits, every possible means had been used by the forces of darkness to discourage, tempt, divide, and deceive.

The Bookseller had been approached by other networks and publishing companies that offered him a quick fortune for a signature that would have made him their exclusive property and enabled them to control his access to the world stage. The forces of darkness had orchestrated this effort and they followed up by flooding his mind with the deception of all "the good" that could be accomplished for God's service with the millions he was being offered. Fortunately for America, the Bookseller responded even as Jesus did when tempted by Satan and rejected the lie as a lie.[92]

"Mr. White," Pastor Wilson spoke quietly when there was a pause in their prayers. "I sense that God wants to use you further to open people's eyes to the importance of Friday and to draw people to Him. We have this website that is available worldwide and through which God has been working amazingly.[93] We have reports from numerous nations that when believers go to this website, they have been able to understand it even though it's not in their own language. God is working mightily! Perhaps posting a message there from you is what God would have us do. After all, from the first day, you understood that the issue is for believers to decide. The question is whether they will return to the Lord so that He may bless and protect America. He has made communication with believers possible through this website and has called you to be His spokesman."

"Why me?" the Bookseller asked, like Moses, sincerely humbled.[94] "I am nothing, just an old man who has struggled with his faith at times just like other people. I have no great following and for the most part, I have been rejected throughout my ministry. There are so many others who appear much more capable than I to be out-front calling the people back to the Lord. No one on earth wants to be used by God more than me, but I am not special."

"That is true, Samuel," Pastor Scribes observed, "it is true for all of us, but the Lord does not look on a man as we do. God looks at the heart and as He took David as a simple shepherd from the hills of Judea to become the great king,[95] He has obviously called you. The key is for you to keep the heart of David. Remember what God said about David's heart? 'I have found David son of Jesse a man after My own heart; he will do everything I want him to do.'[96] He knows your heart, and thus He can and will use you.

"I agree that God wants us to put something out on the website.

Let me pray and then I will write. Perhaps God will provide me another opportunity on ITN to speak to the nation before Friday. I sense that is a possibility. Whatever He wants."

"Then call them, Mr. White. They have made it very clear that they would be glad to have you on again anytime," Paul said excitedly.

"No, no. It is not for me to seek an opportunity to speak," the Bookseller responded quickly. "That is God's providence. If he wants me to have that opportunity, He will provide it. My place is to be ready to speak boldly what He gives me to say, if He gives me the opportunity to speak."

"I am confused by how God works and how I am to work for Him," Paul answered.

"Good, welcome to the crowd," Chaplain Forrest answered. "I am fifty-two years old and I don't know either. He acts as He will because He is God and we are not."

"Listen, Paul, often the most active place for us is not in doing something but in waiting for God to show us what He would have us do and how He wants it done. His work is too important to simply do something that seems logical or reasonable based on our knowledge and experience. God is not limited by logic, reason or our experience and what we may do 'for Him' because it seems right to us could mean we miss what He really wants us to do. We could actually be in rebellion against God while thinking we were doing something for Him. That verse where Jesus says, 'My sheep listen to My voice; I know them, and they follow Me'[97] means just what it says. Listen, and then follow. We never lead in any way other than by following Him."

"Wow," Paul responded, "that is a head full. I have so much to learn."

Acceptance Acknowledged – The Game Begins

In Washington, the majority party reacted with glee when they heard the newly broadcast tape recording of the Sheik acknowledging their acceptance of his invitation to meet and discuss the causes of hate. Former President Cox was instructed to check into the Cham Palace Hotel in Damascus, Syria, by March 7th at which time he would be given instructions on the location of the meeting. Their apparent good fortune encouraged the majority party to step up their hearings on the amendment to the Hate Crimes Act and the investigation of the administration's interference with Harkins College. Only one fly in the ointment appeared. The Together Tomorrow crowd was insistent that the open roads proposal had to be effective by March 7th or they were through funding campaign activities.

"I don't get those folks," Senate Majority Leader Howard said, expressing his frustration. "Who really gives a flip about trucks coming into and out of Mexico and Canada? Why does it have to be by March 7th? If these people didn't have real money, I'd investigate them."

"Yes, but they do have real money and a lot of it has ended up in this party's coffers," Chairman Crow responded. "We need their money, so they get to make the rules. That's politics in America."

"Fine, call the secretary of transportation and see if he is prepared to issue regulations that would effectively open the roads on March 7th," the majority leader agreed reluctantly. "I am not sure it is 100% legal but who cares if it works. We would never be able to accomplish that legislatively. We cannot get a bill passed in time and if we did, it would only get vetoed. He can go public on the 7th after the trucks are rolling and then it will be hard for the President to undo that which is already done. Even if he does, we will have demonstrated our willingness to comply, and his actions would prove we need the cash to get the White House and a super majority in Congress. If they are serious about their agenda, the cash will flow."

"Life is sure going to be different when that boy in the president's office has to retire. No more vetoes and no more of this religion crammed down everybody's throats."

"It can't come soon enough," Crow agreed, "but we have to defeat his protégé, this vice president."

"That should be no problem since he has publicly aligned himself with religious excess and against peace," Howard replied.

Elsewhere in Washington, Baqir Dawood arrived from Saudi Arabia with the envelope for Ahmad Habid from the Sheik. He had a flight already set up to take him to Phoenix, where he would arrive Thursday afternoon. For now, he had a few days to enjoy Washington in all its glory in the final days before MD.

The Search for Targets and Weapons Continues

Officially, Washington was a hub of activity as the Joint Chiefs, the Survival Commission, Senator Lieberman, Attorney General Rodriquez, David Barnes, Darrell Reed, Kayla Walker and others raced to find answers and prepare a response to the MD threat. It was non-stop activities after Darrell Reed's interpretation of the meaning of the video message was heard. The window for preemptive action was rapidly closing. Time was short.

"Do you know how many refineries, power plants, dams and water and electric systems there are in the United States?" General Hedge asked with great frustration.

"How are we to know the specific targets? We can't defend them all."

"There are over 75,000 reservoirs and dams in the United States alone," Barnes answered.

"Someone has been doing their research," Tom Knight commented.

"I have and I've learned a lot about the possible target list the Joint Chiefs have suggested," Barnes continued. "I agree it is an impossible job without more intelligence on specific targets."

"Don't lose your focus," the president interrupted. "Obviously, we prepare first for the largest and most critical of the possible targets and we must have a national strategy. If their goal is to cripple the country, they have to hit us everywhere. Divide the country into manageable sections and prepare for the most damaging targets in each."

"What about the weapons? How are they going to do that much damage?"

"I got a report this morning from Darrell Reed on the truck issue," Barnes began again. "The terrorist training camp was an oil terminal operation; they were training on gasoline delivery trucks. I know from a source that some of the many calls to report suspicious activities involve large trucks being used to transport people throughout the US who have gotten across the Mexican border. Something is definitely going on with trucks and I am sure that is not all. Lest we forget, gasoline explosions and fires brought down the World Trade Center and also caused significant damage to the Pentagon. One cup of gasoline has the explosive power of two sticks of dynamite and then it burns. Trucks, I believe, are one of the weapons."

"You could be right," General Hedge agreed. "We have been testing that possibility and the capacity of fuel trucks to do substantial damage if positioned properly. But how could they get that many trucks filled with gasoline and what kind of explosive mechanism could be used for maximum effectiveness?"

"I don't care how you divide this up," the president said, "but I want answers to those questions and a way to protect the major possible targets from a gasoline bomb whether driven over land or launched from the air." Pausing in frustration he said, "Look, we have to be missing something here. These people cannot possibly hijack enough aircraft and gasoline delivery trucks to do this. They have to have access to the vehicles and airplanes, but how? Also, have you looked into the ammonia bombs like the one that brought down the federal building in Oklahoma City?"

"Mr. President, we are looking at everything," General Hedge assured him. "Can we have a minute to discuss troop deployments here and abroad? We have to reposition our forces to address what may happen here and in the Middle East on MD."

"Absolutely, General," the president said. "We want maximum flexibility to deal with the danger here and in the Middle East."

"Eric, you need to be in this meeting to coordinate with Israel. The vice president will be called in when we have our plan in place."

"Mr. President, before you leave, I want you to know that we have moved quickly to impanel a grand jury to investigate the Harkins student or faculty terrorist. Subpoenas have been issued and we have also noticed the deposition of Harkins' president on an emergency basis for tomorrow and have issued subpoenas for the records they will not give us that may disclose not only the identity of the J-14 leader but perhaps the whole gang if the plot really was hatched at Harkins.

"One more thing, we have found some unusual business activities in the US trucking and aircraft industry as well as in Mexico. We may be onto something about how they will get the weapons of choice without having to hijack them."

"Great, everyone, stay with it," the president said excitedly, "We have to find out before they can strike."

"General, Eric, let's retire to my office and discuss troop redeployment. After we are through, I would like a little time with you two," he said pointing at Tom Knight and David Barnes. Then he rose and excused himself for the next meeting.

Varvel Returns to Williams

Back in Williams on Wednesday, Carl Varvel was again on the move looking for the Bookseller. He had another message from Iran and as he walked to the warehouse, he still wondered what this could possibly have to do with the National Security of the United States.

Opening the envelope, the Bookseller's whole countenance changed. He understood immediately what was meant by the message from the Iranian brothers. "Margaret, come here and look at this," he said walking into his study away from the ears and eyes of the waiting Varvel.

"Every message is more intense and more direct. Whether this threat is against America, clearly it is increasing in urgency and the battle for the hearts and minds of the people is where it will be won. There has never been a comparable period in our lifetime where the spiritual issue has so clearly been drawn. These messages from the Iranian brothers seem to affirm what God has been showing so directly that it almost appears to be from the hand of God Himself."

"I think, you're right, Samuel. This seems to be clear guidance from God," Margaret said as she read again:

Brother, the days are now much shorter and God's protection is essential to prevent disaster and open eyes to deception. Don't believe what you see. Ezekiel 3:17, Jeremiah 8:11, 15.

"When I read this, I almost want to turn off all the news channels and throw away the newspaper," the Bookseller responded.

"Don't be silly," she answered tenderly but forcefully as only a wife can. "You must hear and read what the public is hearing and reading to know how to pray and how God would have you respond when He gives you the opportunity to speak. How can you identify the deception if you hide in a cave? Clearly, this message refers to the false video offer of peace which some have already foolishly embraced, and the verses are instructions to you. Please don't start the 'why me' stuff. It is you because God has called you."

"I surrender to you and to God," he responded. "The verses are clear. I am accountable to God as a watchman appointed to warn the people and I am not to be out there like others saying 'Peace, peace,' when there is no peace.

"The one that really troubles me is that last one, Jeremiah 8:15." He read, "'We hoped for peace but no good has come, for a time of healing but there was only terror.' Hope is not going to get us through this time. God will protect us or we are finished just like biblical Israel and Judah. Whose side is America on? That remains the question."

Taking paper, the Bookseller paused to pray as he prepared his response for return delivery to the unknown brothers in Iran. He wondered at how God used them to encourage him and hoped that the day would come when he would meet them in this life.

The note read:

My dear brothers, please pray as Epaphras in Colossians 4:12 that I be as the man described in Jeremiah 23:22.

Once again, Carl Varvel was off for the return trip to Iran.

Preparations for the Morrow

In the physical world, those under the influence of the competing powers moved for good or ill accordingly. What was seen in the Bookseller and others with the light inside was contested by the actions of those whose minds were directed by Keepers for the forces of darkness. From Cambridge, Massachusetts, and major US cities, the leadership coordinators for MD traveled to Phoenix, Arizona, under the cover of the American Teachers Society's annual convention which was being held at the Kierland Resort in Scottsdale. There, in a secret gathering, final plans would be made for the March 11th attacks.

In Washington, the president had made his final plans for the secret trip to Williams for the memorial service. The Secret Service had objected with all the authority and influence they could muster, but the president had reminded them who was president and that was the end of the discussion. Covertly, David Barnes and Tom Knight were to travel with the president and Janet, under the cover of darkness. The president was strangely at peace as the journey began, looking forward finally to an opportunity to meet the Bookseller yet still unsure what he was to say at the memorial service.

In Williams, another kind of final plan was being made. The three surviving terrorists from the original group of eleven were preparing themselves for what they hoped would be a series of attacks beginning in the morning at Kingdom Day Care. As they readied themselves to kill and die, darkness descended upon them and anger and hate flooded their hearts. Their motivation was no longer their reward – they wanted only to hurt and kill and cause pain. Had they known of the president's plans to attend the memorial service, they would have shifted their target but they were ignorant even as the rest of America. Pastor Scribes, the Bookseller, and Paul Phillips had felt a strong compulsion from the light inside to guard their knowledge that the president was coming to Williams. The secret had been kept and that alone would preserve the president's life in the coming day.

Elsewhere, Susan Stafford still could not sleep. It was that sound, the crying of the children. She could not shut it off. She had heard it before and knew what it meant, for The Curtain again had opened briefly and she heard the sound of the children's angels crying out to the Father for their protection. In her compulsion, she had called the office of the Citizen's Militia and begged to be assigned to guard Kingdom Day Care. There, she sensed was the risk and that was her assignment from above. After much argument, Sam Will gave in and authorized her to be a part of a two-person team in the morning assigned to Kingdom Day Care. Knowing the physical limitations that resulted from her wounds, he assigned himself as the second member of the team and arranged to pick her up so they could travel together.

Susan had finished her letter. She sealed it in a plastic bag and then placed it carefully in an inside pocket of the new red jacket she had been given to replace the one in which she had been shot in. She felt a peace that was ridiculous when she considered her circumstances. She was a woman with no hope, a killer who now understood the full measure of the evil that had so dominated her existence in those months of the shooting spree. She deserved nothing but a slow and cruel death for all the pain she had caused. That she knew, but she no longer feared the second death for she had come to believe that even her could be forgiven and be born again – and she did, the light glowed brightly in her heart.

In the invisible, there had been great rejoicing among the forces of light when God did that which only He could do and changed Susan's heart by the new birth. "These humans do not understand God's holiness or God's love," Barnabas began. "Because God is holy all sin merits the second death, but when Jesus died it was to offer the opportunity of forgiveness even to the vilest of all sinners.[98] Remember Saul of Tarsus who became Paul. He was a lot like Susan. He killed and imprisoned innocents simply because they were believers and yet God forgave and used him.[99] God did the same for Susan because she like Paul came to the place of understanding her sin and God's choice.[100] She chose wisely."

"Glory," Lucius replied. "Even now I am still overwhelmed at God's mercy which is available to all."

"Yes," Manaen replied, "but she still faces the earthly consequences of her sin. I wonder how God will allow that to play out?"

"We may see tomorrow," Barnabas answered.

Another post had been completed earlier that day and was uploaded to the Together We Pray website. It had taken some time but the Bookseller finally completed a short piece to send to the believers of the world. As he prayed and wrote, he was mindful of everything the Iranian brothers had said and the verses they had directed him to. He felt insufficient because he was insufficient, but he knew God was more than sufficient and that if he had been called, he would be enabled, so he released what he had done and had peace resting in that knowledge.

The Defining Question

There was great activity in Heaven this night as the great cloud of witnesses joined with brothers and sisters on earth in bringing America in prayer before God. Their prayers were directed by the light within and paralleled the prayer offered by Daniel, who while living in captivity in Babylon had stood before the Lord and prayed for himself and for his nation. The prayer in the 9th chapter of the Book of Daniel had been the subject of the Bookseller's posting. Daniel had prayed:

O Lord, the great and awesome God, who keeps His covenant of love with all who love Him and obey His commands, we have sinned and done wrong. We have been wicked and have rebelled; we have turned away from Your commands and laws. We have not listened to Your servants the prophets, who spoke in Your name ...[101]

Daniel's conclusion is the reason God was able to answer the prayer, for Daniel's request reflected the truth that they were not worthy of an answer. He closed praying,

Now, our God, hear the prayers and petitions of Your servant ... We do not make requests of You because we are righteous but because of Your great mercy. O Lord, listen! O lord, forgive! O Lord, hear and act! For Your sake, O my God, do not delay, because Your city and Your people bear Your Name.[102]

America, the "Christian" nation, whose people had proclaimed to the world to be "one nation under God" desperately needed to repent. The only question was, would they? America's future hung on the balance just like the Jewish nation living in the Babylonian captivity, dependent upon their answer to that single question.

ENDNOTES

1. Mark 11:15-17
2. Matthew 21:33-44
3. Luke 19:41-44
4. Revelation 12:17
5. 2 Timothy 4:14
6. Acts 17:1-10
7. James 4:7
8. Revelation 1:17-18
9. Philippians 3:2
10. 2 Corinthians 5:8
11. Revelation 20:11-15
12. Romans 3:21-25
13. Revelation 20:6,14
14. Luke 12:5
15. Philippians 2:9-11
16. John 1:1-14
17. John 8:58, John 10:29-33
18. John 17:14
19. John 18:36-37
20. Matthew 10:34-36
21. Luke 9:51-56
22. John 14:6
23. Luke 19:41-44
24. 1 Peter 4:17
25. 2 Chronicles 7:12-15, Deuteronomy 28:15-68
26. 2 Chronicles 20:20-25
27. 1 Kings 18:20-39
28. John 8:44

29. Acts 13:22
30. 1 Samuel 16:1-3, 12-14
31. Luke 4:5-6, Ephesians 2:2
32. Leviticus 18:22
33. Matthew 18:10
34. Ephesians 5:25
35. 2 Corinthians 6:14
36. 2 Corinthians 4:4
37. Ezekiel 36:26-27
38. John 3:3,5
39. 1 Timothy 2:3-4
40. 2 Peter 3:9
41. Isaiah 6:1-3, Revelation 4:1-8, Revelation 16:7
42. Romans 3:23
43. Romans 6:23
44. Philippians 2:5-8
45. 1 Peter 1:17-21, Revelation 5:6-10
46. John 1:29, Colossians 1:13-14, 1 John 3:5, Revelation 1:5-6
47. Acts 16:31
48. Ezekiel 36:26-27
49. John 14:15,21,23
50. Matthew 7:27-23, Luke 6:46, Hebrews 5:7-9
51. Joshua 5:13-14
52. Joshua 5:14-6:5
53. Matthew 12:30
54. Acts 19:23-29, 20:1
55. John 11:45-53
56. Matthew 18:10
57. Acts 2:1-11
58. Matthew 18:19-20
59. Mark 10:13-16
60. Luke 9:28-36, Matthew 26:36-38
61. Matthew 26:39
62. Matthew 26:47-56
63. Matthew 10:32-33
64. Matthew 6:9-10
65. Matthew 6:14-15
66. John 13:34-35, Matthew 5:43-45
67. Matthew 5:43-45

68. Galatians 5:22-23
69. Jeremiah 35:15-17
70. Ephesians 4:26
71. 2 Chronicles 15:1-2, Isaiah 63:10, Revelation 2:16
72. Jeremiah 31:31-34, Hebrews 10:12-17
73. Matthew 26:26-29
74. John 14:8-9)
75. John 10:30
76. Luke 19:41-44
77. 1 Timothy 1:2
78. Genesis 1:28
79. Genesis 1:26-27
80. 1 Peter 5:13
81. 2 Samuel 11
82. 2 Samuel 121-23
83. Matthew 27:1-5
84. John 17:12
85. Psalm 51:1, 4, 7, 10-12, 17
86. John 14:15, 21. 23
87. Acts 11:26
88. Romans 10:9
89. Neville Chamberlain was the Prime Minister of England who when Adolph Hitler threatened war over portions of Czechoslovakia, rather than confronting a not yet fully armed Germany negotiated a peace agreement to grant Hitler the portions of the country he wanted in exchange for a promise of no more territorial demands. Chamberlain immediately claimed that he had achieved "peace for our time," but within a year Hitler invaded Poland and the Great War was on. World War II was the deadliest conflict in human history with between 50-80 million fatalities.
90. John 5:18
91. Matthew 10:34-36
92. Matthew 4:1-11
93. Acts 2:1-12
94. Numbers 12:3
95. 1 Samuel 16:1-13
96. Acts 13:22
97. John 10:27
98. Romans 6:23

99. Acts 22:4, 1 Timothy 1:15-16, Acts 9:10-16
100.　　Romans 10:9-10
101.　　Daniel 9:4-6
102.　　Daniel 9:17-19

After a 40 year legal career as a civil litigator and decades of prayer for revival, all the while teaching God's Word and making disciples, a cancer diagnosis interrupted David T. Maddox and gave him time to finalize a book he had written 7 years earlier, but shortly after publication of the first book of The Curtain series, David passed through the curtain himself to his heavenly home. He left wife Janet, 4 adult children and 8 grandchildren and volumes 2 & 3 of The Curtain series.

CPSIA information can be obtained
at www.ICGtesting.com
Printed in the USA
BVOW08s0958160218
508345BV00001B/83/P